Broken Biscuits: The Blantyre Girl

Ian Colquhoun

Contents

This book is dedicated to everyone who has lost someone to addiction or who has suffered due to their own addiction or that of someone that they love.

About this Book

Broken Biscuits are the ordinary people from working-class housing estates, or schemes, as we call them in Scotland. Some of us born into the neoliberal wasteland don't make it to adulthood, our lives cut short by violent crime, drugs and poverty. Some of us, the lucky ones, get away, be it via marriage, work, or study. However, most of us Broken Biscuits have made our lives still in or near the schemes in which we were raised, despite the constant battle against hard drugs, organised crime, inept policing, out-of-touch politicians, poverty-level wages, insecure employment, shite housing, and ever decreasing public services that we, and our parents, have had to fight over the years.

The billionaires, corporations, and oligarchs make merry whilst we fight for life's basic necessities.

Broken Biscuits isn't a derogatory term – remember, Broken Biscuits are usually the best and have the most character – like us. Despite the hardships that we face, we still know how to make the best of things.

This second instalment of the Broken Biscuits series is very different to the first. I decided to set this one in Lanarkshire rather than my native West Lothian, as things are much the same in all working-class communities the length and breadth of the country, nowadays.

Everybody from Blantyre that I've ever met was a great person, but I don't know the place very well, I just wanted to use its name as some of my ancestors were miners. Though I don't say exactly where in

Lanarkshire this new story is set, you'll probably notice bits and bobs from several towns in its two counties. As ever, nobody in this book is based on a real person and no events in this book are based on real events. One of the protagonists has an amusing name. I had a warehouse supervisor with that same name when I was a teenager and my ADHD brain found that funny. The guy was sound and his namesake in this story is in no way based on him, I just borrowed the name.

This one's a bit darker than The Wood Fairy, by the way. As with The Wood Fairy, this story appeared in my head in full, all at once, one night...

Acknowledgements

For their help, inspiration and encouragement I'd like to thank my amazing editor, Lindsay Drummond and also my family, Tony, Maggie, Jenny, Davie, Kerry, Mad Gerty, Heather, Josie, Paul, Gemma, John N, Ellie, my cat, Angie the raver and Eddie Anderson.

CHAPTER ONE

Mr Vain

Hailing from the small former mining town of Blantyre, Georgia Dooley and Hugh Mann had first met each other at school but were neither friends, nor enemies. Hugh had been the stereotypical angry Scottish teen from a fractured family. While Georgia had heard stories about him, she had generally kept her nose clean and given him a wide berth. She and her friends had spent their school lunch hours revising, talking about music and boys, and eyeing up lads from the years above them. Hugh and his pals spent their lunchtimes hanging around the chippy, smoking cigarettes, buzzing lighter gas and talking about raves.

In his early school years, Hugh's name was a source of great amusement to most of the other kids his age, though understandably not to him. Imagine having to go through the whole of primary and secondary school if your real name was Hugh Mann. Every time a teacher mentioned humans or the human race, folk were laughing. In the playground, it was even worse. Hugh-Mann Nature, Hugh-Mannity, or his least favourite, on account of his large, flabby physique, Hugh Mann-Boobs.

His father had given him the name with the intention of toughening him up. His father, an overweight, bigoted, bullying, wife-beating habitual drunk and former miner, had died of a lung condition when Hugh was just 17, leaving little behind for his long-suffering wife, Yvonne, other than three kids, a mountain of debt, psychological wounds and physical bruises. The only things Hugh had inherited from his father were his bad lungs and worse temper. Hugh's older sister had run away to London to escape her father when Hugh was just 15. She had done ok down south and had never returned. His other sibling, an older brother, had also left to find a better life, joining the police force in Manchester. Like his sister, he too never came back up the road. Just like that, Hugh had become the man of the house and quickly learned how to defend what was his.

This, combined with his affinity for watching gangster movies as a child, while his mum and dad argued downstairs, meant that by around the age of 15, nobody was calling him Hugh anymore. Nobody was mocking his chubby physique, and nobody who knew him dared to use the Hugh Mann/Human gag in any context. Those who did ended up savagely beaten, sometimes even hospitalised. Almost overnight, pudgy Hugh became the all-powerful Shug. However, Shug's harsh upbringing had made him not just tough, but sadistic, too. He didn't just beat up his victims; he absolutely terrorised them. In his years at high school, he became his own crime wave. Weak kids, even older ones, were 'taxed' – their dinner money or pocket money stolen, usually in front of everybody – nobody wanted to fight him. Refusal to pay up always meant a severe beating, whether the victim fought back or not. He would tell his victims he'd kill their parents if they blabbed, and they believed him. His favourite targets tended to be the most handsome boys, the autistic boys, and the poorest boys, due to a mixture of jealousy and lack of empathy. He tended to avoid bullying the children with richer parents as they were more likely to have the capacity to do something about it. Shug soon had a wee gang of other kids at his back, teens from similarly desolate family situations, kids smart enough to know that it was wiser, more pragmatic, to join psychopaths like Shug than it was to try to beat them. After all, in a housing scheme, when you're young, it's all about survival.

Shug had left school at the age of 16 and had taken a painting and decorating apprenticeship – though not academically gifted he had been dragged up the hard way and was streetwise, cunning and astute, even at a young age. The apprenticeship didn't pay very well but it taught him a trade, while also providing him with a great cover for selling bits of hash. Colleagues bought from him, his supervisors bought from him, and pretty soon most people in the scheme bought from him, too. By 17, he had come to the attention of the police, due to his small-time cannabis dealing – he'd started off with a nine-bar he bought for £350, this provided him with 36 quarters, of which he sold 34 at £20 a deal, keeping two for himself, earning himself £680 – a profit of £330 plus his own supply for the fortnight, too – quite the Thatcherite entrepreneur.

Georgia's exposure to the drugs, clubs, and parties scene in her late teens hadn't been huge. Like most young Scots at that time, she had dabbled with party drugs, but had mostly grown out of it over time. Those who didn't grow out of it more often than not ended up on the harder drugs, involved with crime or the underworld to varying degrees, in prison, dead prematurely or just generally fucked up for life. Shug Mann, fell into most of that latter category.

The first time Georgia and Shug crossed paths after Shug left school came a few years later in 1996, at a mutual acquaintance's 18th birthday bash in The Stuart Hotel function suite. It had been around then that Georgia's breasts and body had finished blossoming from skinny wee lassie to full-on Jessica Rabbit's sister mode, and Shug, himself at the time somewhat hunky and dashing though clad head to toe in Stone Island, had wanted a piece of her – that night, he became smitten.

It's weird when you become an adult, when you're aged around 18-21 and are suddenly surrounded by all your old schoolmates who are also now adults, too. It's like everybody gets a clean slate. Lassies or guys who gave you the boak for years at school suddenly become fanciable; previously unattainable guys and girls are suddenly on your level, even the school hotties can start to appear very ordinary by then, as everyone else has caught up, so it can be a wonderful stage in life, when you all, as newly qualified adults, have a fresh start, a reset.

The 18th birthday party had been a great night for all concerned. Everyone drank and danced and sang – the atmosphere was electric. Finally, at around 2am, the party wound down and the partygoers, all a little worse for wear, began to trickle away home. There was always a shortage of taxis at that time of night in the town back then, so, Georgia and her friend, Isla, had decided to walk home. Shug, who had been eyeing Georgia all night, insisted on accompanying them on the near-two-mile walk in the dark and the two girls had graciously accepted. Shug was an utter gentleman as they walked up the road together pissed, laughing, talking about the party, and reminiscing together. They reached Isla's parents' house first and said goodnight, with Shug making sure that Georgia got home safely, next. As he and Georgia walked side by side and went down into an underpass, Shug reached out his right hand to gently hold Georgia's left hand as they walked, and she let him. They carried on walking and talking, laughing together. Georgia was giddy with the drink and buzzing from the lovely party, while Shug, it seemed, was actually quite a nice lad. She'd heard a lot of dodgy stuff about his antics, but he was being fine to her, charming even, so, she took him as she found him, and Shug liked that. As they walked along the footpath through the scheme chatting away, they passed a big, jaggy hedgerow, which looked menacing in the dark, lit only by a streetlamp. They both noticed that the hedge was full of torn-up porno mags – true Scottish scheme art!

They both laughed at this, Georgia playfully ripping Shug, asking him if they were his, which he strongly denied, laughing that one off. When they reached the bench and lamppost at the entrance to Georgia's street, she stopped, turned to Shug, and thanked him for walking her home. He smiled and said, "It's awright."

Georgia leaned forward to give Shug a thank you hug, and kissed him on the cheek, but as she tried to pull away and say goodnight, Shug put his arms around her waist and tried to kiss her on the lips. Georgia tried to laugh it off and dodged his kiss, giving him another hug instead, but he kept trying to kiss her, making her wriggle free and step back. At first, all she could say was, 'Woah, Hugh, no' that, man," while still smiling.

Shug replied, "Look, Georgia, I've always fancied you from afar. I think you're pure dead gorgeous, you were the most beautiful lassie at school, I thought. C'mon-"

He stepped forward as if making to kiss her again, but this time Georgia took another step back and raised her hands, palms facing Shug, saying more firmly, "Look, Shug, it's been a lovely night, thanks for walking me home. It's been great to see you again. Sorry if I gave you the wrong idea, man. I'm no' wanting a boyfriend right now."

Shug stared at her for a second, glanced at the floor, then answered.

"It's awright, I get it, sorry, I must've picked up the wrong signals. I'm really sorry, Georgia."

She answered warmly. "Don't worry about it, man, look, that's me just about home, thank you, you're a great guy, I'll hopefully see you around."

Shug smiled and nodded. Georgia turned and walked in the lamppost light towards her parents' house, and Shug turned to head back to his place.

After about 30 seconds, Shug called her name and she spun around, saying 'aye?' still in a warm tone.

"You've got an amazing body, by the way," he said loudly, smiling.

Georgia blushed and replied "Ocht, away, thanks Hugh, night night." Then she turned and walked home.

Georgia's inner monologue spoke to her as she locked the house door behind her.

'He's actually quite sound, a nice boy, he's maybe no' the selfish bad guy that folk say he is. Still, he's not my type. I hope he sorts himself out.'

On his solitary walk home, Shug's inner monologue was talking to him, too, as he puffed on a pre-rolled joint that had been in his jeans pocket.

"Bitch, snobby cow, cock-teasin' bitch. Who does she think she is? She was a dog at school. I walked her and her daft pal home, and all I get is a fuckin' cuddle? Bitches. I'll have her one day."

Shug hadn't taken Georgia's rebuff as well as it had seemed to her that he had. He was fucking livid, experiencing a mixture of frustration, self-loathing insecurity and anger, as all psychopaths do when they don't get what they want. Though just 18, Shug had been dealing drugs for a couple of years by then, he was used to women in the scheme who took drugs falling into his arms, or at least, not making him work too hard for it as long as he had gear and money. This rebuff had wounded his pride and his ego immeasurably, and he'd never forget it – the girl who told him 'no'.

CHAPTER TWO

The Good Life

The second time their paths had crossed had been in the town's shitey *Paps Nightclub,* almost a year later. They'd both been pretty melted when they bumped into each other at one of the club's bars that night. Shug had been pleased to see that Georgia was on eccies, as in his head, this surely meant that she was just like the other women from the scheme that he knew now, a drug user, vulnerable, more amenable, more accessible to the likes of him, but he didn't steam straight in. The two of them ended up having a fairly long eccied-up chat, catching up, though by then, their lives had diverged somewhat. Georgia had a really good new job and career prospects, but she was considering studying nursing or accountancy part time too. Shug couldn't exactly answer that with 'oh that's nice, I'm a drug dealer and I'm making a fortune. I keep a gun in my house!', so, he talked briefly about completing his apprenticeship and his plans to start a decorating business, then went off on an eccy-fuelled tangent, by which he apologised over and over again for trying it on with her that time, after the 18th birthday party, outwardly out of politeness, but in reality trying to gauge her receptiveness to him, now that she was, in his mind, a junkie skank – albeit one he genuinely fancied.

They both laughed about the incident, and Georgia reassured Shug that it was all in the past, and wasn't a big deal, and that it was good to see him again. Shug, wasted, lust-crazed, his lust-ometer actually off the scale as he was dazzled by Georgia's beauty and trying desperately hard not to be *too* transfixed by the curvaceous contents of her low-cut short black dress, and still internally smarting about her rebuff that time, decided to try the direct approach and leaned in to kiss her, his left hand reaching around to squeeze her arse through her dress.

Georgia showed remarkable restraint, taking a step back while brushing away Shug's hand.

"Naw, man, no that. C'mon Hugh, we're just pals."

Georgia didn't find him ugly, but she'd heard more about his general antics with drugs, women, and violence in the last year, and knew she had to be more assertive, this time. Shug didn't realise that most men and women who take drugs aren't automatically an easy-whore, and he certainly couldn't see that Georgia had been nice to him simply because she was a genuinely nice girl who didn't mind him, after all, he'd done her no real wrong, well, until he then spoke.

"Are you taking the piss, doll? Think you're something special, do you? You're in a club melted dressed like a fuckin' slapper, practically beggin' for it, leading me on but then knocking me back? Who do you think you are? I really liked you, ya cow."

Shug's shattered, fragile ego had spoken.

Georgia was upset, not angry, she said, "Right, I'm away," and turned to go back to her friends. Infuriated, Shug followed her and tapped her on the shoulder, to get her to turn around, which she did, but before Shug could say anything else, two large bald bouncers appeared and frog-matched him off the premises, holding his arms behind his back as they expertly ejected him. In his wasted state and taken by surprise, all Shug could do was curse, swear, and threaten the doormen.

The incident spooked Georgia but a female bouncer came over, asked her if she was alright and told her that 'that nutter' was now permanently barred from the club.

Georgia and her friends didn't let it spoil their night, in fact, she hardly gave Shug a second thought thereafter.

Two days later, one of the club's doormen was attacked by some youths wielding baseball bats, right outside his front door. His injuries kept him in hospital for six weeks, and afterwards, he was never physically able to work as a bouncer again. Nobody was ever caught or charged for the baseball bat attack, but everybody in town seemed to know who had ordered it. The nightclub owner used the local newspaper to offer a reward for information leading to a conviction in the case. Nobody was brave enough to come forward.

But, you see, Shug didn't really blame the bouncer for his humiliation that night – in Shug's mind, it was all Georgia's fault.

CHAPTER THREE

Love's Great Adventure

For Georgia, the two brief encounters with Shug Mann were little more than blips on her timeline. She went on with her life without a backward glance, and a few years later, she met Keith.

It was during the time of the late-90s 'E and Ibiza' explosion as superclub culture and its music had started to become mainstream, even being used on TV shows and in adverts as continuity music. That's right – tunes such as *Cafe Del Mar* by Energy 52 or *For An Angel* by Paul Van Dyk were regularly pumping away as Sportscene highlights of the Edinburgh Derby flashed by on screens, or as those new mobile phone thingy companies tried to brainwash the masses into joining the latest really annoying fad – I mean, mobile phones? What a daft idea.

Keith and Georgia's eyes had met across the cigarette-smoke-choked dancefloor of *Paps Nightclub* in the spring of 1998, and it was love at first sight. Georgia found herself reeled in by the handsome, dark-eyed man in the blue Ralph Lauren Jumper, just as Keith was by the voluptuous, red-headed Georgia in her woolly turquoise dress. It helped, of course, that they'd both been absolutely smashed on those brilliant multi-coloured flying saucer eccies that had been in circulation. Alas, those pills had been so good that one ambitious local dealer had ordered 100,000 of them from a guy in Rotterdam, only to be caught with them by the drugs squad when collecting them off the back of a lorry at Harthill Services one night, leading to the confiscation of the merchandise and the suicide, by hanging, of the dealer involved near the beginning of his 12-year prison sentence. Flying saucers, thus, weren't a thing for very long.

The first night that they met, in *Paps,* both of them had heard bells ringing, they had heard fanfares of joyous angels singing, they had both briefly felt the dry mouth, inner nervousness and butterflies in the stomach that you get when you meet someone that you *know* is going to be so, so special to you. Of course, they had then spent most of the rest of their evening, in that most dreadful of venues, snogging and slobbering all over each other on one of the manky sofas in one corner of the club, as one does when they are nineteen and loved up, before making their excuses to their friends, and leaving together to get a taxi up to Georgia's – she had an *empty,* her middle-aged far-too-trusting parents were away in Lanzorote for a fortnight . En route to her place in the taxi, they had attempted to engage the taxi driver in conversation, but were both so wasted that they just kept asking him his name, to the point that the driver, an older guy who was disgusted at the local upsurge in drug use that decade, had eventually stopped engaging with them, relieved to get them out of his car in the end.

Once back at Georgia's, the two had raided the fridge and started on Georgia's mum's Bacardi Breezers and her dad's stock of Labbats beer. Both in need of a chill after subjecting their ears to several hours of loud, constant chart dance and Eurodance tracks back at Paps, Georgia had gone to the wooden full-wall shelving unit in the living room and loaded five more chilled but still absolutely quality CDs into her dad's hi-fi's CD multi-changer. Massive Attack, Faithless, the *Trainspotting* soundtrack, a compilation album simply named *Adrenalin* and an album by *The Seahorses* – a newish but profoundly mediocre indie-rock band started by John Squire, formerly of The Stone Roses.

Keith, a big and strong, 19-year-old with brown hair in a wedge haircut, and Georgia with her big blue eyes and pale, porcelain-esque complexion, sat together on the sofa together, sipping on Labbats and on Bacardi Breezers, taking in the tunes. Keith tried to build them both a much-needed joint to take the impending edge off those flying saucers that they had taken earlier.

The joint-building wasn't going well, partly because Keith was wasted and struggling to focus visually, but mostly because he was having a hard time trying to burn the solid soap-bar weed using only one of those crappy plastic throwaway lighters you get, the ones that are only useful for lighting cigarettes. Keith cursed and shook his head as the lighter gave up after staying lit for too long, exploding in his fingers with a *PING*, small components of the burned-out lighter flying in all different directions. Though slightly annoyed, they both laughed off that little disaster – Georgia said that her dad kept a cigar lighter in the kitchen anyway – and the two were both back to snogging on the sofa, their mouths locked together and their hands nervously exploring each other's bodies, as the sweet strains of the *Trainspotting* soundtrack CD filled the room. That CD was one of two albums that were, inexplicably, in absolutely everybody's house at any afterparty you went to in Scotland in the late 90s, no matter how geeky or cool the host was. The other CD was 'The Party Album' by The Vengaboys, by the way. Don't try to deny it.

By the time that Bedrock featuring KYO's epic house anthem *For What You Dream Of* was playing, Georgia was out of her dress – she'd been wearing no underwear except her tights – and Keith was down to just the red Adidas tee-shirt he'd been wearing under his jumper.

When the taking and the giving starts to get too much
Let the music hit you with its healing touch
Last night's just a way of marking time
Everybody must express the feeling some time
They say a tree is as tall as its many branches
But not all God's children have the same chances

Their loved-up, eccied, passionate heavy petting had stalled for three reasons: the first and most obvious one being that all 19-year-olds are intense pods of utter insecurity. Secondly, Georgia and Keith were both a little dizzy from the Es. Thirdly, and crucially, Keith's knob just wasn't playing ball – at all. He was horny as hell, he really fancied Georgia, even more so now that they'd seen each other naked and both clearly liked what they saw. During the taxi ride to Georgia's house Keith had noticed that his dick had started to recess back into his body – an often-soul-destroying side effect of dehydration, made even worse by some types of Ecstasy pill, and by too much drink. They'd tried everything to get him going. Georgia had used her hand, and then her mouth, to no avail; the best that she got out of him was a semi, which was of no use to anybody, really. Inside, Georgia was experiencing what many insecure young women go through in these embarrassing, frustrating situations.

Does he like me?
Am I too fat?
Maybe he's gay?
Am I too fat?
Am I doing something wrong?

Maybe he has a girlfriend he never mentioned and she's much hotter than me?

However, Georgia wasn't daft, or naive. Via the holy trinity of listening to her parents arguing in their bedroom through thin partition walls one night, the X-rated post-weekend chats that she had at work with other young women, and the sex-tips section of *More* magazine, she knew that this type of thing usually happened to all guys at some point, and was almost always caused by anxiety, blood circulation problems or over-indulgence in drugs and/or alcohol.

She reassured Keith that it didn't matter, even though it still did a bit, after all, that's why they'd left the club early. Keith was deeply embarrassed but was glad of the reassurance, so, instead, the two of them had got busy with Georgia's dad's cigar lighter, rolling not one, but three joints. They smoked the first one out in the garden, leaning against the wheely bins, because Georgia was adamant that *hot-rocking* the family sofa with falling crumbs of red-hot soap bar was simply not an option, her mum and dad would go absolutely mental. Once the first joint was finished, they went back inside the house and turned on the TV. MTV's late Saturday night dance music show replaced the music from the CD changer on the hi-fi.

MTV were actually doing a live outside broadcast from a superclub in West Lothian - Room at the Top in Bathgate - and it was hilarious watching. Their glamorous, all-smiling star presenter, June Sarpong, was trying to interview clubbers live, but very few punters wanted to talk to her, so she sat on her own at one end of its dancefloor, waiting for any bold clubbers who wanted to be famous to sit beside her, and thus have their face beamed into millions of homes all over the world. There weren't many takers, but that was no reflection on June Sarpong – it's just, well, when you're absolutely trashed on drink, E, and Christ knows what else in a busy nightclub, the last thing you want is a bloody video camera shoved in your face.

Georgia and Keith had both been to that nightclub before, separately, and they found this MTV spectacle both interesting and amusing. They both recounted tales of their own trips and exploits to that particular club, and they laughed together, a lot. This helped ease the slight disappointment that hung in the atmosphere regarding Keith and his untimely case of Mr Floppy. They ended up just sitting together for a few hours on the sofa, half cuddling, nipping out for a joint again, and then another. As the cannabis took effect and the grinding comedown and jaw clenching caused by the flying saucers started to ease away, they ended up switching from bevvy to cups of sweet, milky tea, cuddling up together on the sofa and watching some utterly dreadful dating show, on the other MTV channel, called '*Singled Out*'. Georgia had thrown on her mum's housecoat and Keith sat with her in his red t-shirt and his Calvin Klein trunks – obtained at the Barras in Glasgow some weeks earlier, three pairs for a fiver. It was during this dating TV show, snuggled up to Georgia, with the scent of her perfume in his nostrils and the warm, intimate feeling of having her pressed against him that Keith noticed a stirring in his trunks – it was working again, thank fuck!

Keith made a playful '*hem hem*', took her right hand and gently placed it on the burgeoning bulge in his shorts. Georgia hadn't looked away from the screen, but she let out a soft but encouraging moan as she felt his hardness and started to use her fingernails on said bulge, gently, through his trunks. As Keith moaned softly, she turned to face him and the two were soon necking once more; weed, tea and relaxation having rekindled their fiery sexual tension from earlier on. Within five minutes they had disrobed and were entwined together on Georgia's parents' big king-size bed – Georgia still only had a single in her room.

Keith was harder than a quadratic equation, Georgia was wetter than October. They did about ten minutes of foreplay but were both so desperate to truly feel one another that all they wanted was to fuck – so they did, their mutual lust and drug-fuelled wantonly cravings beginning with Keith going on top, as Georgia wrapped her shapely, slender legs around his waist.

Keith blew his load within 30 seconds and collapsed on top of her, sweating, panting, and sweating some more, his body shaking. As he remained on top of her, still gripped by the dying embers of his humiliating, untimely orgasm, in her head Georgia was again experiencing her own inner monologue.

Fuck's sake, what a useless cunt!
Does he always do that?
Was that my fault?
What a loser, haha.
Now I know why he's single!
That's surely a new record!
Was he a virgin?

Keith's cum was everywhere, between her legs, on her thighs, on her belly, all over the duvet, there were even a few drops on the ceiling. She made her excuses and headed for the toilet, where she cleaned herself up, then sat down on the closed toilet, letting out a disappointed sigh.

When she returned to the bedroom, Keith wasn't there. She headed downstairs and found him hurriedly getting dressed in the living room, his cheeks reddening with embarrassment as he saw her coming down the stairs.

Keith tried to explain. He apologised, then he said that had never happened before. That's the worst thing that a guy can say in such a situation, as it makes the woman think that the problem is *them.*

Georgia put aside her disappointment and tried to ease the tension that Keith's early explosion had caused – he was a nice guy, despite the early splatting. She asked him if he was going home.

Then Keith unwittingly used a trick that, since the dawn of time, all men have had trouble performing at such times – he was honest - he truthed it.

"Look, Georgia, I'm sorry about that, I really am, total anti-climax, excuse the pun, one extreme to the other tonight in the sex department, and that's on me. See, when we were upstairs there, I just lost control. You're just so fuckin' beautiful, I *really* like you, and seeing you naked underneath me, looking up into my eyes like that, all dreamy and lustful, I couldn't help it, I just couldn't control myself – it's you, you're just perfect."

Georgia smiled, all embarrassed by the compliments, and glad she hadn't been a bitch about either the Mr Floppy thing or the early explosion thing. After all, inside, her heart was pounding, and her soul was singing – she'd finally found her man. Love was in the air. He was handsome, funny, good craic and, most importantly, had been honest with her – honesty is one of the greatest aphrodisiacs in the world. She persuaded Keith to stay the night – and after she had changed the spunk-sodden duvet cover, they went upstairs and fell asleep together in her parents' bed. Keith left in the morning feeling rough, but their parting kiss had compelled him to ask if he could call round that Sunday evening, which he did. They ate pizza together, they watched some rank rotten sci-fi film on Sky called *The Fifth Element,* no drink, no drugs, and then they kissed on the sofa for hours, before going upstairs to make love for a few more hours. Keith made her explode in joyful ecstasy with his fingers, with his mouth, and when inside her, before he eventually came himself, collapsing next to her on the big bed, both of them breathless and sweaty, overcome with post-orgasmic glow and warm, fuzzy loved-up buzzes in their souls.

Georgia was sure glad that she'd allowed Keith a mulligan regarding their first night together. The relationship was a veritable young adult whirlwind romance. Georgia herself was quite a catch for Keith, too, she looked like Jessica Rabbit's tidier sister and was very minimal in the head-nipping department, compared to many other local women her age. Throughout the rest of 1998 they went clubbing together, they drank together, they went to the cinema together, they went on holidays together, they did almost everything together. By early 1999, they had bought a two-bedroom semi-detached house in the scheme together - costing a whopping £38,000. They both had good jobs: Georgia was a supervisor at Vantanan Blinds and earned decent money, while Keith was a team-leader in the nearby Coca-Cola distribution centre. They shared a smart-as-fuck Ford Fiesta RS Turbo, and by May of 1999 Georgia was pregnant with what would be their first child, a boy, Jordan, born in February 2000. Their family got along well, they had enough money to live comfortably, and by then they had seriously cut back on the drugs, drink, and clubbing, only partaking on special occasions and only when they could get a babysitter. As far as unskilled working-class young couples in post-industrial central Scotland go, they had it all. Another child arrived in December of 2002, a wee girl whom they named Olivia. There was a Labour government, meaning that most working-class people had a bit more money and hope than they had enjoyed growing up under Thatcher and the Tories, and their economic devastation of much of Scotland.

By 2004, they had moved to a larger, three-bedroom house in a private development on the fringes of the town - £85,000, this time. They were now away from the scheme and had a big garden to enjoy with their kids. Life was sweet. With family help and some assistance from the state via Working Tax Credits, they were able to juggle parenthood and full-time work, and make it work. They had good friends - a mix of new people met through their having children, and a few loyal old pals from the scheme, who they had known since the clubbing and madness era. Towards the end of 2005, Keith proposed to Georgia, and they set the wedding date for the following year. For Georgia, it all felt like a dream come true; her life was a fairytale.

CHAPTER FOUR

Somethin' Goin' On

Georgia was out with friends for lunch one Saturday afternoon, one of those reasonably priced but fuckin' soulless Brewers Fayre type gastro pub places. 'Having lunch' – real meaning a bite to eat and far too much wine over a catchup – had gotten enormously trendy among young women in Britain back then, largely thanks to the TV show *Sex and the City*. Women everywhere were 'doing lunch' – but of course, a chain pub in Lanarkshire with a sticky carpet, mingin' toilets and young staff suffering dreadful comedowns is a far cry from a glitzy elite restaurant in New York . Nevertheless, on one Saturday of each month, Georgia met up with her old pal Isla for a bite to eat, to drink copious amounts of wine and to set the world to rights.

That particular Saturday, both of them at 1pm were dressed as if their itinerary consisted of a high-end business meeting and then an upmarket wedding reception. The post-1997 economic boom had made decent fashion cheaper and more widely available, and the red-headed Georgia and her brunette pal, Isla, were dressed to kill – not for any reason, just because that's what fashion dictated by the mid-00s, and they both liked to look nice, not for men, but for themselves. *New Look*, and other such fashion shops, had changed weekends, and many attitudes forever.

Neither Isla nor Georgia went full stereotype, though, the chicken Caesar salad on the menu was completely ignored, in place of delicious 'home-made' linguini – home-made, in pub-grub trade speak, actually meaning, 'the chef had to actually stir it at some point', but that didn't matter. They ate, they drank Blossom Hill, they moaned about their men, talked about their kids, bitched about their jobs, shared local gossip, then they waxed lyrical about their lovely men, they expressed their love for their kids, mentioned the good or funny aspects of their jobs, and reflected upon how much their lives had changed over the years, for the better. The young waiter was lovely, though he looked a bit wide-eyed and sweaty – he'd clearly had a good Friday night – but his service was still second to none. James Blunt songs were being played through the speakers, and the two girls were having a great time but were both looking forward to going home to their families later, too. When it was time to order dessert, they both ordered the chocolate fudge cheesecake, using the *fuck it* rationale. When the waiter brought the desserts, Georgia looked up to thank him and out of the corner of her eye noticed that one of the three young men sitting two tables away was none other than local hardman, Shug Mann. Georgia and Isla were sitting at a small table in a booth, so they weren't really visible to Shug and his co-diners, but Georgia could see them. Shug and his companions, one a skinhead who was even bigger than him, the other an older guy in his 40s with a cringey blonde mullet haircut, were dressed in business suits and were stuffing themselves with the Brewers Fayre's legendary all-day breakfast. They were drinking cups of coffee and each had a pint of Irn Bru, too, which calmed Georgia a bit as that meant that they weren't on it and likely to be a nuisance, more likely they'd been on it since Thursday but were now winding down, or had some business to do that day. Georgia hadn't given Shug much thought since that incident in *Paps* nightclub back in 1999. Over the years she'd heard his name mentioned a lot, mostly in work-canteen gossip, or on nights out, and, well, let's just say that what she had heard hadn't exactly extolled Shug and his minions' better virtues. On the other hand, Georgia had also heard that Shug had settled down with a younger lass named Karen and that they had kids now, so, Georgia hoped that had helped Shug in some way – there was nothing like having kids and a missus to turn edgy guys into boring twats, after all.

As Georgia and Isla ate their cheesecakes slowly, savouring every delicious mouthful of the 'home-made' dessert which the chef had actually bought frozen from his wholesaler, Georgia's eyes wandered to the table where Shug was sitting. *'Beautiful'* by James Blunt filled the Saturday afternoon air as she watched him eat his enormous afternoon fry-up, his elbows on the table, dipping his face towards the plate in order to shovel more food into his mouth with his fork, rather than using cutlery properly, like a real person. Baked bean juice and runny egg ran down the sides of his unshaven, flabby chin. He chewed with his mouth open while talking at the two guys who were eating with him, every so often a tiny piece of food would shoot out of his mouth as he spoke, landing on them, but they said nothing, didn't even seem to acknowledge that it had happened, in fact. Shug would occasionally stop eating and gesticulating, to take a huge swig of coffee, or his Irn-bru, or both, and as he guzzled, the excess drink from his mouth would run down the side of his face, as he was belching, loudly and often. Sometimes he'd stop and wipe his mouth on a napkin, but then the revolting gluttony would continue – his mates weren't that much better mannered, either.

You're beautiful
You're beautiful
You're beautiful, it's trueI
saw your face in a crowded place
And I don't know what to do
'Cause I'll never be with you

Georgia thought that they looked like a bunch of greedy, disgusting pigs, gathered around a trough. No matter, though, they were nothing to do with her, thank goodness.

Isla and Georgia ordered a couple of lattes from the waiter, then Isla went away to the toilet to freshen up. Georgia reached into her handbag and took out her new-fangled Samsung flip-phone – it had an actual camera on it and everything. She was pleased that there were no missed calls or texts, as this meant that nothing was wrong at home – Keith hadn't managed to burn down the house or accidentally open a time portal to another dimension during his afternoon alone with the kids, so, all was well.

Georgia sensed the waiter go past and turned to receive the two lattes, but it wasn't the waiter. Shug was standing there next to their table, in his suit, holding a pint of Irn-bru and having wiped all of the food away from around his mouth and chin.

"Well, well, how ye doin' Georgia?" he said, in a warm, welcoming, friendly tone.

Georgia, a little taken aback, put down her phone and answered.

"I'm good, Hugh, doing well – how are you?"

Georgia had assumed that, like most real actual adults, Shug had abandoned using his childhood nickname by now – guys who don't are invariably weirdos, after all. But the grimace on his face as she addressed him by his given name told her she'd got that wrong. Yet he answered in the same, friendly tone.

"It's Shug, mind. It's no' Sunday, Georgia. So, how's life treating ye?"

Before she could say anything, Shug had plonked himself down in Isla's seat, opposite her.

"Well, Shug, I'm still working at that same place, we've got two wee weans now, a boy and a girl, me and Keith are doing well – we're getting married next year. How about you?"

Shug just stared silently at her for a couple of seconds, then smiled broadly.

"Aye, daein' well, business is good, me and Karen have twins now, I've got responsibilities now, you know?"

"That's great Shug, I'm really happy for you, what are the twins' names? What about Karen? Where did you meet her?"

Shug continued speaking, ignoring her question.

"Oh aye, that's right, you and that Keith Smith, and you've a wee boy and a younger daughter, Keith works in the ginger warehouse, you work for Vantanan blinds. And neither of you parties hard anymore, is that right? Still livin' up in Lindsay Crescent?"

Georgia was unsettled but not surprised that Shug knew her business – she knew what he was, as it was in his nature – remembering the tale of *the scorpion and the fox* – but that didn't bother her too much. She gave him the benefit of the doubt.

After a brief pause, Shug then told her all about the twins, Karen, and how they'd helped him grow up a lot. Isla then returned, just as the waiter brought the lattes. Shug shuffled along so that Isla could get a seat and asked the waiter to bring him a latte, too. Soon the three were enjoying shallow but fun chit-chat about what having young kids in the house is like, and they were getting along just fine, though Shug's eye was firmly on Georgia almost the whole time that they were chatting. Isla's phone rang – one of those cringey dreadful polyphonic ringtones blaring *'Come with me'* by techno outfit, Special D.

At the end of every week each one of us becomes a freak.
Tonight, the DJ makes us move and then the sweat drops from the roof
Each time you let the bass beat hard to know we all spend now apart.
Just activate your energy lets sing the song and come with me...

Isla apologised and said that she had to take the call, then headed outside with her phone, leaving Georgia sitting with Shug. Georgia was pleased that Shug seemed to be more settled and she was glad that his ejection from that nightclub five years earlier hadn't been brought up. Shug spoke.

"So, it's all going well for you, Georgia? You're nice and happy." As he finished that sentence, he burped loudly, turning slightly away as he did so, but immediately turning his head back to face Georgia. He exhaled, filling her nostrils with the vilest of aromas, a mixture of stale drink, fried breakfast, coffee, alcohol and tobacco – absolutely minging.

Georgia tried not to wince at the pungent stink.

"Aye, Hugh, we've got a lovely wee life – I wouldn't swap it for anything."

Shug didn't appreciate that answer, at all, but he hid his anger at being called by his given name. He continued.

"Does it never get a bit stale, bein' with the same man all the time?"

Georgia knew exactly what he meant but the comment had taken her off-guard. She blushed, took a sip of her latte, and then a gulp of the wine that she had earlier decided not to finish.

"No Shug, I love Keith, I couldn't imagine being with another guy."

Shug smiled and nodded in agreement. Unconvincingly.

"Look, Georgia, that last time we met, in that disco, when you got me thrown out, I just wanted you to know that, as far as I'm concerned, it's all water under the bridge."

Georgia had been praying in her head that he wouldn't mention that, but now that he had, gangster hardman or not, she wasn't taking that from him.

"Eh, look, Shug, that wasn't my fault, I didn't do anything, in fact I didn't even see what it was you did to get chucked out," she lied, slightly, remembering what had subsequently happened to one of the doormen who had chucked him out that night.

"Georgia, Georgia, Georgia, it's fine, all forgotten, no need to mention it again," said Shug, trying to sound warm and magnanimous.

Somehow, the revolting psychopath had turned that incident from 1999 around in his head so that Georgia was in the wrong, and thus, by implication *he* was accepting *her* apology for his behaviour that night. That's what all deranged nutters do – a kind of mental gymnastics. Yet, in Shug's head, he had just offered a contrite, heartfelt apology.

Georgia knew that was about as close to an apology that she was ever going to get from him regarding that incident, but something about Shug's manner was now unsettling her.

"I wonder where Isla has gotten to," said Georgia, rising from the booth, but before she could walk away, Shug grabbed her forearm with one of his huge hands, and prevented her from leaving. Still seated, he looked up at her, fixing her with a greedy stare.

"You're looking hot today, hen, dressed to impress, and lookin' good for a lassie that's had two weans. Doll, if you ever want a real man, come to me, any time you want. You'll no' regret it. I've always been hot for you,

Georgia". Shug then winked and let out a loud rippling fart, still gripping her forearm with his hand.

Georgia's stomach did a somersault, and she felt her very flesh creep with disgust, made worse by the utterly stinking eggy fart that was now wafting up into her nostrils. Other diners had also noticed the stink, some covering their noses, others looking around accusingly. Georgia hoped that nobody was blaming her for the utter honk.

"Erm, look, Hugh, naw, we've had this conversation before, that's never gonnae happen, I'm happy, and I'm so glad that you're settled, too," she said, warmly but firmly, the second part of that statement partly aimed at reminding Shug that he had a partner and kids, too. Shug let go of her arm as Isla returned, Isla blurting out "Sorry, I need to go, shall we book a taxi?"

Georgia had scarce ever been so pleased to see her. They said hurried goodbyes to Shug, and then turned to leave, but as they did, Shug spoke again.

"You'll come round, they always do, you'll see." Shug then took out and puffed on a blue Ventolin inhaler several times. He then headed back to the table where his two henchmen were still seated.

Georgia didn't acknowledge what Shug had just said, but she heard it, clear as day. As she and Isla approached the pub cash register to pay their bill, they were told by the young Polish waitress that somebody had already paid the bill for them, but she didn't know who. Georgia and Isla knew exactly who had paid. They talked briefly about it in the taxi home, but used no names, as half of the town's taxi drivers were involved with Shug's dealings, one way or another. Georgia had gone from thinking of Shug as an absurd relic of her past to seeing him as being a disgusting, frightening menace in the present – and she was right. Both agreed that this man was best avoided.

CHAPTER FIVE

Never Gonna Let You Go

Georgia decided against telling Keith about her encounter with Shug; he would only worry.

Before she knew it, 2006 reared its head, and wedding bells rang for her and Keith. Georgia was from a Protestant background, while Keith came from Catholic roots – Scots Catholic, that is. Religion was never really a big deal to either of them, but their wedding reception disco had seen '*Simply the Best*' and '*You'll never walk alone*' played to accommodate both the Rangers and Celtic fans of the family. The pair danced and laughed and drank into the early hours of the morning. As they lay in bed together that night, Georgia thought back to the night they met. That dizzy, E-fuelled mess of a night that had brought them together. It felt like such a long time ago; so much had changed since then. Neither of them had touched an E for two years, and all they did now was a little bit of social drinking – pints while out watching football, wine together at home after work on a Friday, a drink or two at a work night out – and the odd joint on occasions where the kids were away staying with grandparents for the night. Georgia and Keith loved having stoned sex whenever they had the house to themselves, that's where they got their real buzz – a far cry indeed from that first night they had met, back in 1998.

By 2010, Keith and Georgia Smith, their ten-year-old son, Jordan, and their seven-year-old daughter, Olivia, were still going strong as a family, though there were challenges.

"Mum, do I have any clean school trousers?" asked Jordan, shoving an over-filled spoonful of cereal into his mouth.

"I thought you got everything ready last night?" Georgia replied, suddenly noticing that he was still wearing pyjama bottoms under the kitchen table.

"Yeah, but I couldn't find any." Jordan said, giving a shrug, not seeming to care that they only had ten minutes left before they had to leave the house.

"Have you looked in your cupboard?" Keith chimed in, sifting through a pile of folded clothes sitting on one of the chairs.

"Yeah, I've looked there."

"What about in your chest of drawers?" Georgia suggested.

"I don't know."

"Well, could you go and look, please?" she asked, trying hard to keep her cool at her son's nonchalance.

Jordan tipped the rest of the milk from his cereal bowl into his mouth and ran up the stairs to check. Meanwhile, Georgia began pulling the washing she had just loaded into the machine back out to see if there were any school trousers that would do a second day. Keith ventured cautiously into Jordan's schoolbag in case he had any spare ones jammed in there.

"Mummy, Daddy, look what I can do!" Olivia cried from the living room, oblivious to her parents' rising panic and frustration.

"What is it, love?" Georgia called, still rummaging through the dirty laundry.

"Come and see!"

Georgia let out a heavy sigh, but she knew Olivia wouldn't quit until she got her audience, so she peeked her head around the living room door and said, "Ok, I'm here, what is it?"

"Where's Dad?" Olivia asked, refusing to start without him.

"Keith!" Georgia called, failing to mask the bite in her voice.

Keith appeared and Olivia took her position at one end of the living room. She raised her hands, leaned forward, and did a cartwheel. Although impressed by her daughter's gymnastic ability, it really wasn't the best time to showcase it, and Georgia couldn't help but notice how close she had come to knocking the lamp off the coffee table.

"That's great, darling, but can we save cartwheel practice for the garden where there's more space?"

She didn't wait for the reply, still acutely aware of the 'missing trousers' crisis. She darted back into the kitchen and back to the laundry pile, which was now spread across the kitchen floor. There had to be a pair of school trousers somewhere.

"Did you find any?" She called upstairs to Jordan.

No reply.

Georgia lifted a scrunched pair of trousers from the pile and gave them a shake. They were no good; they were caked in dry mud again, obviously Jordan had been playing football with his friends at lunchtime.

Keith came back into the kitchen and began stacking the breakfast dishes beside the sink.

"Any luck?" He asked Georgia.

"No, there's no way he can wear these." She held them up for Keith to see, and as she did so, she noticed a large rip down the back of one of the legs.

"Oh, for fuck's sake! Not another pair of trousers! That's the fourth one since August!" She raged, inspecting the hole and wondering if she would be able to repair them rather than forking out for yet another pair.

Keith looked at his watch. "Shit, we're going to be late," he said, then he urgently called, "Jordan, did you find your trousers? Remember to check under your bed!"

There was a scuffling noise from upstairs, and a few moments later, a voice called, "Found them!"

Just as Georgia was ready to breathe a sigh of relief, there was a crash from the living room. She and Keith rushed through to find Olivia, red-faced, trying to hide the broken lamp under a cushion.

"Olivia, I thought I told you to save your cartwheel practice for outside?"

"It wasn't a cartwheel; it was a handstand!" Olivia protested.

Georgia rubbed her forehead and took a deep breath to stop herself saying anything she would regret. Sensing her rising anger, Keith tactfully instructed the kids to put their shoes and coats on, while Georgia did her best to clear away the shards of porcelain. 'Great, now I have to buy a new pair of school trousers *and* a new lamp!' Georgia thought to herself.

In the background, as if to add insult to injury, the TV news reporter said, "Families everywhere are struggling with rising costs, and now they are waiting with bated breath to see whether the new Conservative government will do any better than its predecessor."

"Oh, fuck off!" Georgia groaned, grabbing the remote and stabbing her thumb into the power button.

As she got to her feet, on the verge of tears, Keith stepped back into the room and put his arms around her.

"We'll be alright," he said, knowing that her stress was less to do with the kids' chaos and more to do with their tight finances. Things had been tough since she had been made redundant from Vantanan Blinds. The new job at the Sky TV call-centre was ok, but it was a longer commute and a smaller pay packet. She never complained about it, but Keith knew it was taking its toll.

Georgia hugged into him, feeling the tension begin to drain from her shoulders as she drew in a deep breath and let it go. Somehow, he always seemed to know how to make her feel better.

"Yeah," she agreed, "yeah, we'll be ok."

Olivia looked up at them with sad eyes as they walked into the hallway. "I'm sorry, Mum," she said sheepishly.

Georgia looked at her daughter's apologetic expression and her heart melted.

"It's ok, sweetie, it's just a lamp," she replied, smiling, then added, "But please ... no more gymnastics in the house."

∽⤳

While Georgia's redundancy had been a huge blow for the Smith family, there had been one up-side. Georgia had been able to follow a wee dream of hers and started studying part-time to become an accountant – she had always been good with numbers. While working full-time and studying, Georgia still did her best to spend as much time as possible with her beloved children, and with her man, Keith.

The banking crash of 2008/09 and then the resurgence of the Conservative Party were indeed bad news for most families in Scotland. Mortgages went up, the cost of living increased and wages flatlined, unable to keep up with soaring inflation. Georgia and Keith had bought their first house at just the right time, though, so, while their repayments skyrocketed, they were never in any real danger of losing their home, during those tough times – the saying at the time seemed true – if you bought before 2005 you were fine – if you hadn't, you were fucking finished. Things still got much tighter for them financially, though, and the cost of the family, the house, the bills, debts, and running two cars left them far less money at the end of each month. But, they were able to keep things steady – as long as they both had full-time jobs, they were fine.

However, 2010 was not done messing with the Smith family. As part of a global 'restructuring' drive, Coca-Cola had that year announced that they were downsizing the local depot, allocating around a third of the customers that it currently served to their North of England depot, instead. Around a third of the workforce at the Scottish depot was no longer needed, so, 150 workers faced redundancy. The restructuring also comprised of the depot changing shift patterns and getting all employees who were retained to sign new contracts, in essence making them new employees. 'Restructuring' is big business speak for callous firms utterly shafting their employees to preserve their profits.

Keith and Georgia talked it over and decided that, as Keith had been there for over a decade, it would be best for him, and for the family, if he took the voluntary redundancy package on offer – over £40,000. Keith was a good worker and would easily find something else, and the lump sum would really help to provide the family with a security buffer in the bank, in case life threw anything bad at them.

Keith finished up with Coca-Cola on the Friday and started his new job the very next Monday. His new job was working as a van driver and labourer for his old pal Neil's small building business.

Keith and Neil had known each other since school, in fact, Neil had also worked in the Coca-Cola depot beside Keith for a while some years back, driving forklifts, but had been sacked for gross misconduct after dropping a full pallet of Sprite from height-level 12 on the racking, which had almost killed him, falling onto the top of his forklift. The sturdy truck roof saved his life but he had ended up drenched through with the fizzy drink and had had to be sent home. That wasn't the real reason that he was sacked, though. Neil had been writing hilarious insulting poems about depot supervisors and other employees in the staff toilets and the bosses had it in for him for that, but couldn't catch him for it, despite all but knowing that it was him. On one occasion, not long before the Sprite incident, they had all gotten together and decided to make Neil repaint the toilet, thinking that would teach him a humiliating abject lesson about the graffiti, most of which targeted overweight supervisors and managers who all supported the same football team. This backfired spectacularly, when Neil happily accepted the painting task, but not before warning the bosses that he had no experience of painting at all. The bosses were insistent that he complete the task, so, he did, and he made a right cunt of it. Paint on the floor, paint on the mirrors, paint on the bog seat, the walls weren't done properly, there was paint on the light, and the task took him all day, a whole shift. Furious managers hastily arranged a disciplinary meeting, but Neil took the warehouse USDAW union representative to it and the union rep was quick to point out that, though Neil's contract did specify that he could be used for *ad-hoc* duties – boss speak for *'you'll do what we fucking say'* – Neil had no experience as a painter, he was employed as a forklift driver, so, he couldn't have been expected to have carried out the task competently. Moreover, the union rep suggested that whichever boss had chosen Neil for such a task must surely be incompetent. Livid, but unable to take the matter further, the bosses were forced to back down. Neil then took three weeks off on the sick, claiming to be suffering from a chest infection, caused by the fumes from the painting job, and the union rep insisted that Neil be paid a full wage for those three weeks, as he had acquired his illness because of poor management. So, Neil had won that battle, however, the bosses really had it in for him after that – he was a marked man, and the absence from work over the paint fumes thing was his fourth absence in 12 months, so, when he returned to work, the pricks gave him a 52-week final written warning . That meant that the next time that he did anything wrong, at all, like dropping a pallet of juice from Level 12, endangering himself, others and company property, he was toast. So, he'd bought two vans with savings and set himself up as a building maintenance company, doing janitorial work, grounds work, repairs, landscaping, gardening, and anything else he fancied. Property maintenance, management consultancy and being a top football player agent – three jobs that any cunt can make a killing at without needing a single qualification.

So, Keith went to work for Neil and was soon earning more than he ever had at the warehouse, and most of the work was Monday to Friday day shift, too, much more preferable to working shifts in a warehouse on an 'any five from seven' days basis. His switching to days really helped, as now Keith was always in the house of an evening, meaning they needed to rely on childcare a bit less whenever Georgia was backshift at Sky.

Keith was also able to start going to the football again now and then with Neil and the rest of the folk who frequented the local Celtic Supporters Bus. He started going to their social functions, too, which ranged from charity discos to rowdy Irish rebel music concerts. Keith had never really been into the political side of being a Celtic fan before, after all, his beloved wife was a nominal Rangers fan and a Protestant, and he himself had no Irish ancestry in his family, but he liked the catchy songs and the banter. Sometimes Georgia would even come to the rebel gigs with him, as she knew a lot of the punters at them, too.

CHAPTER SIX

You Don't Know Me

The second consequence of the 2008-10 banking crises and the return of the Tories was far more destructive for Scotland as a whole. At some point in 2008-2010, beginning under the outgoing Labour government then tacitly continued under the Tories, the state stopped giving a fuck about the drugs trade. Big dealers were left alone, as long as they didn't bother or harass legitimate businesses or law-abiding members of the public – for many dealers, it seemed, it was boom time – they had a free pass, and they knew it.

Georgia and Keith had, of course, partaken of drugs when they were younger, a few Es back in the day, and they still liked weed – like hundreds of thousands of other Scots did, too. Most people under 40 had very liberal attitudes towards these drugs and saw no problem with their decriminalisation or even their legalisation. At some point, the state, too, realised that it was fighting a losing battle against the drugs trade, but it wasn't E or Hash that it decided to quietly ignore. No, the state, or the global elite, or whoever controls such things in the world, seemed to have made a quite different, chilling, devastating decision about drug liberalisation.

"If the plebs want drugs, we'll give them fucking drugs. But not these fiver-a-pill Es or this hash stuff, no, if they want drugs, we'll let them have

cocaine. *Expensive, addictive, life-ruining cocaine. We'll flood the country with the fucking stuff. It's far more profitable, it might even save the doomed edifice of western capitalism. Rich and middle-class folk will lap that up, and if they get addicted, fuck them, they can afford it, they can go to rehab, or lose their house. And as for the poor, well, who cares about them? If the drug causes havoc and misery in the schemes, it's only the schemes, right, it's only the poor? How can they afford it in the first place, anyway? Fuck them. As long as the scheme's problems are confined to the schemes, who gives a fuck? We'll keep it illegal, though, at least technically, then the police can still deal with any traffickers or dealers who break the unwritten rules." (Sic).*

The above may not have been by anybody's direct design, but that's still basically what happened, in the UK and beyond. Cocaine had always been around, but from the mid-2000s it seemed to be everywhere, though often in very poor quality. However, by around 2009, there were two types of marching powder available – 'Pure' was decent quality stuff that had only been cut or diluted 20 or 30 times since leaving Latin America. It was still full of crap, but was still also very strong, and when it arrived around 2009 it cost around £100 per gram, a far cry from 'Council', the white powder that had been doing the rounds in the UK since 2001, which only cost around £35 per gram. It got people wasted but contained precious little actual cocaine, being bulked up with baby teething powder, dental anaesthetic, ground up nicotine lozenges or caffeine pills, laxative powder, farming chemicals, and basically any old crap that traffickers, and then dealers, had cut it with to maximise their profits.

One very nasty side effect of the explosion of the cocaine trade in the UK was the return of feudalism to the country's housing estates. People in schemes who were addicted to cocaine and other drugs became little more than cash cows, serfs used for profit with impunity by their quasi-feudal untouchable local baron, the dealer. The 'Baron' no longer required of the serf his or her labour, nor their military service – these new barons, they only wanted your fucking money – all of it, and if that ruins your life and destroys your community, well, tough luck, fuck you, he's the untouchable baron and there's precious little that you can do about him. There was one such dealer in the town where the Smith family lived – Shug Mann.

By 2010, aged 30, Shug had a small drug-dealing empire and a successful decorating business, HM Decorators. His company vans were painted in claret and amber, the colours of the family's favourite football team, Motherwell. Karen and the kids were gone by then, Karen initially to a women's refuge, the twins into care with social services, as, sadly, when it came to family life, Shug was just like his dad. He had cheated on Karen multiple times during their time together, was rarely sober or straight and even when he was, he was still unstable, regularly beating Karen to a pulp. The young family hadn't been short of money and yet, to Shug, every penny was a prisoner. His domestic skinflint tendencies were poles apart from the lavish lifestyle that he led outside the family home. Frequent late-night cocaine and alcohol sessions with his henchmen were the norm, usually in pubs, in houses or at strip clubs in Glasgow, always with a gaggle of younger women in tow who were there primarily for the drugs, and for the street cred of hanging around with gangsters. Many a night, Shug would get home at 4am absolutely wasted and would then explode with rage when Karen asked him where he had been. These confrontations invariably ended up with Karen getting a sore face while the twins cowered in fear among their freshly pissed sheets upstairs. Shug also limited Karen's access to money, so that she couldn't leave him, a common tactic used by psychopaths to keep their partner in line since time immemorial. Karen had seen that it all wouldn't end well for her or for her children, so fearing that when they grew older the twins would become Shug's next victims, Karen had saved up what little cash she could over the space of 12 months, then run for the hills. Shug blamed her for it all, like all abusive narcissists do. Social services had arrived at his door on the afternoon of the same day that Karen had run – it had been Karen who had phoned them, and Shug was, for once, helpless as his children were taken away from him by social workers backed up by the police – ironically, on that one day that he had actually promised to spend some time with the kids, while Karen was out 'shopping'. However, convinced of his own innocence in the whole situation, Shug soon went back to business as usual as though nothing had happened.

One of his lackeys ran the decorating business for him while he continued to run the drug-dealing enterprise, selling weed, ecstasy, speed, and later cocaine. Shug was a clever bastard in that he never used the telephone to conduct business of that nature – a tip that he had picked up from watching the movie *Goodfellas* one night as a teen in his bedroom, with the volume up loud to drown out all of the screaming from downstairs. He had lackeys doing his distribution, his collections, his dealing and even his enforcement in the schemes. The years 2000-08 had been a boom time for drug dealers, and by 2010 Shug was a millionaire – although he had to appear to be living the life of a successful business owner, rather than that of a drugs baron, so, his cars remained impressive but not excessive. He stayed put in the same house, resisting the temptation to go full-on Tony Soprano by buying a big fuck-off mansion somewhere– because it was idiot dealers who went splashing cash about like that who always got caught. His decorating business could only launder so much of his ill-gotten gains every year, nowhere near enough to remain plausible, so, much of Shug's wealth remained hidden, in cash, stashed discretely on his property, or hidden in Paypal accounts that he had coerced his lackeys into opening for him – always in their names.

He did, however, move his elderly mother into a luxurious private sheltered housing complex in Glasgow, the city she'd originally hailed from, where he visited her twice a week and always made sure that she was ok and had everything that she needed – after all, horrid gangster types always seem to love their ma, no matter how much they seem to despise other human beings.

Having failed miserably at the whole 'woman and kids' setup, in the years after Karen left, Shug had used his wealth and power in order to fill that particular void in his life. There was no shortage of beautiful, naive young women who found hard-men devilishly attractive in the central Scotland clubs, drugs and parties scene, after all, and Shug used his name, his money and his limitless supply of gear to bed as many of them as possible. On the odd occasion when no such young women were easily available, he was no stranger to using other sometimes darker methods, to sate his increasingly voracious carnal desires and need for basic human company. If a young woman from the scheme owed him tick for drugs, he could use that debt as leverage and work out 'an arrangement' with them. If they refused, he usually either added extra money to their bill, or, if they remained steadfast in refusing to sell their bodies to him in such a manner, he could make a few calls and suddenly that particular lass wouldn't be able to buy any sort of gear within a ten-mile radius – sometimes that brought desperate, craven women who had previously spurned his advances into his bed at the second attempt, sometimes it didn't. With all the drug money he'd rinsed from everybody in the schemes, he could easily afford to splash out on hookers, too, when all else failed, but only as a last resort, as he found confident, empowered escort girls, whom he had no control over outside of the agreed meeting time, to be a bit intimidating, particularly as the girls' boss was a notorious Glasgow gangster who was far higher up the food chain than he was.

Shug used his power, his drugs and his money to mess with ladies and young men, too. He knew exactly who was addicted to what in the schemes. He told his minion dealers to raise prices for certain guys whom he viewed as threats, or who dated women he knew, or whom he merely suspected didn't respect him enough. He used young laddies as drugs couriers, and gave them hash instead of money as payment, thus guaranteeing their future custom, and their loyalty. He'd also get the ones he trusted to do some of the more petty dirty work that he didn't want his regular minions doing, things like smashing somebody's window, or torching their car, or putting fireworks through the letterboxes of the elderly parents of people who owed him money. Nobody ever grassed on Shug, fear of him and his minions kept the schemes in line, and because his affairs, indiscretions and crimes deliberately didn't target the well-off or the well-connected, he operated with relative impunity. He was on the police's radar for years, but he was clever – no phone calls, everything done in person, so he largely flew under their radar.

Though a proud womaniser, Shug was certainly no Adonis and never had been. He'd always been a bit chubby, though he had stretched and became more muscular as a young man, but as the 2000s became the 2010s, all those late nights of lager, drugs, takeaway food, sleeping in all day and not doing very much actual work - beyond having meetings and dishing out beatings - had caught up with him. He wasn't an ugly man; he was just mediocre in the looks department. He had 'number 4' shaved black hair, with a receding hairline, was just over six feet tall and was a bit overweight – about 18 stone all in, with a beer belly and a big arse. He was muscular and bearish, menacing and imposing in stature, with huge hands and feet. His eyes, which many in the past said were his best feature, were big and brown, and he wore designer stubble. He could usually be found wearing either a snappy business suit, custom made due to his size – most fat bastards have to go down that route – or a Motherwell FC trackie top and loose fitting jeans, with a Stone Island baseball cap – the latter outfit was usually worn during the day if he was out checking on the decorating business or going to the shops. He looked somewhat ridiculous in that particular getup, but nobody would ever be daft enough to say that to his face.

He was the size that he was because of his lifestyle choices. Often during his nasty, abusive deprived childhood, there hadn't been much food in the house and what there had been hadn't been great, at all. So, when he metamorphosed from troubled teen into local gangster with plenty of money, he was able to buy whatever he liked to stuff his face with, like a starving Russian peasant in a French patisserie, and as the years went by, it showed, and yet, the overweight figure, double chin and his ever-swelling arse didn't seem to put off the type of women he pursued – whatever his faults, damaged young women flocked to him, like flies around shite.

Shug had grown up to be wealthy, powerful and an alpha male within the schemes; he was a product of his environment, both his home environment as a child and his wider local environment, the housing schemes. He was not to be fucked with. However, in spite of it all, he still couldn't get the one thing he really wanted – Georgia.

He was used to getting his own way, manipulating himself into unwilling women's beds, using his dominance in the schemes to do as he pleased. But, he didn't have control over Georgia like that. She didn't seem to work the same way other women did. She had refused him on more than one occasion, and that didn't sit well with Shug's ego. In his mind, he deserved her, and she had no right to turn him down. His mind ran wild with fantasies of all the things he wanted to do to her.

He would get her one day. He knew it. He just had to figure out how.

CHAPTER SEVEN

Bullet In the Gun

Oblivious to Shug's continued obsession with Georgia, she and Keith went on with their life as usual. Georgia was relishing the challenge of her Accounting course, and Keith was enjoying being able to actively engage in his love of football with his new workmate, Neil.

In 2012, Celtic's city rivals, Glasgow Rangers – a great Scottish sporting institution – hit financial trouble and ended up going bust, much to the mirth of many fans of other Scottish clubs, and to the great despair of Rangers fans, who were themselves blameless for the debacle. In a way, the whole episode was a tragedy for a large swathe of Scotland's working class, after all.

The once-mighty Govan side ended up starting again in the 4th tier of Scottish football and Celtic became the undisputed kings of Scotland's dreadful domestic football setup.

Because of Celtic's dominance and a renewed interest in all things rebellious, republican and anti-establishment in Scotland caused by the looming 2014 referendum on Scottish independence, there were a lot more of these Irish rebel and Celtic concerts happening all over Lanarkshire, Glasgow and beyond. Keith and Neil started going to a lot of them, sometimes with other folk off the local Celtic bus, sometimes just the two of them. Much chatter at these types of nights inevitably turned to the

2014 referendum. Like most Celtic fans, Keith and Neil weren't opposed to independence, but as socialists they didn't like the idea of splitting the working class on the island of Britain along ethnic grounds, as had been the case in Ireland since 1922. Moreover, they were both homeowners with pension pots and with wives and kids and didn't want to take the risk of Scotland ending up as Greece or the Republic of Ireland had after the 2008 global banking crash.

Nevertheless, they both gave it big licks at the rebel nights they went to, and on the Celtic bus, and they had a bloody good time. They were only really there for the beer, the football and the companionship. On the night of September 18th 2014, though, while at a Christy Moore Tribute Artist show in Carfin Hibs club, things changed.

Don't forget your shovel if you want to go to work.
Oh don't forget your shovel if you want to go to work.
Don't forget your shovel if you want to go to work
Or you'll end up where you came from like the rest of us
Diggin', diggin', diggin'

It had been polling day in the independence referendum and someone from the Celtic bus had brought along a large bag of cocaine. Keith had taken coke once or twice in the early 2000s and wasn't that impressed by it, but the stuff available by 2014 was far purer, far stronger, and that night, Keith really enjoyed spending half of the evening in the toilets snorting the stuff with his football friends, as did Neil, before spending the rest of the night at a house party in Motherwell, where the host had a set of DJ decks. The party went on until around 4am, with Neil deciding that the next day would be an impromptu holiday for Keith and him. Keith got home at around 6am, just as Georgia was getting up to get ready for her dayshift in

Livingston. She wasn't best pleased with the utterly embarrassing, melted state of her husband but he was in good fettle and was pleased to see her, so she wasn't angry. The kids would both be off to Georgia's mum's when Georgia left for work, anyway, as Keith was supposed to have been working dayshift that Friday, too, so, he got a good few hours of half sleep in his bed once Georgia and the kids left, and later felt bad about the state that he had come home in, so that afternoon he cooked the family's favourite meal, home-made lasagne and chips, with salad, plus a Vienetta for after, which they all devoured together that evening. Later on, when the kids were asleep, Georgia took advantage of the fact that she knew Keith would still be feeling really horny after his wild antics on the coke, and the two made passionate love in their big bed, Georgia riding Keith like he was Seabiscuit as they both struggled to remain quiet amid their lustful shagging.

The next night, the Saturday, wee Olivia was away at a sleepover at one her friends' houses and young Jordan was away to a late cinema show with friends from school, so, Keith and Georgia had the house to themselves for a few hours. They drank a bottle of Blossom Hill, finished off the small amount of cocaine that Keith had found in his jeans pocket and danced around the living room like teenagers together to Avicii.

So, wake me up when it's all over
When I'm wiser and I'm older
All this time I was finding myself, and I
Didn't know I was lost

As they danced and laughed with each other to the sweet music, the four to the floor beat regressed them both back to when they had first met, and soon they were kissing passionately on the living room carpet, before scrambling upstairs to the bedroom to have unbridled, loud, epic cocaine-fuelled sex, both of them cumming like express trains before collapsing, exhausted in bed together. That certainly put a spring in their step the next day, which they spent with the kids at home, watching movies and finishing off the lasagne, after all, home-made lasagne is always better the day after. That evening, as Keith and Georgia lay content in bed, cuddled up watching *Father Ted* on *More4*, Georgia spoke to Keith.

"You were in some state on Friday morning, by the way. Still, last night was amazing, eh?"

"Too right it was," said Keith, with a smile. Georgia continued.

"That coke was fun, but we really shouldn't be doing that anymore, we've got the kids to look after, and our jobs, I don't mind a wee joint every now and then, but don't you think we should stay away from the class A stuff from now on? Look at the pure state of everybody else our age who still does it, I mean, we're in our mid-30s now, shall we quit while we're ahead? I don't need that stuff, I just want you, and the weans, Keith."

Keith pondered for a second then replied "Aye, it was good to relive the auld days, but you're right, lets consign that stuff to the history books – we don't want to get into taking that stuff all the time."

Georgia gave Keith a big kiss and then smiled, looking into his eyes, before rolling back to her side of the bed, where they both laughed out loud watching Bishop Brennan being kicked up the arse.

They were happy, so happy. They'd been together for 15 years by then. They'd met on a drink and drugs bender and were still going strong. Now they had jobs, cars, two beautiful children and a lovely home, as well as each other. They had everything. Georgia had been concerned that Keith had taken coke quite a few times in the last two years, even though it was only at special nights out, and he was never out of order on it. She was relieved that he agreed that there would be no more cocaine in their lives as when

Keith said he'd do something he always did it. That night she drifted off to sleep, happy. Content.

CHAPTER EIGHT

Music Sounds Better With You

Keith didn't stop taking cocaine.

What he did do, at first, was to try to ration his use of it and keep control of it.

He'd have a wee sniff at nights out or at Celtic bus functions, or at the football, or at work, because Neil always had some on him.

Yes, Keith tried to stay in control of his cocaine use – just like millions of others have tried and failed to do – coke doesn't work like that.

Through the rest of 2014 to 2016, Keith, Georgia and the kids still enjoyed a pretty sweet life. By 2016 young Jordan was in the army cadets and getting ready to start 5th year at high school, he was outgoing, popular, and sporty. Wee Olivia was 14 by then and a fiery but sweet redhead, just like her mother. She was sporty, too, and had been signed by Hamilton Accies' newly formed girls football team, so Keith and Georgia were often busy driving her to and from training, and back and forth from matches.

Georgia's mum, Janice, a formidable, loving, warm woman, had a heart attack in the summer of 2016 and almost died. This hit the family hard, but they got through it, and all four of them became involved in doing more to help out Georgia's mum and dad, as her mum couldn't do much around the house anymore.

Throughout all, Georgia and Keith kept up their full-time jobs, knowing that they'd have the mortgage paid off by 2025. They had plenty of money put aside for if the kids wanted to go to university, too.

Things changed in January of 2017. Neil's building maintenance business was in trouble, partly because of the soaring cost of his cocaine habit, partly down to uncertainty in the commercial property market, caused by the 2016 UK referendum on leaving the European Union – the narrow margin vote in favour of *Brexit* had really made the business community shite their pants, big time, and it had made the banks miserly when it came to lending money to small businesses once more.

Neil had enough work to keep Keith on, but to stay afloat and to cut costs, he cut a deal with a local businessman that would see Neil's tiny operation henceforth come under the umbrella of a local firm called *HM Solutions*, who specialised in all sorts of construction, refurbishment and maintenance work. One of the other companies under that firm's umbrella was HM Decorators – Shug Mann's painting and decorating mob...

CHAPTER NINE

Dreaming

March of 2017 brought some good news for the Smith family, as Georgia, sick of commuting to Livingston every day for work and also now a qualified accountant, secured a new job with Lanarkshire Council, as a statistical procurement officer – whatever the fuck that is.

The money was better and the location was only a ten-minute drive away.

Georgia found out through a colleague at the council who oversaw public tenders for council contracts that the firm who had absorbed the small company that her husband, Keith, worked for, *HM Solutions,* was bidding for many council contracts – everything from school maintenance to landscape gardening. That would've been good news, were it not for the unsettling additional information that HM Solutions' CEO was a local businessman by the name of Hugh 'Shug' Mann. Georgia's husband was now an employee of a rather nasty piece of work, and Georgia didn't need to do very much digging at work to find out just what a big man that Shug Mann had become, since she had last encountered him some 12 years earlier.

She learned that Shug now had numerous businesses throughout Lanarkshire and beyond, most of them bearing the 'HM' moniker – HM Decorating, HM Landscaping, HM Cleaning, HM Couriers, HM

Removals, and half a dozen other firms, all indirectly under the umbrella of HM Solutions. He had a head office in Hamilton now and had moved to a big posh house in Bothwell back in 2012. Only when she learned this did Georgia realise that she had, in fact, seen the various HM vans all over the place in the last eight years or so, she just hadn't given any thought to who the HM in the company names referred to.

At home one night, as they were eating a pizza together, Georgia confronted Keith and asked him if he knew who he was really working for. Keith stared at the ground for a second then confessed that he knew, it was Shug, though he said he had only met the guy twice. To Georgia, that was the first time that Keith had ever lied to her – withholding information can be as bad as lying, after all. She told Keith how hurt she was that he had not told her who his new real boss was. Keith filled in the rest for her, telling quite a tale.

Around 2008, as the banks had crashed, and the new stronger, more expensive 'pure' cocaine had hit the streets of central Scotland, Shug had gotten out of the E and speed trade altogether and had delegated the running of his weed empire to one of his lackeys - a lanky, dangerous streak of piss by the name of Thommo – the weed business was, at that time, in the process of transitioning from solid to grass, which, in time, would treble its value, so there was no way that Shug was going to give that up altogether.

However, Shug's most important commodity was the new strong cocaine. To dealers and criminals, it was simply white gold. Ten times the profit made from weed could be racked up by selling coke. It was far more addictive, too, which appealed to Shug's sadistic nature. He knew full well that heavy cokeheads will keep buying and buying until they've spent every penny that they have in the world, and then they'll try to start on other people's money. Eventually, men who succumb to it fully end up involved in crime to fund the habit, in jail, or hanging themselves, while women who develop a long-term liking for the 'marching powder' and need to keep obtaining it usually ended up on their knees sucking cock just to get some, one way or another. Those were just the kind of customers that Shug wanted, so he had quickly established a local monopoly on selling the drug, using a mixture of intimidation and downright thuggery. His diverse array of local businesses gave him good means by which to launder the cash, too. After all, who really checks to see if a painting and decorating job listed on a company's accounts was real? Who really checks to see if a series of lucrative parcel deliveries and collections were genuine? The answer is simple – nobody.

Shug's businesses were real businesses, and on paper they were near FTSE levels of finance, but in reality, they were really just twenty-odd vans driving around doing various jobs here and there to make his tax return, and those of his lackeys, look good.

Keith also confessed to Georgia that Neil's wee firm being taken under the wing of HM Solutions had been less of an exciting pragmatic merger and more of a hostile takeover. Neil had been into Shug for almost 30 grand in coke debt. Shug had continually allowed Neil to keep getting bags of coke on tick, knowing that the higher the tick bill became, the less likely it was that Neil would ever be able to pay it back, which would put Shug in a position where he owned Neil, and his company. One afternoon, Neil's request for a quarter of coke had been suddenly met with Shug saying, "You owe me 30 grand, and I want it, now, or you'll be fuckin' sorry." The terrified Neil thus had no choice but to become an employee of Shug, signing over his vans and other business assets to HM Solutions and thereafter being Shug's bitch, in essence, as Neil still needed coke AND a wage to live off. That was pretty much how Shug acquired most of his other businesses, too – find out which coke customers had something worth taking, let them go crazy running up a huge tick bill, then take everything they had, usually retaining them as a pathetic, but loyal lackey. These unfortunate losers had helped to buy Shug a big house in Bothwell, and there was nothing that they could do about it – their craving for that white powder that he had a local monopoly on kept them in his power, even after he had rinsed them. It's like the scorpion and the fox, that's just what dealers do, it's in their nature.

Georgia was shocked at Keith's revelation but deep down she wasn't really that surprised. Then a terrifying realisation dawned on her – Keith was involved in all this now, too, as he worked for Neil. She looked Keith in the eye and calmly asked him.

"Do you still use cocaine, Keith? Do you?"

"Nooooo, of course not," said Keith, dismissively, adding "Neil does, though, at the weekends."

"But you don't, do you?" Georgia pressed him again.

"Of course I don't, we agreed, remember, no more class As," said Keith, in a reassuring tone.

Georgia was relieved, she knew him after all, he wouldn't have kept doing that.

They both went back to finishing their pizza – a nice Italian one, not a commercial toxic-sludge sugar-fest, as they giggled at a comedy series on BBC about zany metal detectorists.

Chapter Ten

The Bomb

Keith, like many addicts, had become something of a master at hiding his habit.

Since agreeing with his wife to knock the cocaine on the head back in September 2014, Keith had initially tried to do just that. He still went to nights out with friends, colleagues and people from the Celtic bus. He managed a few months of sticking to beer only, but a couple of years of on/off coke use had completely changed the way that his mind worked, forever. He would get to the four- or five-pints stage and his brain, his body, even his soul would start to feel an urgent craving for something more, something to perk him up a bit. There were a few times not long after he had agreed not to sniff the stuff anymore that he was successful in abstaining– he would leave house parties early, and get a chippy on the way home, instead. He would leave the pub right after the final whistle of whatever televised match that it was showing to avoid the post-match lines in the toilets and so as not to end up back at anybody's house after the pub closed. He even took the car to a few of the Celtic supporters functions, so that he couldn't drink, and thus wouldn't be tempted to consume anything else. Sometimes he avoided social gatherings altogether, choosing to go to the gym, or to go swimming, or doing things with Georgia and the kids. These avoidance tactics only worked for a little while, though.

Soon, he was back on it. Peer pressure was the trigger that eventually broke his initial period of abstention, at the local Celtic supporters' club Christmas function. Everybody at that night out seemed to be on it, off their faces, slavering absolute pish, confident, swaggering, empathic, jovial – and having fun, while Keith just sat there with his pint of lager, tops. On one trip to the toilet, two younger lads invited Keith into a toilet cubicle for a line, and he cracked, snorting a pretty stingy, miserably thin line off of a manky toilet cistern. To Keith, that one line made him feel like Asterix the Gaul after drinking his special magic potion – it felt like coming home – he felt invincible, and he wanted more. The Christmas party then became to him what it was to almost everybody else in attendance – a fucking cartoon. He had another three lines that night – snorting Neil's good stuff instead of the stuff he'd had from the young fellas – unsurprisingly, Neil's stuff was like rocket-fuel, by comparison.

Keith had four lines that evening in total, and ended up on the dancefloor, sweating with his shirt off along with all the other revellers, badly singing along to a dance music version of The Fields of Athenry. It's weird how the tune of that beautiful Irish ballad is used as an anthem by both sides of Scotland's ingrained quasi-religious divide. In truth, so called blue nights and green nights aren't really that different – lots of drunk, melted people having a good time, pledging allegiance to one cause and hatred towards another, glorifying the deaths of their ' enemy' while eulogising the lives of their own martyrs, most being completely oblivious to the fact that the way that they're behaving would have Jesus Christ doing a facepalm. Most people who go these types of night, of either side, aren't knuckle-dragging bigots, terrorist sympathisers or religious maniacs, though – it's mostly about simple tradition and having a good time – the minority who take it all seriously and let it infect their everyday lives are invariably sad fuckers, to some degree. While Keith and Neil's 'green' function was in full swing, across town at the bowling club, the 'blue' night, the Christmas party for the town's staunchest Protestants, loyalists and Rangers supporters was in full swing, also, and they were all doing the same cocaine, bought from the same dealer – they'd even booked their DJ from the same local company – HM Discos.

After the green night, Keith and Neil had gone back to a house party, but Keith was exhausted and didn't want to go home to Georgia all wide-eyed and melted, so, he didn't take any of the coke that he was offered at the afterparty and instead just had a few puffs of a joint and drank two pints of tap water, before heading off home. At the house party, they'd been joined by some people they knew who'd been at the blue night in the bowling club, and all present had partied together – drugs, after all, always transcended the sectarian divide.

Georgia was asleep when he got in, as he knew she would be, so Keith got away with his illicit consumption, that night.

CHAPTER ELEVEN

As The Rush Comes

As 2017 rolled on, things still looked rosy for the Smith family. Keith was getting a lot of overtime working with Neil, while Georgia was really enjoying her job with the council – she had a lot of responsibility there now and she relished that. Jordan was nearly 17 and was turning into a young man. He was tall and handsome, bright, athletic and kind. He had his heart set on joining the army, having excelled as a cadet, but his mum and dad didn't want him to do that. Eventually they reached a compromise with Jordan that he could join the army, but only after first obtaining a university degree and only if he went to Sandhurst and trained to be an officer – his parents promising to financially back him all the way through university, if he chose that path – anything to stop him enlisting in the infantry as a private straight from school. Jordan was pleased and his early path in life seemed promising. With the right grades from his highers he planned to go on and do an engineering degree before going to Sandhurst to become an engineer officer – his granddad had been one during the Korean War. Jordan, by then, also had a lovely girlfriend in tow, a lass his own age named Ciara.

Olivia was almost 15 by then and was also a bit of a brainbox at school, she also excelled at gymnastics, football and with computers. She had taught herself computer coding in her own free time and, to be frank, was the smartarse in the Smith household. She was skinny with red hair and blue eyes, just as her mum had been at that age, but even at age 14, her parents, her brother and her teachers could all see that she was destined for great things in life. At school, she was nicknamed 'Sparrahawk' on account of her appearance, but despite her above average intelligence and impeccable grades, she was popular – she never had a bad thing to say about anybody. Neither Olivia nor Jordan were into smoking or drinking, and while Jordan loved spending time with his girlfriend, Olivia never took much interest in romance. She liked school, coding, music, her family, and her small group of friends – she was a sweet wee girl.

Keith's overtime with Neil in February of 2017 involved 7am starts on a job in Paisley, clearing out a disused chilled distribution unit, so he was up and out of the house by around 6.20am each morning, as always, leaving a cup of tea on the bedside table next to the sleeping Georgia before he went out of the door. It was when Keith started these new hours that Georgia noticed that perhaps things weren't quite as rosy for the family as she had thought.

With Keith starting work early and finishing later, too, Georgia, for the first time in years, became the one who was in the house when the postman came each day. About a week before Valentines Day, two letters addressed to Keith plopped through the letterbox one morning. Both looked like junk mail – one was from a company called *Capital One*, the other from *Ocean Finance*. Georgia hated junk mail and spam and with an angry sigh, grabbed them off the inside doormat, tore them up and put them straight into the bin, without so much as looking at them.

A week later, the house broadband and telephone developed a fault, so Georgia phoned up Virgin to see what the issue was. A condescending Indian gentleman in Virgin's Mumbai call-centre, in between his pathetic attempts to prove that he *really* was based in the UK, told Georgia that their household services were on hold due to non-payment of the bill from January. Georgia thought that was strange as the bill should have been automatically paid by direct-debit but, feeling embarrassed and mortified about being cut-off, and needing the internet back on as a matter of urgency, she paid the outstanding balance in full with her credit card, thankful within 24 hours they'd be reconnected to the internet and thus free from their temporary spell in the socially excluded minority of people who weren't online. After all, in the modern era, having no internet is like having no phone, no running water, no heating or no inside-toilet – it's dreadful. When she asked Keith about the internet issue, he said that the date of the direct debit had changed and that there had been a mix-up, nothing to worry about. That made sense to Georgia. She and Keith split the family costs between their bank accounts – the mortgage and food shopping came out of her bank account, the utilities, council tax, insurance and other small payments came out of Keith's. That's how it had always been.

As winter became spring of 2017, life went on for the Smith family much as it had. Keith was doing a lot of hours working with Neil, so Georgia didn't mind that she seemed to be seeing less of her husband, as his weekends often involved socialising with new friends from work, or out with Neil and the other folks from the Celtic bus, and Georgia didn't mind him going out for a pint and maybe the occasional joint, he did a hard physical job and she thought that it was a good thing that he could blow off some steam. The job was clearly tiring Keith out, too, as he'd often come straight in from a long shift and go straight to bed Mondays to Thursdays, exhausted from his day's graft.

Chapter Twelve

Mysterious Times

Georgia and Keith's sex life had waned a bit over the last three years or so – they still fooled around occasionally, usually on the rare night that both of the kids were off out and that they themselves were both at home – which was becoming a less and less frequent occurrence.

Georgia mentioned this to some of her work colleagues and to her friend, Isla. Her workmates were of the opinion that this diminishing of the physical side of a relationship was just something that happened to all couples over time, and that Georgia shouldn't worry too much about it. After all, you might have prime steak in the house to eat daily, but you'd eventually become somewhat underwhelmed by it and wouldn't fancy it quite as often.

Isla, her real friend, asked her over lunch one Saturday in the Brewer's Fayre what was really going on. Georgia, a tear in her eye, confessed that she didn't think that Keith found her as attractive as he once had – he seemed more interested in football, pints of lager and Celtic functions and concerts these days, and when he wasn't absorbed by those things, he was in his bed asleep.

Isla reassured her friend that for 37 years old, Georgia still looked great, and she did. She did gym and swim three times a week, she did yoga at home, she ate properly and still looked in her mid to late twenties. A lot of women like Georgia, who are voluptuous and busty in their prime, struggle to maintain their looks and their figure into their 30s and 40s, growing saggy where once they were pert, and chubby where once they were curvy – not Georgia. Asides the tiniest ripple of a *mummy tummy*, she still had the same curvy but defined figure and was still the same clothes size as when she was 21 – still Jessica Rabbit.

Isla asked Georgia if her sex life with Keith had changed much over the years. Georgia stared into space for a minute, then told Isla that gone was the joy of foreplay, the thrill of seduction, the heated anticipation that they had once shared – things had gotten stale. Often sex for them now involved just mutual oral and then about 20 minutes of actual sex – enough for them both to be relieved, sorted out, but really bottom drawer stuff. Keith didn't seem anywhere near as interested in sex anymore, and Georgia was at a loss as to why. She was no slob or frump, she usually dressed well, she owned a vast array of lingerie and nightwear, she tried to always look her best, not for Keith, but for herself. Often she had suggested steamy weekend nights in to Keith with long baths and mutual massaging, which he'd usually agree to at first, but by the weekend something his end would always come up to mean that such plans had to be shelved – usually things to do with work, football or a night out.

Isla listened to her friend, then gave her some good advice – talk to Keith, ask him what's wrong. Sound advice, even though most people really, *really* don't want to ask a partner who has lost all interest in shagging them, *why* they don't want to shag them anymore. Nevertheless, Georgia resolved to do just that.

When Georgia got home that afternoon, Keith still wasn't home from his Saturday shift, but the two kids were upstairs in their rooms. Georgia glanced at the Saturday post on the inside doormat that none of her tribe had bothered to pick up. Four pizza leaflets, two Chinese menus, some shite glossy flyer from the local SNP MP about his crusade against dog fouling, and two letters, both addressed to Keith.

These two letters comprised of another letter from Ocean Finance and another letter from Capital One – this time both with red warning text on the envelopes. The red writing on those two envelopes made Georgia feel a little shiver of dread – maybe she should have opened the previous letters sent by those two companies – maybe, she thought, she should open these ones, even though they weren't addressed to her – it might be some sort of mix-up, like when the broadband had been cut off for days just recently, and that had been sorted out just fine. Georgia threw her handbag down onto the big charcoal DFS sofa, kicked off her heels and slipped off her stylish red wool jacket, heading through to the kitchen to pour herself a glass of prosecco. Returning to the lounge, she plonked herself down on the sofa and turned on the TV. She went for a music channel. She looked at the various different MTV channels and the niche genre ones like Kerrang and Kiss – that was all shite – stuff her kids were into. She eventually decided on MTV Classic as that was showing a Spice Girls special – she'd loved them when she was a wee girl. She sipped her bubbly prosecco, pondering whether or not to open those two letters and enjoying the Motown vibes of one of that band's last, and best songs – *Stop!*

And we know that you can go and find some other
Take or leave it 'cause we've always got each other
You know who you are and yes, you're gonna breakdown
You've crossed the line so you're gonna have to turnaround
Don't you know it's going too fast (ooh, too fast)
Racing so hard you know it won't last (ooh, won't last)
Don't you know why can't you see

Slow it down, read the sign
So you know just where you're going

Twenty, even fifteen years earlier, MTV or VH1 Classic would have been the types of music channel that she'd have watched at 4am for a laugh when drunk or wasted with Keith, or with their friends, giggling away at early Bon Jovi, guffawing at crap like Level 42 or Sheena Easton – but still having reverence for Kate Bush's *Wuthering Heights,* like almost all women do. Nowadays, the same old-fogey music channels were playing tunes from her own and Keith's youth and that irony wasn't lost on Georgia, at all. Life moves fast.

Her wee trip down memory lane was interrupted as she heard a car pull up outside the house – a taxi, she judged, by the excessive light emanating from the vehicle. She heard a car door slam and Keith's voice shouting 'cheers, mate', then a moment later she heard Keith's key rattling in the front door, which she had left unlocked upon her return. Keith soon came staggering through the front door, and looked very surprised to see her, but still pleased.

"I thought you'd no' be back for a few hours yet," he slurred, trying not to slur, which, of course, always makes the slur more pronounced. He stotted over and kissed Georgia, and she kissed him back, but just a kiss on the lips, like couples do, not a snog. Keith stank of drink, smoke, and something else.

Keith was clearly a little the worse for wear, or as we say in Scotland, absolutely fucking blootered. That didn't bother Georgia too much, it was better than him being wide awake and full of himself, like he used to get back in the class-A days. Keith declared that he was off to get a beer and asked her if she fancied a prosecco refill, to which she replied, "No, I'm good for now, thanks, darling."

Keith threw his own long woolly coat onto the vacant armchair nearest the lounge door then staggered slightly, through to the kitchen, returning momentarily with a can of Budweiser – his favourite. He plonked himself down on the sofa next to Georgia and clicked open the can. His eyes were very heavy. Georgia noted that he had lost some weight, probably from all the overtime he'd been doing with Neil.

"What's this shite you're watching?" said Neil, playfully poking her in the side. She laughed and recoiled slightly, countering with "Hoi, man, these were the tunes when we were growing up, time flies, eh?"

Keith made an agreeing face, but said nothing, as MTV moved onto the dreadful song that ended the Spice Girls as a contemporary force in pop music, 2000's *Holler*.

As the inane, dreadful, over-produced yank-inspired ear-piss emanated from the TV speakers, Georgia took a sip of Prosecco then turned to Keith.

"Keith, are we alright? Financially, I mean?"

Keith answered immediately, automatically.

"Aye, aye, we're sound, I mean, if Scotland had chosen independence, we'd all be better off, but aye, we're sound, we're both working, doll."

Georgia really hated when he called her that, which he only ever did when he was absolutely steaming, she found it patronising and cringe, but she let it go as she was more perplexed by his bullshit nonsense answer, than by terms of endearment.

"That's not an answer, Keith, c'mon. Are we in debt or anything? Is our nest egg safe?" she referred to the near 60 grand that they had put away in an NSI Bonds 90 Day Notice account, Keith's redundancy from his old job plus what savings they'd managed to hold onto in the post-2010 Tory catastrophe that was the UK economy and Brexit uncertainty.

"Aye, aye, everything's under control, Georgia, why do you ask?"

Georgia held up the letter from Ocean Finance and the one from Capital One.

Keith looked disinterested for a second, then reached for the arm of the sofa to put on his reading glasses, before peering at the two envelopes she held out to him.

Georgia noted the colour draining from his face and knew something was amiss.

They were interrupted as young Jordan poked his head into the lounge on his way out of the house, grunting in typical teenage dialect that he'd be back by about midnight.

"Ok, son, have fun," called Georgia after him, as the front door slammed.

"I'm so proud of our laddie, Georgia, that boy is going to do well in life," said Keith.

Georgia didn't say anything in response to that and instead renewed her questions.

"Ok, so, if everything's in control, why do you have these two letters?"

"Ach, Georgia, they're nothing, it'll just be junk mail, here, I'll stick them in the bin."

Georgia flicked the two envelopes out of the way, away from his grasp. "Aren't you curious, Keith?"

Keith seemed agitated "No' really, it's just junk mail, bin it. They're actually addressed to me, by the way, privacy and that, no?"

Georgia wasn't having that as an excuse.

"Well, if they're just junk mail, there's no harm in my opening them, is there? It might actually be a laugh."

Keith took a loud slurp from his can of Budweiser and answered "Aye, sure, go ahead," thinking that would deter her from opening them.

Georgia called his bluff and proceeded to do just that. She opened the Capital One letter first. Keith started moaning, drunkenly.

"Aw so you don't trust me now?"

Georgia didn't answer. She was transfixed by what she was reading.

CHAPTER THIRTEEN

Communication

The Capital One letter was a final demand for over ten thousand pounds for outstanding credit-card debt, on a credit card that Georgia didn't know Keith even had. She felt a sickness in the pit of her stomach as she read. They were threatening legal action and blacklisting. There was also a statement for the card. Some items on the bill were legitimate household or general living payments, utilities, petrol, and the like, but around seven grand of the debt was in cash withdrawals, dozens of them, made over the last year or so, most of the withdrawals being between £200 and £500. There was also a thousand-pound payment to a company called Seventh Heaven, a lap-dancing club in Central Glasgow, dated the weekend that Rangers had beaten Celtic on penalties in the semi-finals of the 2016 Scottish Cup at Hampden.

"What the fuck is going on, Keith? I thought you said we were alright? Why a credit card?"

Keith let out a long sigh. "Can we talk about this tomorrow? I need my bed."

"Can we fuck, Keith! This concerns *us*, the kids, our family, our future. Start talking," Georgia said firmly, trying to hold back her anger and fear long enough to hear him out.

Keith just stared into space, like he was thinking.

Footsteps on the stairs heralded Olivia's entry to the lounge, so Keith and Georgia did their best to seem as if they were just watching TV together. Olivia reminded them both that she had a school trip coming up soon and that it needed to be paid for next week. Georgia had remembered and said that the money was no problem. Olivia, with her red hair and impish grin, chided them both for a moment over their choice of music channel, then went back up to her bedroom.

"Keith" said Georgia. "What will I find if I open this Ocean Finance letter? Is this just *junk mail,* too?"

Keith stared at the carpet for a moment then began to speak in a low, sorrowful, monotone voice, telling quite a story.

Keith had been doing coke on a regular basis pretty much ever since he had been made redundant from the warehouse in 2010. It had started off at the Celtic nights and had snowballed after the 2014 independence referendum into a regular habit, in pubs, at house parties and even at work, with Neil. Often, they would start the working day with a line, then have another at lunchtime, then one early afternoon. At weekends and at nights out their use would be far heavier, and even on a quiet day the pair, with other colleagues, were easily sticking £200 a day up their noses, all pure, no *council* rubbish. It got worse.

Keith and Neil had started buying the drugs from guys at work in recent years, and before long had both ended up owing several small-time dealers thousands of pounds. By 2016 the pair had racked up coke debts in excess of £45,000, a large enough amount for the trafficker who supplied their small-time dealers to become interested. That trafficker also happened to be their main boss, a local businessman and scumbag by the name of Shug.

Idiots like Neil and Keith were bread and butter to guys like Shug, as he could let their dealers keep giving them drugs on credit for a long time, then when the amount owed became large enough to be interesting, Shug could step in, turn off the supply and demand payment in full. The logic behind Shug's tactics was basic but brutal. Both Neil and Keith were homeowners, both nearing the end of their mortgages – Shug was all but guaranteed his money back because both of those men were now addicted to cocaine – they wouldn't be going anywhere.

There was more. Because Neil and Keith had continued playing in the snow, the debt hadn't just remained static, Shug had added on interest. The bastard still allowed them both a reasonable basic wage for their jobs, but all of the overtime that they had done for his company over the last few years had been unpaid – all that sweat and toil unrewarded, used to knock a tiny amount off of an astronomical drug bill.

Georgia was sickened and stunned, not just at Keith and at Shug, but at herself, for not knowing that something so catastrophic had been going on right under her nose – how could she have been so stupid? When she asked Keith why, as a cokehead, he had seemed so tired all of the time when at home in recent years, he looked at his shoes, sighed deeply again, then reached into his pocket and pulled out a blister strip of tablets, handing them to Georgia.

Valium!

The vallies, Georgia could see, weren't pharmaceutical ones from a chemist, but were instead those bright blue large street Valiums that had been all over the news of late, for causing many deaths among drug users. They rarely contained any actual diazepam; they were usually home-made using dye and other sedatives and anti-hypnotics – they were the Russian roulette of street drugs. Georgia realised that Keith had been abusing these 'Valium' in order to function properly after a heavy coke session and to hide his addiction from her when at home. She tossed the blister strip back to him, feeling disgusted about how swiftly and keenly he picked them up and stashed them back in his pocket, like Gollum from 'Lord of the

Rings' with his *precious*. The cocaine epidemic was always going to cause a sedatives boom, too, after all, what goes up must come down.

Georgia fought back tears and tried to compose herself.

"What about this Ocean Finance thing? Are you going to be honest with me, or do I have to open it?"

"I'm so sorry, Georgia, it has just got so out of control. I raised 20 grand of the mortgage as a secured loan."

Georgia was momentarily confused. "How the fuck did you manage that, Keith? That needs both our signatures." She already knew the answer as she spoke, but Keith answered.

"I forged your signature. I told the bank it was for home improvements."

Georgia kept her composure.

"How did it come to this, Keith? What else are you hiding? You've got one chance, one chance to tell me, now."

"Nothing else, honest, I'm so sorry." Keith was starting to cry. Georgia's mind was racing. She thought of all the football nights, pub sessions, house parties and concerts that Keith had been to in recent years, how had she not known? Then another, even darker thought entered her head, and she automatically blurted it out.

"Is there somebody else?" She asked, directly.

"Aw no, no way, it's no' like that, Georgia, I love you, you know I've never been much of a ladies' man. I've had opportunities to go with women at coke parties and nights out, but I'm not interested. It's just a social thing, the coke, but I know it's got out of hand. I need help, Georgia, professional help. But even if I get off all that, I'll still owe Shug a fortune."

Despite all the lying about the coke and the vallies, Georgia believed that he was telling the truth and had remained faithful – he was right, he was no Lothario – that's why she had fallen for him, back in the day.

The two stayed up talking in the lounge all evening, switching from alcohol to sweet tea, at Georgia's insistence. Georgia was livid at being deceived for so long and about such a huge thing, yet on the other hand she kind of admired her loyal but fucked up husband for admitting, finally, what was going on. They were married and when Georgia had taken those wedding vows back in 2006, she had bloody well meant it. For better or worse, in sickness and in health.

Things now made sense to Georgia. The unpaid broadband bill, Keith's tiredness and his long working days, even his loss of libido and the deterioration of their sex life could all be traced back to his starting work beside Neil - Neil who was a nice man, but also an incurable cokehead. Georgia, satisfied that there was no other woman involved in her husband's descent into becoming a drug addict himself, made several demands of Keith, demands that he was in no position to quibble about or to refuse, demands to which he readily agreed to. Those demands being:

Keith must find a new job – not with Neil or at any place linked to Shug Mann.

He must stop the drugs immediately and go to Narcotics Anonymous.

No more football nights or social events – unless Georgia was going with him.

And last, but crucially, they see a debt management counsellor and in future all of the family's bills and finances would be handled by Georgia alone – even Keith's wages were to be paid into her bank account – at least until he sorted himself out.

She was, metaphorically cutting off his balls and she had every right to do so, you see, when there are kids involved, the parent with the expensive addiction isn't just an embarrassment, they are a clear and present danger to the family.

Georgia and Keith agreed to stay together and to try to make this new way of doing things work, after all, they loved each other, they had two beautiful children, they had a home – a life – neither of them wanted to lose any of that.

So, with the family now some 50 grand in debt but with a strategy planned to escape the morass, Georgia and Keith felt relieved. Georgia knew she could handle being a lone parent, but she didn't want to be one – Keith, despite his faults, was her man, after all. Keith had that evening expected to be asked to leave the family home, becoming one of those miserable dads who only see their kids at weekends, but the couple, and the family would, it seemed, face their current problem together. They agreed to tell the kids what was going on the next day, over Sunday dinner. It had been quite a Saturday, for the Smith family.

Before Georgia and Keith went up to bed that night, they flushed the street Valium down the toilet – as much a symbolic gesture as a practical measure. They both went straight to sleep that night, emotionally and physically drained.

And so, Georgia gave her beloved husband a chance to sort himself out, and vowed to do all that she could to help him, Georgia wasn't naive, she knew that all sorts of people, good and bad, can lose their way with cocaine and other drugs. But Shug Mann would be getting a visit from Georgia Smith, very, very soon.

CHAPTER FOURTEEN

Fool's Gold

G eorgia turned off the engine of her old but faithful Renault Clio, unplugged her phone from the USB charging point and with a deep sigh sat back in the driving seat for a second, her eyes closed. With her phone now unplugged from the car console, the radio came back on, unexpectedly blaring *Despacito* by Fonsi. She turned down the volume but let the catchy yet annoying track finish, only switching off the radio when the irritating radio DJ called the track 'the sound of the summer'.

Despacito means 'slowly' in English. Georgia was regretting how slowly she'd cottoned on to the extent of her husband's drug problems, yet she was determined to try to put things right for her, for him, and for her family, quickly.

> *Despacito*
> *Quiero respirar tu cuello despacito*
> *Deja que te diga cosas al oído*
> *Para que te acuerdes si no estás conmigo*
> *Despacito*

Georgia was sitting in the carpark of Hamilton Academical FC's stadium, New Douglas Park, that Monday morning. She wasn't there to see a match; she was there for a meeting.

Much of the space beneath the stadium's main stand was rented out to various local businesses. There was a gym in there, some shops, a crèche, and some offices. One of those offices was rented out to HM Solutions, and she was there to see that business's CEO, Shug Mann. She'd been surprised earlier that morning when the receptionist had granted her a same-day appointment over the phone, so she had called the council to request a half-day holiday because of a family emergency, which had been granted by her boss.

Georgia was wearing her bog-standard but classy office wear and her long wool coat – it was still a bit chilly for spring, the old adage was true – never cast a cloot until May's oot.

She sat in the communal waiting room that the business offices shared, sipping a revolting latte from the vending machine. The others waiting beside her clearly had appointments with different business. There was a young lass in her 20s, chewing bubble-gum loudly whilst glued to her smartphone. There was a big guy in his 30s wearing rugby gear, and there was a young gentleman in a wheelchair who had no legs, who was also glued to his phone.

A blonde woman in her late 20s wearing tight black leather trousers and a white blouse walked into reception and called out "Georgia Smith" in a loud, well-spoken Glaswegian accent. Georgia looked up and smiled. The blonde woman smiled broadly and shook Georgia's hand, introduced herself as Alana, and asked Georgia to follow her. The pair walked down the carpeted corridor to an elevator, then took the lift up to the first floor.

In the bright lights inside the lift, Georgia was struck by Alana's appearance. The woman looked good, Georgia thought, but had clearly undergone several cosmetic procedures. By the looks of it she'd had J-Lo style implants put into her arse, had a boob job, and had work done on her nose, too. The lassie looked amazing, Georgia thought, her curves straining at her blouse and leather trousers, her skin flawless, her long dyed-blonde hair tied back – all that work had clearly cost some lucky guy a lot of money.

Upon exiting the lift, Alana led Georgia past two smaller offices before they came to the door of a larger one that had HM Solutions on the door.

With a warm, friendly tone, Alana asked Georgia if she fancied some tea or coffee, which Georgia politely declined, then Alana said, "Shug's in there, just go in." Alana then headed off back along the corridor as Georgia pushed open the wooden door and went inside.

The office comprised of two medium-sized desks facing each other, on the right just inside the entrance door. To the left of the door were two new-looking red chesterfield sofas with a coffee table in between them. There was around eight feet of floor before the room's main feature, a huge walnut desk, behind which sat a man in his late 30s with 'number 4' shaved black hair. He was muscular and bearish, menacing and imposing in stature (even sitting down), with huge hands. His eyes were big and brown, and he wore designer stubble. He was clothed in a stylish Marc Darcy business suit – he was Shug Mann.

"Georgia, Georgia, it's good to see you, pal, it's been a while, has it not? What a nice surprise this is. What can I do for you?" Shug had stood up to shake Georgia's hand, before sitting down and gesturing for her to do the same.

Georgia looked around the office – it was a bit Spartan in appearance – not much to it. A few HM Solutions things on the walls, an enlarged framed photograph of Shug wearing a high visibility vest and a hardhat while sitting on an excavator, and on the wall behind Shug was a large workforce rota, and a whiteboard with a marker pen on string hanging from it. Writing had been scrawled across the entire thing – Georgia wanted to wipe it clean, but she stuck to the task in hand. She ignored Shug's asking her what he could do for her, even though he sounded warm, helpful, and genuinely pleased to see her.

"This is your HQ, Hugh? Did you just move here or something?"

Shug decided to ignore her use of his given name and answered.

"I've got builders in at the main unit doing the place up at the moment, this is just a temporary measure while the guys drag my current HQ kicking and screaming into the 21st century – you know how it is, Georgia. It's no' the Ritz but it'll do for now. But, shhhh, please don't tell anyone I'm renting an office from the Accies, I'm a Motherwell FC man, remember."

Georgia nodded and smiled, feigning sympathy for his *very* first-world problem. Shug seemed in a good mood, which was good news for her, she hoped.

"How are you getting on, Shug? I heard you'd moved to Bothwell? Someone's did well for himself."

Shug smiled and replied, briefing Georgia about how he'd had to move to a bigger house to match his newfound status as a paragon of the local business community, and that he'd been glad to leave the old house as it held too many bad memories for him. Those were clearly memories of him beating the living daylights out of his ex, Karen, before she and their twins had departed, but Georgia wasn't going to mention that. Shug then told Georgia that he was engaged to 'wee Alana', the lassie who had just escorted Georgia from reception up to the office, and that he'd finally found happiness and inner peace with her in 'oor wee love nest'.

Georgia wasn't at all surprised that the nice but very plastic, impressionable, beautiful, insecure young woman she had just met was Shug's new woman – it was probably him who had paid for all her surgeries as part of whatever weird pact their relationship was silently predicated upon – the younger lassie gets money, security, protection and probably a daddy substitute, the older guy get a younger woman to fuck and to control, both to boost his ego and to make his associates jealous – as with most gangster love stories.

"You're looking well, Georgia, still working for the council? How are the kids and the husband?" Shug asked, sounding genuine. He then tore open and started to eat one of those triple-decker all-day breakfast sandwiches that you can buy in supermarkets or petrol stations.

"Listen, Shug, that's why I'm here. Look, my kids are fine, but my husband has some drug issues that we're trying to help him with. Part of the problem is who he works with."

Shug reclined back in his office chair, loudly chomping on the remnants of the first of the three big sandwiches, before swallowing, then belching loudly, like a hippo.

"Oh, I'm sorry to hear that, Georgia, so, are you wanting me to give him a job? Where does he work just now?"

Georgia kept her cool. "Keith works for one of your companies, Hugh."

Shug scratched his head, looking genuinely perplexed for a moment, then answered.

"I think there is a Keith, he works as a driver and a labourer for wee Neil Conroy, in my decorating outfit. I can't say I know the guy, though. Is that your husband?"

Georgia, unsure if Shug was attempting levity or was just being a typical boss who didn't know much about his employees, pressed the point.

"Aye, that's him. Look, Hugh, we've known each other since school. I'm really glad you've done so well for yourself, I really am, you didn't have it easy as a kid."

That statement seemed to irk Shug, he displayed a split-second scowl, but his face quickly returned to having the expression of a helpful boss in an office.

"So, Georgia, what's the problem?" he asked, before starting to eat the second all-day-breakfast sandwich, loudly.

"Shug, I need you to put my Keith in a different squad, or another part of your business, away from that Neil. Neil is a nice guy but he's a bad influence. Keith can work hard wherever you put him. Please, Shug, we need this, urgently. Neil is a cokehead. His influence on Keith is hurting our family."

"Right, I see," said Shug, still chewing on the sandwich loudly. Some of the mustard and tomato sauce from the sarnie had dribbled down onto his shirt from his flabby chin, but he hadn't noticed.

"Right, no problem, I get it, Georgia, I really do. So, you want me to move yer man to my landscaping business or my tar-laying squad, or maybe even send him away on a training course for a week, to give him, and you, a bit of breathing space? That all sounds reasonable, I'd be happy to help, Georgia. Family is important, after all."

Georgia was pleasantly surprised.

"Thanks, Hugh, you're a good man. Thank you."

Shug didn't acknowledge her thank you, he instead swallowed the last part of his second sandwich then cracked open a can of Irn Bru, greedily guzzling the juice to wash down the sandwich. He looked vacant for a second, then grabbed the third and final sandwich from the packet and held it out to Georgia, offering her it.

"No thanks, I'm going out for lunch after."

Shug belched loudly again, and again, putting the sandwich piece back into its packet.

"What are you doing on Wednesday evening, Georgia," Shug asked, looking at her with eyes like a cold arctic wolf.

"Ehm, I've no plans, Hugh, why?" The question had caught her off-guard.

"Have you ever been to the Sheraton Hotel in Edinburgh, Georgia? I'm staying there on Wednesday night due to a work meeting early the next morning, do you fancy coming?"

A familiar revulsion began to stir in the pit of Georgia's stomach, but she gave Shug the benefit of the doubt.

"What, to your work meeting?"

Shug shook his head. "To the hotel for the night. It's a lovely hotel, big beds, a nice pool and spa, decent grub. I've always had a wee thing for you, Georgia, and I can't think of a lovelier place for us to finally to get it together. You're the only woman who's ever refused me, so it would be nice to finally put that right, would it not? Be like finishing a love story, in a way."

Georgia was disgusted. 'A love story'. This cunt hadn't changed at all, and she knew it. She didn't doubt that in Shug's head their 'relationship' had been like a long-drawn-out 'will they/won't they' soap opera romance, but to her he was just a creepy, dodgy sleaze she'd once felt pity for and had already rebuffed several times.

"You want me to come and spend the night with you at a hotel in Edinburgh?" said Georgia, seeking clarification.

"Aye, that would be great. You'd love it. Listen, I'll even get you some new sexy underwear and shoes for the occasion. What do you say?"

Georgia couldn't believe the nerve of the bastard, who was now smiling, a sleazy look in his eye. She stayed calm – she still needed his help with Keith's job.

"No, Hugh, I've told you before, that's not going to happen, that's never going to happen. I'm married. The answer is no!"

Shug scoffed and replied.

"Well, there's your answer, Georgia."

It was then that Georgia fully realised the implication. If she didn't spend the night with Shug, he wouldn't help with Keith's problem. 'Fuck that', she thought. She would fix it another way. Angry, she rose from her chair and looked down at Shug, her big blue eyes ablaze with rage.

"Fine. My family and I will sort this out another way. Thanks for nothing, Hugh. And for the record, I wouldn't fuck you if you were the last man alive."

"Be careful what you wish for, Georgia." said Shug, coldly.

"And what the fuck is that supposed to mean? Go on, spit it out."

Shug gestured to her with his hands, to sit down again. "Listen, Georgia, I wish I could help you out, but I really don't see there being anything in this for me. Besides, I couldn't redeploy your husband to another one of my squads even if I were inclined to."

"Why not?" Asked Georgia, sitting down again.

"Because, Keith Smith, your husband, hasn't been at his work since the turn of the year, he's on the sick, stress issues, apparently, I have his sick line somewhere here, if you'd like to see it?"

Georgia, upon hearing that, felt like she was falling through the air at 100mph. She didn't need to see the sicknote, now it all *really* made sense. It was April and her husband hadn't been at his work since before Christmas. This begged the question about where the fuck Keith had actually been, but Georgia sensed that Shug had more to say.

"He's your husband, I thought you two told each other everything. Clearly not. Likes a sniff does our Keith, likes a vally too, and a pint, and a joint. But you knew that, right? What he doesn't like, though, is paying for those things. Fuckin' waster still owes me a fortune."

"No, he paid you that back, he took out loans to do it, I've seen the paperwork," said Georgia, grasping.

Shug looked smug. "You've seen the paperwork for the money he borrowed, aye, but did you see a receipt from me? "

"Drug dealers don't give out receipts," snapped Georgia.

"Very funny, Georgia. No, you're half right, he did pay off about half of that debt him and Neil owed for that Charlie – fucking Dyson hoover noses, the pair of them. Trouble is, that loser Neil Conroy was arrested yesterday on the M74 while bringing a package up from Manchester, you see, he was remanded in custody this morning, so it's unlikely that we'll see him in the near future. This means that Neil's share of the debt now falls onto his fellow nose-merchant, your husband, Keith, it's actually about 50 grand he owes me now, and interest increases that amount each week."

Georgia sat there, livid, burning with fury, her world in tatters. She needed to get away from this horrible cunt across the desk from her.

"We've money put by, still, Hugh, if I pay you the 50 grand will you forget the interest?"

"Will ah fuck," laughed Shug, adding "and don't be thinking that you're going to leave town, or tell the polis, or even find Keith another job. Until all that debt is repaid, that cunt's arse belongs to me – if he's fit enough to work again soon, he comes back to work for me – he was one of my better couriers. I'm running a business here, not a charity, it's nothing personal."

"Couriers? I thought he was a driver and labourer?" asked Georgia, in desperation.

Shug laughed again. "Well, he's my gopher, they all are, he delivers what he's told." Shug belched loudly again, then winked at her.

Georgia was stunned. She'd not even considered the possibility that Keith had been picking up and collecting cocaine and other drugs – this changed everything for her.

Shug continued.

"Your husband has spent most of this year hanging about down at that Neil's flat, pretending to be at his work, taking drugs, drinking, smoking, but timing it all so that when he comes home to you, he just seems a bit woozy and tired. He's been getting full wages, mind, I'm no' a complete bastard. Dafty thinks I'm his mate because I'm his dealer, he even took me and the other lads to that lap dancing club in Glasgow a while back, 7th Heaven, what a night, he spent thousands, private dances, extras, blow, drink, the works. Oh, yer man likes a bet, too, he's never out of Ladbrokes, go down and ask them at the bookies if you don't believe me. If I were you, I'd be most worried about who else hangs around that Neil's flat when he's there – all sorts of riff raff, I hear. Nae wonder the cunt is skint."

Georgia was taking all of this in, silently. She instinctively knew that it was all true, every word of it.

"Fuck you, Hugh," hissed Georgia, her world falling apart around her, her hands tightly gripping the arms of her office chair. Shug raised an eyebrow and answered.

"Aye, we'll get to that eventually, Georgia, how about we still do Wednesday in Edinburgh at the hotel as planned? Then a few more nights like that, we could work out an arrangement to pay off this debt. C'mon Georgia, would that be so bad?"

Georgia stood up and spoke in an accusing tone, now it all made sense.

"Oh my god. It's you. All of it. You engineered this whole fucking situation. You knew Keith was my husband, you let him and Neil run up all that debt, you knew we owned our house, you knew that eventually, because we knew each other in the past, that I'd come to see you to try to get you to let Keith off the hook, and then you'd pounce – you probably set up that daft Neil to get lifted, to make this all happen more quickly, too, didn't you?"

Shug answered more firmly.

"Hello! HELLO! You know what I am. You know I always get what I want. I didn't set out to trap you like this, but I confess, it's been a buzz watching it all happen anyway. Why wear a hairshirt for all this debt and suffering when you could wear some sexy gear for me a few times and make it all go away? So, Wednesday, Georgia, the Sheraton?"

Georgia snapped, "Fuck off, I'll never go with you, Hugh, ya fat bastard, never. I'll get you your money. I will, even if I have to crack our family nest egg to get it." Georgia turned and made to storm out. Shug shouted her back and she turned angrily, snarling, "Whit?"

"You should never have knocked me back all those times, Georgia. Still, you'll come to me begging for it, eventually, they always do. 50 grand, by the end of the month. Clock's ticking. Oh, and a bit of advice – be wary of life's bonds." He then took two huge puffs from his inhaler and went back to typing on his computer as if nothing had happened.

Georgia stormed out of the building and jumped into her car, distraught, livid, holding back tears as she drove home, to wait for Keith to return from 'work'.

CHAPTER FIFTEEN

I Feel Love

As she pulled up outside the family home and turned off the engine of her Renault Clio, her phoned bleeped and she picked it up, the phone still plugged into the car dashboard console. It was a WhatsApp message from a number she didn't have stored in her phone. There was a video clip in the message, and a one-line text reading 'OMG recognise anyone?'.

Georgia assumed that it was spam or a message from a friend who'd changed number, but curiosity got the better of her and she opened the clip as she sat in the stationary car. There was buffering for a few seconds then a clip started.

There were voices, several Scottish voices, male and female, and the centrepiece of the video was a big fat young woman with short brown hair, sitting on a sofa touching herself, clearly out of her face but really enjoying herself. She wore only a suspender belt without stockings and she had a huge saggy belly, rolls of fat around her thighs and huge unattractive pendulous breasts. She had a Celtic FC tattoo on one bicep and was snorting a line of cocaine from a bank card. After snorting the fat line of marching powder, she reclined back further then dumped a small lump of cocaine onto her breast, before slurring "c'mon then babe, get a move on." Georgia liked porn but not this sort of dead-eyed junkie trash she was watching. Whoever the lass in the video had summoned then appeared in the video, his face away from the camera, he was topless. Whoever he was, he laughed and drawled "OH YES" before bending down to snort all of the cocaine off the woman's huge tits. Several voices could be heard laughing in the background as he did. The lassie herself giggled playfully as the guy made more snorting noises, then the lassie turned around onto all fours and the guy stepped to the side so that he could get closer to fuck her from behind. It was then that his face was revealed – he was Neil Conroy! The pair rutted away on camera for a moment then the lassie again called out, in between her moans, calling, "You too, handsome." A pale-skinned, wiry-built naked male with thinning brown hair loomed into view at the opposite end of the woman from Neil, he looked absolutely wasted and he too was snorting cocaine from a bank card. Then, the lassie giggled and started to suck this guy's cock, as all the three in the ménage à trois moaned like the whores that they were. The guy getting the blowjob was Keith Smith. Georgia was sobbing as she watched her husband cavorting with this foul woman, she felt every emotion – revulsion, shame, anger, desperation, insecurity, foolishness and, of course, betrayal. Watching someone you love having drugged-up sex with someone else isn't most people's cup of tea, but Georgia watched all 12 minutes of it, her face wet with tears – after all, this was evidence, now. She saved the video to her Google drive and deleted it from WhatsApp. She already knew who'd sent her the video – Shug must have had her number from when she'd phoned the stadium reception to request a meeting. The video had clearly been made in Neil's flat. She felt glad that Neil was in jail now. She'd eventually find out who the junkie lassie in the video was, and she'd deal with Shug, somehow, too. However, first and foremost in her mind now was confronting her lying, cheating, bastard junkie of a husband when he got home, which would be in around five hours. Georgia went inside, poured herself a large Laphroaig whisky and sat down on the sofa. She texted the kids and told them both to go to their granny and grandad's after school, after phoning her mum, Janice, to ask if she would give her and Keith a few hours to sort out 'an issue'. Her mum and dad were all too happy to help.

Georgia couldn't bring herself to watch the video again, so she just sat on the sofa with her whisky, watching MTV classic and waiting for that piece of shit to get home. An old classic Fleetwood Mac video was playing on the big family TV. It had been a traumatic few hours for Georgia Smith.

Tell me lies, tell me sweet little lies
Tell me lies
Tell me, tell me lies
Oh no-no, you can't disguise
You can't disguise
No, you can't disguise
Tell me lies, tell me sweet little lies

Humiliated and justifiably seething with rage as she pondered her next move while sitting on the sofa, Georgia went over and over the last few years in her head, trying to decide what course of action to take. She almost re-watched the video on her phone but managed in the end to resist. All of that solidarity and compassion that she had shown Keith the other day had just made her seem weak – one thing was certain, there'd be no more 'aw poor you' treatment for her dissolute husband. She would see what he had to say when he came in, first, after all, she still loved him and he was her kids' father – Georgia caught herself when that particular thought entered her head – hitherto she'd always thought of Jordan and Olivia as 'our kids', or 'the kids', not *her* kids. Oh the kids! The kids were both old enough and well-rounded enough to understand that parents are just human beings and that they make mistakes, so if she decided to put Keith out of the house there'd be tears but perhaps not future maladjustment for the kids – after all, at school, kids whose parents were still together were actually a minority, these days. On the other hand, were she to let Keith remain at home, the kids would hardly benefit from absorbing what was doubtless going to be a horrible atmosphere within the family home for the foreseeable future – plus, that option helped neither Keith nor Georgia. The other day when she and Keith had the long chat about his issues, Georgia had been every inch the loving, loyal wife, offering sympathy and solutions – making sure they faced this together as a team, as husband and wife. However, now that she knew that Keith had been fucking junkie lassies behind her back while also leading a secretive life of cocaine and betting since Christmas and almost destroying the family finances and security in the process, Georgia was far less inclined to play the supporting spouse. Her husband's habits and newly unmasked lifestyle made him a clear and present danger to the Smith family's welfare, even though he was a part of that family. The more that Georgia thought about it, the more she became convinced that she really didn't want Keith around her or the kids, not in his current state, anyway.

However, mindful of her wedding vows and of the kids' feelings, she resolved to give Keith one last chance to come clean. Georgia's mind then turned to that bastard, Shug, and his indecent proposals. 50 fucking grand, on top of what had already been blown by Keith. See, the thing with coke dealers is, they can decide whatever an amount of debt owed is worth. They can inflate it or deflate it on a whim, but you can't exactly take your local scumbag dealer to a tribunal or report them to trading standards, can you? She had no choice, so she decided that she would use the family nest-egg from NS&I to pay off all of that fucking coke debt in one fell swoop – at least then, whatever happened, they would be free of the debt and free of Shug Mann's influence.

Georgia was on her third strong whisky and was curled up almost in the foetal position on the large sofa when Keith arrived home. He was wearing his work jeans and boots, with his Celtic home top, which looked as if it needed a wash. Georgia sat up as he entered the lounge – he looked surprised to find her there. He was drinking a can of Coca-Cola as he sat down on the end of the sofa, which made Georgia instinctively shuffle to the opposite end of the sofa, clutching her phone in her left hand.

MTV classic was still playing. The channel was playing a selection of hits now, entitled "90s top 20", though the actual chart tracks were probably just chosen by some smug poser in an office somewhere who thought they were the bees knees because they worked for MTV.

'Torn' by Natalie Imbruglia was playing.

There's nothing where he used to lie
The conversation has run dry
That's what's going on
Nothing's fine, I'm torn

I'm all out of faith
This is how I feel
I'm cold and I am shamed
Lying naked on the floor

Georgia took another sip of her whisky and asked Keith. "So, how was work today?"

"Acht, the usual, same old slog. Whiskey at this time? That's no' like you," he answered.

Georgia ignored the comment about the whiskey, reaching for the TV remote to turn the volume down a little.

"How are you feeling coming off the gear?" she asked.

"Ah it's not so bad, work takes my mind off it, no? I think I'll grab a drink, too-"

Georgia interrupted him. "Keith, man, we need to talk. You've been lying to me, haven't you?"

Keith looked a tad confused. "Eh? No, we've been over all that, straight down the middle from now on, darling."

Normally Georgia loved it when he called her darling, but today it just rang hollow, in fact, it broke her fucking heart.

"So, there's nothing you forgot to tell me? Nothing else you think I should know?"

"No, darling, I told you the lot, warts and all, why?" Keith didn't seem nervous when questioned.

"Nothing? Really?" said Georgia, as with her left hand she pressed 'cast' on her phone, and a disgusting sex tape started to play right in front of them both on their huge 65-inch TV with surround sound.

"Oh my god," said Keith, holding his head in his hands, his fingers covering his eyes.

"Watch the video, Keith, you fucking watch it, watch it!" growled Georgia, using an aggressive tone that she'd never used before.

Keith removed his hands from his face and stared at the dank, soulless sex film on the TV. His cheeks were scarlet as he sat there, beginning to squirm.

"So, who's she? One of Neil's coke skanks? Or is she a hooker, a stripper, maybe, I know you like strippers, too. Well, come on, *Mr Loverman*, who is she?"

Keith was quiet for a moment then simply said, "She's a friend."

Georgia's voice grew louder as they began to argue.

"A friend? A fucking friend? Where did you meet her, ya fucking sleaze? She doesn't look much older than our Jordan, ya manky, cheating, lying cunt! What's her name? Is it love?" Georgia's last question was loaded with sarcasm, of course.

"I'm sorry, Georgia, I really am. I was in a bad place. No, of course I don't love her, she's just a friend."

"A bad place, Keith, *a bad fucking place*? Really?"

"Aye, you know how things have been recently, but that's all behind me now. It was just a blowjob, that's all, the gear makes me horny sometimes."

"What, so you couldn't just come home to fuck me, instead? Is it me, Keith? Don't you fancy me anymore?"

"Naw, it's not that, you're beautiful, Georgia."

"So beautiful that you'd rather stick your dick inside any old fat junkie slag, instead? I mean, look at the fucking state of her, man, do you realise how hurtful and insulting this is for me?"

"I'm sorry. I really am. It just kind of happened."

"Bullshit. Just a blowjob? Do you really expect me to believe that? Fuck's sake, Keith, I want to be sick."

Keith let out a long sigh, a sorrowful expression on his face. "It'll never happen again, I promise."

Georgia drained her whisky glass and stopped casting the video to the TV. MTV came back on, playing MMMbop by Hanson – probably the least appropriate song to have such a pivotal argument to.

Georgia did her best to appear angry but focussed, calm and collected, but she was surprised by what Keith said next.

"I'm guessing you know that I've no' been at my work since Christmas, too, right? I mean, Neil wouldn't have sent you that video. I suppose Shug sent it? And that means you've been in contact with Shug, how else would he have your phone number? Am I right?"

Georgia remembered that while her husband may be a lying, cheating addict, he wasn't an idiot.

"Aye, I went to see Shug, to try and help you, to try and help us. He told me all about you being off your work, and about your other habits. 50 fucking grand, man! Fuck's sake, man, how could you do this to us?"

"I'm sorry."

"Stop saying that, prick, you're not sorry, you're only sorry that you've been caught." Georgia realised that this conversation dynamic could probably go in circles all evening.

Keith scratched his head and then spoke.

"Look, Georgia, I am sorry, truly sorry. What else do you want me to say?"

"Wait a minute, Keith, how on earth did Shug have that video to send me in the first place?"

"He was there when it was made, he filmed it."

It was then that Georgia realised that Shug had made an arse of her all along. He had known all about the video, and Keith's infidelity, all throughout their meeting at his Douglas Park office – he'd been playing with her all along.

Georgia was growing angry again, not just at Keith, but angry all the same.

"He filmed it? He fucking filmed it? Oh, so Shug Mann was partying with you and Neil, was he?"

Keith shook his head, sitting forward on the edge of the sofa.

"Not exactly. We were partying in Neil's, we ordered more gear, but Shug brought it round himself instead of sending a laddie round to post it through the door, like usual. He brought his new bird, Alana, with him, and her pal Louise. He put out some lines of rocket fuel, we all had some, things got a bit messy and Shug kind of manipulated us all into doing what you saw in that video, he filmed it, then he just got up and left with Alana, leaving that Louise lassie partying with us."

"So that's her name, her from the video, Louise?"

"Aye," said Keith, staring at the floor again.

Georgia took a deep breath, then spoke.

"I feel sick, Keith. You've really broke my heart. You're a fucking mess."

"What will you do?" asked Keith.

Georgia then realised that Keith actually seemed relieved, so she asked him why that was. Keith told her that he was glad everything was out in the open now, because the stress and the guilt were killing him and he didn't like the lying, but his next words were a surprise.

"Look, Georgia, I like a party, I'm a cokehead, I like a bet, these are just things that I like to do. I love you, and the kids, and our house and all that, but I need a bit more from life, some excitement, some danger. The whole Narcotics Anonymous thing and maybe doing rehab, that's not for me, I only said I'd do that for you. Georgia, this is who I am, now. Aye, I got in with a dodgy crowd, but I love the buzz and there's nothing I can do about that. So, what will you do?" he asked again.

Georgia wanted the ground to swallow her up. She'd heard about and read about idiots who choose a life of drugs over a family and a partner, but she'd never in her darkest dreams thought that her Keith was one of those people. Until recently he'd been a good husband, he was a good dad – the coke had got him, though, bigtime. Georgia wasn't naive enough to think that anything she said in that moment would somehow counter the addictions in him, so she made a suggestion.

"Wow, ok, I suppose I should thank you for your honesty." As she spoke, she was signing into something on her phone. "Right, here's what we'll do.

We use the NSI bonds to pay off that cunt Shug, with what's left we can put a deposit down on a flat for you – somewhere nearby but not too close – there's the kids to think about – 2 secs..."

Georgia was logged into the NSI banking app, typing in a password. The bond account was in Keith's name, but she knew the login details. She felt reassured when she saw the figure £59,272.48 at the top of the screen, until she saw the word TRANSFER next to it, and her blood ran as cold as ice.

Transfer £59,272.48

Remaining Bond Balance £17.50.

Georgia then had a flashback of Shug's voice in her head, smugly saying "beware of life's *bonds*".

"What the fuck is this?" she snarled at Keith, holding the phone screen up to his face. Keith didn't look surprised.

"I'm sorry, Georgia, I needed it."

Georgia was incandescent with burning rage, standing up.

"YOU needed it? You fucking needed it? 60 fuckin' grand, ya fucking waster. Your family needed it, we needed it, your fucking kids needed it". Georgia looked again at the website and saw that the transfer had been made to ... HM Solutions.

"Please tell me you didn't send every fucking penny that we have to Shug Mann?"

Keith stood up and paced up and down. "Fuck's sake, aye, awright, I get it, I'm fuckin' sorry. But we'll get it back, Shug's no' that bad really, he's got some new jobs lined up for me that'll fix all this, he's a mate-"

"Your mate, your fucking mate?" screamed Georgia, hitting Keith with a left hook which sent him sprawling onto the carpet. "Your mate? That's a fucking bad joke. That must be near a hundred grand that bastard has had off you these last few years, off of *us,* are you totally fucking stupid?"

Keith stood up, shaken, but otherwise unhurt. "He is ma mate."

With anger and derisory laughter, Georgia replied.

"He's your fucking dealer, he's not your mate, he's never been your mate. Do you know that when I went to see him, he tried to get me to pay off your fucking coke debt by shagging him at hotels? Did your *mate* tell you that, did he? You stupid, junkie loser cunt. That's it, we're fucking finished, the kids will be home soon so you can stay the night, but I want you out of this house tomorrow – I'm not exposing the kids to any more of your shite. Sleep in the fucking box room tonight, don't you fucking come near me – got it? You blew it, Keith, you had it all, and you fucking blew it, and for what? Some fucking white powder? You're pathetic, Keith. I'm going to my bed; we can sort details out tomorrow." And with that Georgia stormed upstairs to the bedroom, where she collapsed onto the bed in tears, putting the TV on to hide her sobs. She texted the kids to say that she wasn't feeling well and was in bed.

Keith went through to the Kitchen and made himself an Irish coffee to take the edge off, then popped a fake blue Valium from his pocket, to totally obliterate the edge. Soon he was spaced out, watching an endless loop of Sky Sports News on the little TV as he sat at the kitchen table.

Wee Olivia and Jordan were dropped off by their grandparents about an hour later. Olivia went straight up to her room to resume an online chat with a buddy from Japan. Young Jordan, knackered from playing 5-a-side football earlier, went into the empty living room, glad to get the TV and the remote all to himself, which was rare in their house.

Jordan took off his tracksuit top and started flicking, then he opened Netflix, then closed it, then the BBC iPlayer, but closed it scoffing. Then his attention was drawn to a thumbnail on the TV screen, and being an inquisitive young man, he opened it. To his delight it was porn, so he turned the volume right down – volume being the secret porn-watcher's greatest enemy. The porn looked shit, home-made, but it had a profound effect on him.

Within two minutes he was through in the kitchen, waking up his gouching dad before giving the dazed and confused patriarch of the family a right good doing. Jordan, by then, was the same size as his dad but was infinitely fitter and stronger. The disgusting clip of his dad cheating on his mum and taking drugs had confirmed a few silly rumours about his old man that Jordan had heard around the schemes and school, and Jordan let his fury flow. As he kicked and punched his dad, who lay helpless on the tiled kitchen floor, Georgia and Olivia both came flying down the stairs to split them up.

Georgia hadn't realised that casting videos to Smart TV's sometimes leaves a thumbnail on the home screen.

Jordan wouldn't hit his sister or his mum, and they stood between him and his battered father. Jordan ranted.

"I knew something bad was going on. Some dad you are, you're a fucking joke, drugs, and that fat slag?" Jordan turned to his mum.

"Put him out, Mum, or I'll knock him out, I'll fucking kill him."

Faced with that choice, Georgia glared down at Keith and said, "You better go, *now.*"

Keith, visibly shaken and silent, did just that, not even pausing to pack a bag. He exited the family home into the night, disappearing into the darkness, looking for a party.

CHAPTER SIXTEEN

There's Nothing I Won't Do

Georgia and the kids sat up together for several hours, drinking hot chocolate and having a frank, adult, family conversation about what had been going on. Both Olivia and Jordan had heard dodgy stories about their dad's exploits on the local drugs circuit, but neither had said anything in case it caused trouble at home. Georgia was taken aback by how much her beautiful children knew about the local drugs scene. They had even heard of Shug Mann, though they only knew he was their dad's boss and a drug dealer - nothing else. Nobody got much sleep in the Smith household that night.

The summer of 2017 came and went. A General Election that summer saw the hated Tory party cling to power, though they were run very close by a Labour party under a genuine socialist, Jeremy Corbyn. The Tories, under the uninspiring Theresa May, lost their parliamentary majority from 2015 and were forced to form a parliamentary pact with Ulster Unionist minority parties, in order to remain in power. Corbyn's Labour had been the first party in generations to both inspire the young and to offer hope to people who live in housing schemes – the broken biscuits that Neoliberalism leaves behind. Britain's establishment thus resolved to ensure that if Labour were to contest another election with Corbyn as leader, they would lose, very badly. A hatchet job of epic proportions began against Corbyn and against the left in general – this would be catastrophic for working class people in housing schemes, in the long-term. One group of people who relied on the so-called working poor for their income – drug dealers – weren't too fussed which party was in power after the 2017 election, as no major party had mentioned a single policy about drugs and organised crime in their manifestos – the underworld's vital revenue streams from the poor would thus continue, uninterrupted, in fact, for dealers and criminals like Shug Mann, continued lack of any challenge to the neoliberal consensus meant that the good times, for them, would continue to roll.

Georgia and her two kids soldiered on through the rest of 2017 as best they could, following Keith's departure from the family home. By Hogmanay, none of them had seen Keith at all since that horrible night with the dirty video. He had returned to the family home a few days after that depressing drama, doing so when nobody else was in. He'd taken some of his clothes, a few of his belongings and had left his house keys and his wedding ring on the kitchen counter.

Georgia had been left quite literally holding the babies, albeit grown up ones. She also now had almost £40,000 in secured debt – loans and credit cards spunked away secretly by Keith before he was rumbled - linked to the family home to pay off, in addition to the mortgage, the bills, food, petrol and all of life's other necessities. Jordan, almost 18, got a part-time job in ASDA to try to help, but Georgia didn't want him working to pay off his absent dad's drug debt, so she refused to take any money from him when it was offered. Olivia, too, wanted to help out, but would need to wait until she turned sixteen before she had any chance of finding a job.

Georgia's ingrained Protestant work ethic compelled her to both seek promotion in her current job and to look for a part-time job elsewhere – to supplement her income and to keep the family afloat. She wasn't initially successful in getting promoted at the council, but she was welcomed back as a weekend worker by Sky TV in Livingston – that brought with it a 60-minute-per-day commute, but that was a necessary evil in the Smith family's new predicament. That new job, though, did have one other drawback – Georgia would get far less time to spend with her kids and with her elderly parents, for the foreseeable future.

Young Jordan Smith turned 18 in February of 2018. By the time of his 18th birthday party in The Stuart Hotel, which was like most 18ths usually are – vomiting, embarrassment and mayhem – nothing had been heard from Keith, his dad, at all, though a birthday card from him with £50 inside it did make its way to the family home two days after the bash.

At first, Georgia was pleased that her son had found a part-time job that he liked in the local supermarket. The money wasn't bad for him, he was learning a lot on the job, and he seemed to have made a lot of new friends since starting work there, too. Jordan rarely spoke about his dad to his mum, or to anyone for that matter and Georgia knew that it was unwise to press him to open up about that whole episode while the lad seemed to be doing so well otherwise. Jordan had even acquired a bit of a reputation in the scheme, too, as the man who had given his own dad a kicking and threw him out of the house, but Jordan wasn't bothered about that kind of fame. The lad, now a young man, still wanted to become an army engineer, but told his mum that he now wanted to earn a bit of money before applying for university – in essence, once school was over in May, he was going to work full-time at ASDA for a year. This was a major change to what the family's plans for Jordan had been, but Georgia respected his wishes and, as ever, said she would support her son in whatever he chose to do. Jordan was a bright, handsome lad, just like his father had been at that age, though Georgia thanked her lucky stars that her son hadn't dabbled in drugs, like she and his dad had at that age. Georgia desperately wanted her son to go to university and to become an engineer, even if that were to eventually be in the army. But she, like most mums, prioritised her child's happiness, besides, she had a strong hunch that a year working a dead-end job in a supermarket and being ordered around by all sorts of halfwits would deter her eldest from ever wanting to work an unskilled job ever again. So, young Jordan had his job, good friends and his wee girlfriend, Ciara, with his engineering studies on the horizon – it seemed that despite the family upheaval, Jordan was on a good path.

Wee Olivia, it seemed, had been a tad more impacted by the marital breakup of her parents. She became a bit more introverted and spent more and more time coding in her room alone or talking to online buddies in foreign countries while playing elaborate MMO RPG video games. Georgia was just pleased that she wasn't out in the scheme taking drugs or getting up to other mischief with kids her own age. Olivia still played football twice a week and was still into physical fitness, in a big way, but by the time she turned 16 that year, she had become bored of the gymnastics thing and had packed it in altogether. She still maintained her small group of friends and still seemed largely disinterested in boys, or in alcohol – she still loved coding and professed to her mum that one day she would be the female Mark Zuckerberg. Georgia, upon hearing that, had no idea who the fuck this Zuckerberg guy was, but she googled him, and was pleased that her daughter wanted to emulate such a tech giant.

Money was tight for the family, still, as 2018 moved into autumn. Jordan had passed his driving test that summer but with all the bills and Keith's debt repayment, even with her second job at Sky TV, there was no way that his mum could help him to get a car. Georgia was able to put him on the insurance for her ageing Renault Clio, but as she used the car for both of her jobs, Jordan didn't get to use it himself very often. Sometimes at weekends, though, he would drive his mum to work at the Sky TV call-centre in Livingston, and would pick her up again in the evening, meaning that he at least got the car during the day at weekends, to go for drives with Ciara, or to pick his little sister up from the shopping centre or from football.

Georgia had moved the weekly family shop from ASDA to ALDI, in an attempt to save money. There had been a bit of grumbling from the kids about not getting their favourite branded products anymore, but they had quickly learned that most products from the discount supermarkets are more or less the same as the branded ones, so they all got used to it. To save more money, she also switched all three of the family's mobile phones from O2 to Smartie Mobile, saving the household around £80 per month. The kids didn't like that at all, as suddenly they experienced the occasional phenomenon of disappearing texts and unexplained drop calls, but again, the kids and Georgia sucked that up. The house and car insurance were moved to cheaper companies. The gas and electric were switched, too, in an effort to save a few more pounds each month. As a family, they went from having one takeaway meal together per week to just one a month. Georgia's long liquid lunches in town on a Saturday afternoon with her friend, Isla, also had to be curtailed, partly because of work, mostly due to the cost. Instead, Georgia and Isla would have a wine and movie night once a month at home, instead, taking turns to host each other for a much-needed girly catchup.

Even with all these cost-cutting measures, the crippling repayments to the credit card companies and to Ocean Finance on the secured loan taken by Keith out against the family home meant that after all bills, expenses and essentials were taken into account, Georgia was left with barely £200 each month, even working two jobs. She now lived in fear of little things, like car maintenance or washing machine breakdown, as such things as these would now be financially catastrophic for the Smith family.

There was one kind of 'win', though. Shug Mann had never been in touch in 2018 about the 50 grand Keith still owed him. Georgia assumed that particular debt had followed her loser husband when he had left the family home, and she was right, though that had little to do with the benevolence of a scumbag gangster drug dealer and more to do with Shug's desire to maintain his financial grip over Keith for the long term – that debt, Georgia was sure, would hang around her estranged husband's neck like a yoke for eternity, and it wouldn't end well for him – she was certain of that.

As for Keith, he made no attempt to contact his family in 2018 at all. Georgia heard on the grapevine that he was living in a rented one-bedroom studio flat in Bellshill with some younger junkie lassie called Louise – probably the girl from the filthy video she'd been sent on WhatsApp that time. It seemed that Keith was living the life of a much younger man – football, drink, parties, drugs, betting, you name it. She also learned that Keith was still working as a driver for HM Solutions, and a simple Google search showed Georgia that her dissolute, waster of a husband was renting his little drug-den love nest from, that's right, you guessed it, HM lettings. Keith had sold his car, too, presumably to fund his pathetic new start in life.

Georgia still cared deeply about Keith but had fallen out of love with him soon after seeing that now infamous sex tape on her phone. As 2018 became 2019, though, she became increasingly upset at the fact that her husband had made no attempt to contact her or their children – for the children's sake. She tried to look for him on social media but could find no trace of him – he'd clearly pre-blocked her on all of his socials. To Georgia, and the kids, it was like he'd simply vanished – the only word that they ever got of him was second-hand information that Georgia sometimes heard from work colleagues, or rumours that the kids heard from people in the scheme – and those tales seldom brought good tidings, in fact, the stories were usually sad, or embarrassing, or both.

CHAPTER SEVENTEEN

Tell Me Why

March of 2019 saw Georgia apply for, and receive, a promotion at the council – she was now head of procurement. The promotion came with a pay-rise of almost £4000 per year and brought with it far more responsibility – something that Georgia relished. The extra dough from her main job meant that she could have packed in the weekend gig at Sky TV, but Georgia chose not to, she liked to be busy and the extra money still provided the family with much needed security – after all, the household was still being run on a shoestring because of all the debt that Keith had left behind.

Georgia, by the spring of 2019, was getting lonely, too. She was over the loss of Keith and ready to dip her toe into the world of dating for the first time since her teens. Georgia found this daunting, yet also strangely exciting. On one of her girly nights in with Isla, Georgia did her hair and her makeup and put on her best cocktail dress, with Isla acting as photographer, until they had a decent mini portfolio of photos and selfies. Isla then made a basic Tinder profile for her and uploaded the best photos that they had taken to the account. That evening, the two of them drank wine, ate pizza and swiped through the world's biggest dating app. They giggled and scoffed at the guys' profiles who had gym selfies or topless mirror pics – losers. They hastily swiped left on the profiles of men that had Red-Hand of Ulster memes or Bobby Sands photos in their profiles – bigotry just isn't attractive, neither are people who openly flaunt their allegiances on dating apps. They both fell about in guffaws of laughter when they came across the obvious fake profiles – 'guys' with catalogue model stolen images who were probably really scammers from Nigeria. In their frenzy of swiping, though, Georgia and Isla did find plenty of profiles that had potential, Isla swiping right on them on Georgia's behalf, before Georgia reclaimed her phone and started to browse herself once more. That night, the two of them had a great laugh together and Georgia swiped right on around 40 decent-sounding good-looking guys within a 50-mile radius – it was the most fun that Georgia had enjoyed since Keith had left the house two years ago.

Georgia was no innocent or naive woman, but she had been with Keith and Keith only since 1999 – apart from an illicit drunken snog with an Italian builder she'd flirted with one night while on a hen-do in Glasgow back in 2010, which she had instantly regretted. Dating had changed somewhat since 1999, and when Georgia opened her Tinder profile later that evening after Isla had gone home, she realised the true extent of that change.

She had matched with nine men, but had notifications saying that another 78 men had 'liked' her – she could see all 78 of those profiles if she opted to upgrade her Tinder membership by paying £10 a month for the 'free' app. Though the thought of having almost 90 men interested in her was exhilarating, she decided to first message the nine guys whom she had mutually matched with. Georgia was excited! In the past, internet dating had been seen as sad or sleazy, but now it was the norm. With giddy trepidation, she opened the first message from one of her nine matches. It was from a guy called Gary, aged 42, from Glasgow. His pics showed him in various cheerful poses, one in a business suit, one on a jet-ski, one wearing a tool belt and rigger boots, one in a bar on a night out with two other guys who were as handsome as him and one of him cuddling his Alsatian dog. His profile stated that he owned his own building business, liked golf, snooker and reading, and that he had never been married or had children. Georgia had smiled as she browsed his profile – he sounded lovely -maybe he was *the one*? She read his introductory message.

"I want to stick my cock between your big tits bbe what's your number?"

Georgia stared at the message for a moment, feeling sick to her stomach, but she was new to this, maybe this handsome fella was having a laugh?

She replied "Lol. Easy Tiger, tell me more about you".

To her considerable surprise, Gary replied straight away.

"7 inches and hot 4 u bbe, u busy tonight?"

Georgia tutted and blocked Gary, shaking her head. She'd been told by friends and girls at work that some men were like that online, so she moved onto the next message, after all, a girl sometimes has to kiss a frog before she finds her prince.

The next profile was an older guy, Drew, 50, from Alloa. In his pictures he looked every inch the distinguished silver fox – suited and booted, with a nice smile, looking fit for his age. His profile said he was a widower who worked as an accountant. Georgia liked his profile, maybe an older guy was just what she needed. She gazed at his profile photo for a moment, imagining sharing a meal with him on the shores of Loch Lomond, or holding his hand atop the Eiffel Tower. She read his message.

"Hi Georgia, you look really lovely, have you got any more pics? Drew".

She replied.

"Hi Drew, thank you, yes, I have a few, mostly just selfies at home, would you like me to send them?"

Drew replied within 30 seconds.

"Yes please, you're so beautiful, send topless/nudes, please. Drew."

Georgia uttered a 'fuck's sake' under her breath but tried to give him the benefit of the doubt. Maybe he was just having a laugh. She was typing a witty rebuke when a picture appeared in the chat, from Drew. It was a picture of a man's penis, with the pubic hair around the base and balls all neatly shaved away. Accompanying it was another message from Drew.

"Well, you like that?"

Georgia felt sick again, deleting her witty rebuke and instead messaging him.

"You dirty auld cunt."

That, too, got a near instant reply from Drew.

"Oh yeah babe I love that dirty talk, don't stop, send topless pic."

A disgusted Georgia closed the message and blocked Drew. She wondered if it was something in her profile or photos that had made these two men think she'd enjoy being serenaded with such filth. She saw that one of the profiles that Isla had taken of her did show quite a lot of her ample, firm cleavage, so she deleted that particular photo from her profile, and went back to checking the other seven messages.

Roy, a handsome taxi driver from Whitburn, who liked hillwalking, wanted to know if she did anal. Blocked.

Simon, from Motherwell, a fitness instructor, sent a photo of his dick with the caption 'all for you'. Blocked.

Joe from Kilmarnock seemed lovely at first, charming, even, but it soon became clear that he was really an African prince looking for a bank account to send 40 million Ugandan Shillings to. Blocked.

Yannick, a Polish HGV driver from Livingston, who liked heavy metal music and was recently divorced, started off well enough but within ten minutes was asking if he could worship Georgia's big tits. Blocked.

Brian, a business entrepreneur from Denny, sent a naked mirror selfie and a dick pic, but on the dick pic he used a smiley face filter to cover his bellend. Blocked.

Forbes, from Ayr, opened by asking Georgia if she was into threesomes. Georgia had sometimes fantasised about kissing other girls, but still – Blocked.

Billy, from Grangemouth, 38, sounded more promising, though he did open with a long, sad monologue message about how much his ex had hurt him. Georgia replied in turn, saying how she too had been hurt. Billy then immediately sent her a picture of his cock. Blocked.

After these exchanges, Georgia's appetite for and enthusiasm about internet dating was somewhat lessened. She went into the Tinder settings and turned off notifications for it, before posting a rant in the WhatsApp group chat she was in with Isla and her other friends, posting screengrabs she had taken of those filthy messages. Nobody in the group chat was surprised – it was normal, they said. In the end, they all had a good laugh about it in the group chat until the wee small hours, which cheered Georgia up a bit. After that, though, Georgia decided that dating apps weren't for her.

CHAPTER EIGHTEEN

Get Get Down

In April of 2019, Georgia, in her new role as council procurement head, was called to a meeting at work because one of the companies who provided buildings maintenance for the council as a sub-contractor had gone bust, leaving behind a backlog of work that needed to be cleared. The contract was put out to public tender and four companies from the central belt put in bids. Georgia was on the council panel which would decide who got the contracts. The next day, Georgia and three colleagues sat and listened to proposals from three different companies – one from Glasgow, one from Coatbridge and another from a big nationwide conglomerate, one of those parasitic companies akin to Mears or Serco, who often take on big government contracts at a loss, just to get the deal, as its costs can be absorbed by their wider organisation, meaning that local firms can rarely compete with them. The fourth and final proposal was from a new local company run by a woman – AH Repairs. By the time the representatives of AH Repairs were about to be ushered into the meeting room to make their pitch, Georgia was almost falling asleep. It had been a long day – tedious, in fact. The finer points of local government finance and public sector buildings maintenance would bore a statue to tears, after all.

When all was ready with Georgia and her colleagues, they summoned in the final delegation. A blonde woman in her late 20s, wearing a sharp, tight business suit entered first. She made her way along the line of council reps, shaking each of their hands in turn. When she reached Georgia, she smiled. There was something familiar about her, but Georgia couldn't place it. Next up was an overweight younger lassie – early 20s Georgia guessed – wearing a navy-blue skirt-suit. She seemed nervous and her hands were sweaty. Finally, the group was rounded up by a big, balding middle-aged man wearing a Marc Darcy business suit.

Shug.

As soon as Georgia saw him, her stomach dropped, and suddenly she knew where she recognised the blonde woman from – it was Shug's receptionist/girlfriend. Reluctantly, Georgia shook his hand, determined to remain professional in front of her colleagues. Shug smirked slightly as he walked to the middle of the room and stood alongside his group.

The blonde woman seemed to be the group's spokesperson, while the chubby young lassie was clearly their lackey, as she carried a briefcase and a large notepad in her hands.

The spokesperson introduced herself. Her name was Alana Renfield, operations chief at AH Repairs, with years of experience of leasing between the private and public sector. The younger, chubby lass with them, who was there to take notes, was introduced as Louise Hall, the company's administrative assistant, and Shug was introduced as 'Hugh, who some of you may know'.

Georgia didn't really hear the formal introduction for, in her head, she now repeated the mantra.

"Shug Mann, Shug's girlfriend and that wee slag who was fucking my husband on that video."

To Georgia, this situation was as near to a dystopian nightmare as could be imagined. In fact, it was far worse than that. This was humiliation on a grand scale for her – was it deliberate?

How the fuck had Hugh 'Shug' Mann managed to get anywhere near the bidding process for a lucrative local government repairs and maintenance contract? He was a fucking drug dealer, a gangster and a nasty piece of work! These thoughts raced through Georgia's head as she closely examined her copy of the written bid submitted by AH Repairs. Then she saw it – Shug was only listed as a non-executive director. On paper, at least, it was Miss Alana Renfield who ran this particular show. She was the face of the operation, so, everything appeared to be above board – but Georgia knew that it just fucking *wasn't*.

She tried not to stare at the chubby younger lass, Louise, who was taking notes, but it was hard. What the fuck had Keith seen in this decidedly plain, fat wee howk? Sure, she was much younger, but other than that, Georgia couldn't understand it. She then realised how unprofessional she was being – this was work, so she diverted her mind back to listening to the pitch coming from Alana. That just made things even worse, because Alana's pitch was dynamic, well-informed and ticked every box, as far as the contract was concerned. Alana held forth for a full ten minutes, covering every possible angle and outlining just how good a job AH Repairs would do for the council and for the people of Lanarkshire. Georgia's three colleagues on the panel were nodding away, smiling, lapping this up, while Georgia cast her eye on the trio again. Louise, the wee homewrecker, was busily taking notes, her tongue sticking out of one side of her mouth as she scribbled. Georgia didn't want to look at the tongue which had doubtless by now spent many an hour all over her husband's cock, up his arse and fuck knows where else, Alana was too nauseatingly polished and perfect, so her gaze drifted to Shug. Shug was eating a footlong subway meatball roll, almost deep-throating the bloody thing. Marinara sauce was dribbling down his chin onto his suit and onto the floor. Shug looking even more grotesque than usual, not caring about the mess, focussing only on devouring his gigantic, messy snack. When he eventually finished it – two minutes to eat a foot long roll – Shug let out one of his big, disgusting trademark burps, then made a pathetic apology for the burp, as Alana was finishing her pitch to the panel.

Georgia looked at the three of them, the slag, the psycho who had ruined her family, and the psycho's girlfriend. Though Alana had actually done Georgia and her family no wrong, that Georgia knew of, Georgia still hated her, too – guilt by association – it's human nature.

As the meeting was wrapping up, Shug was puffing heavily on his inhaler, clearly having some breathing difficulties, but after a moment the three-person delegation from AH Repairs thanked the panel and were gone from the meeting room. Georgia was relieved to see them go, breathing a huge sigh of relief as the meeting room door closed behind them. When Georgia got home that night her head was in pieces from that last pitch, so to take her mind off it she decided to do some laundry. She washed her own clothes first, realising that she hadn't bought any new clothes for herself since Keith had left the house. While the clothes were on a washing machine cycle, she phoned her mum and dad to check that all was well with them – they'd been greatly supportive to her since Keith's departure but she hadn't seen very much of them recently due to the fact that she was always working – Georgia didn't feel great about that, especially as her mum's health had never really recovered fully after the heart attack that she had suffered back in 2016, but she knew that at least her mum still had her dad. After phoning her parents, Georgia put on Radio 2 and decided to do more washing. She went upstairs. Olivia, now nearly 17, was busy talking loudly through a headset, obviously gaming online with her myriad overseas buddies. Georgia decided not to disturb her, instead opting to go into Jordan's bedroom. Jordan was staying at Ciara's house for the night, so Georgia grabbed her son's wicker laundry basket and carried it downstairs. Jordan usually did most of his own washing – he was a good boy like that, but Georgia needed a task. She got downstairs and plonked his laundry basket down next to the washing machine in the kitchen, beginning to sort out his dirty clothes. As she unrolled sweaty socks and took in the heady aroma of stale spunk, farts and sweat, her blood ran cold, for there was another smell, coming from his blue Lacoste tee-shirt – the one he always wore to parties – it stank of green! The overpowering scent of herbal cannabis soon nullified the laundry's other pungent whiffs, and she unfolded the tee-shirt, sniffing at it to make sure that it was indeed green that she could smell. It was.

Georgia felt a sense of dread creep over her – she didn't want the kids taking drugs. Then, common sense kicked in. Her son was a young man, maybe he had been experimenting, maybe he and Ciara liked to use it to enhance the joys of sex, maybe Jordan hadn't been smoking it at all, but someone he was with had been? Georgia paused for a moment, then put all of Jordan's washing into the machine and turned it on. She would speak to him about it when she saw him – that's all she could really do, after all, it was 2019, now, it was just the smell of weed, that didn't automatically mean that her son was destined for a junkie overdose death in a pool of piss, like in the 1980s, did it? After all, drugs were mainstream now, inevitable, almost. Still, Georgia didn't sleep well that night.

CHAPTER NINETEEN

Light My Fire

T he next day at work, Georgia and her three colleagues from the previous day's panel had to decide on which of the four tenders to accept for the council buildings maintenance contract. Georgia's mind that day was preoccupied about how she might ask her son if he had been smoking cannabis, but she tried to focus on the task at hand.

With every fibre of her being, Georgia wanted to give the contract to anybody other than Shug's outfit, AH Repairs, but Georgia was professional enough, somehow, to put her personal feelings to one side. Shug's girl, Alana, had made a superb presentation and that company had tendered by far the best bid, all things considered. Georgia and her three colleagues soon discounted the bids from the Coatbridge firm and the Glasgow one – both were too expensive, and the companies seemed too inexperienced. This left the bid from AH Repairs – short for Alana and Hugh's Repairs- and the one from the big faceless UK-wide conglomerate - Ashco. After some deliberation, the panel voted to award the emergency contract to AH Repairs – their bid was slightly higher than that of Ashco, but council and Holyrood directives regarding the awarding of local contracts to local firms wherever possible meant that AH Repairs got the gig.

During the panel's deliberations, every fibre of Georgia's being had wanted to scream to her colleagues that AH Repairs was owned by a gangster, that that gangster and his machinations had played a part in the destruction of her family, that his minions with their drugs were destroying the schemes, that an employee of AH Repairs – Louise – had been shagging her husband, but Georgia just couldn't. She had no real proof of what Shug, and his businesses, really were, and her colleagues would want proof, and would doubtless also ask her why, knowing that she had never reported his activities to the police. As for the Louise angle, she didn't want anyone at her work to know about that – she still felt so humiliated by that entire episode of her life, besides, that was hardly grounds to deny the company that the lassie happened to work for a chance at getting a contract – she would look petty, vindictive and unprofessional. Moreover, the bid from AH Repairs was the best bid and was in the best interests of the council and the local populace, too, so, Georgia said nothing. It had been two years since Keith had been thrown out of the family home, Georgia was just starting to move on – she didn't want to have to think or talk about her ex, or Shug, again.

That night at home in the kitchen, Georgia confronted Jordan about the smell of hash that she had noticed on his clothes when doing his laundry. At first, Jordan became defensive, saying that he did his own laundry, and accusing his mum of spying on him, but he soon calmed down and opened up. To Georgia's surprise, her son had a lot to say about the matter.

"Look, Mum, everybody my age tries drugs these days, it's not like when you were my age and being a drug-user meant lying in a filthy squat with a needle in your arm – things are different now. I don't really like the drink, I prefer a wee smoke now and then – after everything that's happened with you and dad these last couple of years, I bloody well need *something*. Ciara and I don't do it that often, only really at parties or when we have time alone together, to our generation, a wee joint or a bong is no different to having a pint. You see that, right Mum?"

Georgia listened and was impressed, though also sad – her wee boy was clearly a man now who could make his own decisions. Jordan continued, reassuring her.

"And look, Mum, I don't buy the stuff locally, I get it from a guy at work, we don't have anything to do with the local junkie circles, and I don't take any other drugs – no coke, no Es, no speed, just weed. I'm not going to end up like dad, Mum."

Georgia wasn't reassured completely, but nor was she naive. Her son had made a clear, well-reasoned argument. He had obviously given it some thought and wasn't just jumping in with his eyes closed.

"Ok, son, look, you can always talk to me about drugs, or anything, you know that, right? I did dabble a wee bit myself when I was your age," said Georgia, impressed by just how much of a cool mum she actually was. "Son, what about Olivia?"

Jordan scoffed, shaking his head. "You're joking, aye? Mum, ma wee sister is a boring wee geek. No, she doesn't smoke weed, or drink, or do anything really, except talk to her weirdo pals online and muck about with her computers – you've nothing to worry about there. If I ever hear that someone has tried to give her gear, I'll fucking kill them."

Georgia believed him and actually felt a bit daft that she'd even asked that about her daughter in the first place.

"So, son, have you got any hash on you right now?" Georgia asked her son in an accusing tone.

Jordan hesitated for a moment then answered.

"Mum, it's not 1997 anymore. Nobody calls it hash, it's weed, or smoke, or green, and aye, I have, I've got a wee bit of Stardog – don't worry, though, I'll not be smoking it here at the house."

Georgia looked at him. "Oh really...that's a shame. Why don't you skin up?"

"Eh? Are you serious? Here? Now?" asked Jordan, in disbelief.

"Aye son, fuck it, I could do with it after the last few days."

Jordan got out his big silver rizla and small plastic bag of weed, and within moments had rolled a perfect wee joint. Georgia was both impressed and disgusted by his skill, speed and aptitude in that department. Mother and son stepped out onto the back patio and sparked up a wee number together. At first, neither of them said much as they took turns puffing on the joint, Jordan laughing at his mum's over-the-top, excessively spluttering cough. Jordan's laugh set his mum off laughing, too, but she was also still coughing and was soon doing a hilarious hybrid cough/laugh which sounded like a walrus arguing with a hyena. Jordan's giggles soon turned to guffaws, which only made his mum laugh louder and cough harder, until eventually they were both in stitches at each other. As a few raindrops splattered the patio at their feet, they decided to go back inside, Jordan stubbing out the joint on the wall. Once back in the kitchen and still in fits of laughter from the strong weed, Georgia managed to stop giggling for long enough to say.

"Right, son, you make tea, I'll shove Netflix on."

"Oh aye, that's a fair division of labour, isn't it?" laughed Jordan, but his mum had already made for the living room and had taken the sofa. Jordan joined her a few minutes later, passing her a KitKat mug of strong tea, then sitting in one of the armchairs with his own brew. They spent the next couple of hours laughing their heads off to old episodes of Peep Show and Father Ted, and eating not one, but three huge share-bags of Aldi's own brand Doritos rip-off. Georgia later sent Jordan to the petrol station to get her a Caramac, too, after they'd had a second joint together in the pissing rain outside. Mum and son had begun the evening with an awkward question and ended up having superb laughs together. Towards the end of the evening, with Jordan almost dozing off in the armchair, Georgia had a realisation – everything was going to be alright for her and for her beloved kids – the past was the past - though she also promised herself not to touch weed again after that evening – this new stuff was far too strong! That night, Georgia had the best night's sleep she had enjoyed in years – certainly the best since Keith had left.

The past was the past – everything was going to be alright.

CHAPTER TWENTY

Anthem

By July of 2019, the country had a new prime minister. Yet another old Etonian, Boris Johnson, became the latest unelected Tory prime minister, ousting previous PM Theresa May in a coup driven by the upper classes' disdain for May's soft Brexit deal and enabled by rampant misogyny within government. By then, there'd been three different prime ministers in three years and uncertainty over whether or not Brexit would go ahead wasn't helping the country's flatlining economy at all, but then again, neither would Brexit itself. For the broken biscuits – that is, the working-class people in housing schemes whom neoliberalism and trickle-down economics had purposefully forsaken – not much had changed. Wages were still low, public services were cut to the bone, the NHS was struggling and, crucially, drug dealers and organised crime syndicates were still operating with impunity, from Land's End to John O'Groats. By now, the drugs industry wasn't even bothering to try to hide its money-laundering fronts anymore. A failing UK economy somehow still had booms in takeaway food and desserts, nail and hair salons, Turkish barbers, Tattoo parlours, magically reinvigorated previously failing local pubs, and a multitude of independent gyms – all cash-only, of course – always *cash only*. By then, the imperialist white powder had, it was rumoured, even begun to infect the corridors of power at Westminster,

Cardiff, and Holyrood, with its use now the norm among politicians, staff, SPADs, reporters and, well, almost everyone connected to those places. The drugs epidemic had reached and infected the very people whose job was supposed to be to protect the people from such blatant exploitation in the first place.

The Smith family were doing ok. With Jordan now 19 and Olivia 17, Georgia was no longer tied to the house, as she once had been. Her, more or less grown-up, kids came and went as they pleased, getting on with their lives. This left Georgia a little bit more time to check in on her mum and dad, to see friends, and to have a bit more of a social life. She still worked two jobs but managed to find time to go to the gym, to do yoga and swimming, and even to have a few dates. Georgia had found a better dating app which required women to send the first message after matching and had actually met one or two decent fellas on it. Nothing serious had come of the dates as of yet, but Georgia had at least sated her need for sex and male companionship, after virtually living like a nun since her marriage had broken down two and a half years earlier.

Jordan was due to start university that September, while Olivia had just decided to stay on at high school into 5th year. Despite the crippling debt left behind by Keith, the family had survived, and the children's futures were intact. Jordan planned to do his engineering degree at the University of the West of Glasgow and to keep his part-time job in the supermarket. Olivia, meanwhile, had recently begun designing apps at home and selling them to tech companies, utilising her natural talent and wealth of knowledge of computer programming – Georgia was proud of her children, they were her world.

The kids' dad still hadn't been in touch with his estranged family, except to send the odd birthday card. Georgia heard wee stories now and then about her AWOL husband, none of them bore good news – they usually involved tales to do with the local underworld and included, as extras, many notorious characters. Georgia was, however, somewhat numb at hearing one rumour that Keith had managed to impregnate a younger woman, and that local business paragon, Hugh Mann, and his partner, Alana, were also expecting a child, too. Georgia, and indeed, half the town, would shudder at the thought of whatever coked-up sex party might have brought about those pregnancies.

In early August, those rumours were confirmed by Isla, when she and Georgia went out for drinks one Friday night, at a mutual friend's 50th birthday bash in the function suite of The Stuart Hotel. The function suite was superbly decorated that night with streamers, banners and even giant photos of the birthday girl, Fiona, at various stages of her life.

As with most 50th dos, most of the younger ones buggered off early to hit nightclubs or house parties, but most of the older party-goers stayed on, badly dancing like the dads and mums that they had all become – the women doing that 80s hip-swivelling and arm swinging routine popularised by the lassies from The Human League back in the 1980s, the middle-aged men dancing beside them mostly doing generic middle-aged white man dance – but all of them loving it and not really giving a fuck. All the classics one might expect to hear at a 50th were played by the enthusiastic DJ. *Stuck in the middle with you* by Stealer's Wheel. *Happy Birthday* by Altered Images. A few songs by *INXS* – the birthday girl's favourites, and some really old house and Hi-NRG tracks, *The London Boys, Yazz* and *Inner City*.

Never forget, inside every middle-aged person lurks the soul of a 20-something – you just need the right tunes and conditions to coax it out of their ageing bodies.

The DJ – a weegie who chose to address his crowd in a mid-Atlantic yank-esque accent, as if he were presenting on the long defunct Atlantic

252 station – took to the mic to ask everybody to head to the dancefloor for the birthday girl's favourite song.

TIME WARP, T-T-T-T-TIMEWARP, T-T-T ... ARE YOU READY? YEAH?
SO, YOU THINK YOU CAN DO THE TIMEWARP, EH?
ALRIGHT! WELL, LET ME TELL YOU ... IT'S ASTOUNDING...

It wasn't the version from the Rocky Horror Show, it was the 1980s disco version of *The Time Warp,* the more upbeat Stock, Aitken and Waterman version, sung by Damian, and it filled the dancefloor of the Stuart Hotel function suite.

It's astounding
Time is fleeting
Madness takes its toll
But listen closely
Not for very much longer
I've got to keep control

Georgia, looking stunning in a figure-hugging red dress, had rushed to the dancefloor when it came on, dragging Isla with her, Isla almost tripping over her longer green party dress en route. Soon, everybody was dancing to the cheesy but popular track and doing all the actions, boy and girls alike grabbing their chests at the 'put your hands on your tits/hips' part. There were a few single men whom Georgia and Isla had already noted and checked out, as well as a few decent married ones, but as the song came to an end and the lazy cunt in the DJ booth went straight onto Damian's other, more shitey hit, *Wig Wam Bam*, the dancefloor began to empty slowly again. Isla was a smoker and gestured with two fingers to Georgia that she was going out for a fag, and Georgia decided to go with her.

The Stuart Hotel didn't just have a function suite, it had a large public bar, too, which took up the other side of the building's ground floor. Function suite and public bar thus shared a foyer, cloakroom kiosk, and toilets, as with many such venues. The two women made their way outside and Isla lit up a cigarette as they sat at one of the tables at the outside seating area. From there, through the big glass doors, Georgia could see that the toilet doors in the foyer, both male and female, were busier than Piccadilly Circus. She mentioned that to Isla, who just shrugged and said "the ching brigade, sad bastards". There were, however, a lot of sad bastards about that evening. Georgia had noticed many people from the 50th that either had chronic bladder weakness or were regularly nipping to the toilets to powder their noses.

"We don't need that, hen, we're bad enough with a drink" said Isla, giggling as she took puffs on her cigarette.

"Och, I know, it's just, it's fucking everywhere now, does everybody take it?" said Georgia.

"Look, I can't stand listening to folk slaver on it, either, hen, listen, it's everywhere now and there's nothing going to change that. They say it's good for having sex, but my Cammy took some on his work night out and came home horny as fuck, but he couldn't do the business, he went Mr Floppy, trying to get him up me was like trying to fit a marshmallow through a fucking piggy bank slot".

They both burst out laughing, Georgia adding, "Aye, it makes them talk the talk, but they cannae walk the walk". The laughter continued, but then Georgia remembered that her husband, Keith, hadn't ever struggled to get hard with coke, either with her or with that junkie skank from that video –

oh fuck. The video. That skank. Georgia sighed. She hadn't thought about any of that stuff all day.

Isla apologised for what she'd said, she simply hadn't thought, but Georgia was quick to tell her that no apology was required.

"Look, don't be daft, it's been a good night and I'm alright, really."

"You've did really well, Georgia," said Isla. "For what you've had to put up with, you're a strong person. Your husband was a daftie, but your kids are amazing, you've a successful career, and, well…"

"Well what?" asked Georgia.

"Well, I wish I was still the same bloody dress size as I was when I was 20, you're such a bitch by the way."

The two of them were laughing again, alcohol and their long friendship keeping them from going melancholic – that's what friends do. Isla was right, too, Georgia did look amazing for someone who was almost 40. Isla had gone from size 8 to size 14 in the last 20 years, but still looked good, too – natural beauty tends to be lasting, and they both had it in abundance.

Isla finished her cigarette and the two headed back inside, the strains of *Dancing Queen* by Abba clearly audible, emanating from the function suite. As they walked through the foyer towards the sound, a heavy wooden door swung open in front of them, coming within about an inch of smashing both their faces in. It was the door to the disabled toilet.

"Haw! You, watch what you're fuckin' daein'," screamed Isla in a course, scheme accent that Georgia hadn't heard her use in almost two decades. A young man and a young woman emerged from behind the door, sheepishly, the man greeting them with a loud, "Oh fuck, I'm really sorry, are you alright?" He was handsome – though young – and wore a grey Armani tee-shirt and smart-casual trousers, his young female companion was all trout-pout and hair extensions, and she wore a short, tight, ruffled halter-neck mini dress.

It was Jordan and his girlfriend, Ciara.

Georgia's annoyance at almost being decapitated by the door dissipated immediately, and Isla instantly switched from fight-mode to drunken auntie mode, too, giving Jordan and his girlfriend a big hug each. Georgia was pleased to see them. She noticed her son's flies were half down.

"Oh, what a surprise, what are you two doing here?" she asked.

Jordan hesitated then spoke quickly. "Erm, we're just having drinks in the bar next door with pals from my work, I didn't realise your night out was here, Mum."

"Naw, son, I mean, what were you two doing in the disabled bog?"

Georgia knew they'd probably been having some cheap sexual thrills together in the disabled toilet, after all, in most pubs and clubs it's the only place with the privacy and the space that doesn't have piss everywhere, but she wanted to embarrass her son a little bit – that was her right as a mum.

Jordan and Ciara both turned scarlet and looked at each other, then Jordan said, "Well, erm ... we were ..."

"I'm only pulling your leg, son, I was your age once, remember," said Georgia, warmly, Isla adding, in a faux-stern tone, "I hope you used protection."

"Well, aye, we did, the lock on that door is well sturdy," quipped Jordan.

All four of them erupted laughing. Jordan and Ciara asked Georgia and Isla to join them in the public bar for a drink, and they agreed.

"You'll like my pals, Mum, they're sound," said Jordan, as he held open the bar door for the three ladies, like the young gentleman that he was. Ciara headed to the bar. It was only when Jordan grinned at her once more that Georgia realised – his eyes were like fucking flying saucers!

Seething inside but appearing calm, Georgia sat down next to Isla as Jordan introduced his five pals to them both, all of them sitting at a large table next to a huge bay window. Ciara soon appeared with four odd-looking drinks, which she announced were Pornstar Martinis.

Jordan's pals seemed ok, nice lads and lassies, but they too had eyes like saucers, and from the amount of nose sniffing they were doing for no apparent reason, it was obvious that they'd all partaken of the devil's dandruff. When you're just drinking and you come into the company of folk who've also been taking drugs, it's fucking weird. Still, Georgia enjoyed having a drink with her son in a bar – it was the first time that they'd really done that and she decided not to pull him up about the coke thing – the last thing she wanted was a confrontation or to ruin her night, or his, though deep down, of course, hers was already ruined the second that she saw the state of her son's peepers.

Later, Georgia and Isla went back through to the function suite to see their old friends and had another wee middle-aged dance, before getting taxis home. As they were leaving, Isla did try to tell Georgia not to worry, that Jordan was a smart lad, a nice lad, and that he was probably just experimenting with the Charlie – after all, all the young ones were at it these days. Georgia knew Isla was probably right, but that didn't matter. After all that had befallen her family because of that drug, her dear son was now a user, too. And, if he was a cocaine user, that meant that he or his friends had acquired the drugs from a dealer, and if that dealer was from within a ten-mile radius, that meant that, one way or another, her son had bought his cocaine from Hugh 'Shug' Mann.

Georgia knew she'd have to have a big talk with her son about this, but she wasn't going to do that when he was wasted or on a comedown, or when his girlfriend was there. She planned just to talk to him privately during the week, he'd been an adult when she'd confronted him about smoking weed, so Georgia hoped that they'd be able to have a similar heart to heart about the ching, too. After all, Jordan was smarter than his dad was.

CHAPTER TWENTY-ONE

He's on the Phone

The day after the 50th bash, Georgia's mind was reeling. The drug that had destroyed her marriage and shattered her finances now seemed to be threatening to take hold of her son too, well, she wouldn't let that happen, not on her watch. Jordan had stayed out overnight, but Georgia knew he would be home that evening. She paced. She cleaned. Anything to give her an outlet for the torrent of feelings threatening to overwhelm her. Her son, her smart, handsome son had taken coke. She tried to calm herself. Maybe it wasn't that bad. Maybe it was a one-off. But she couldn't help her thoughts from spiralling into worst-case scenarios.

When Jordan finally came home, Georgia was sitting at the kitchen table waiting for him.

"Erm … hi, Mum," he said, sensing that something was up. He took off his jacket hesitantly and draped it over the back of one of the chairs.

"Hi, son." She replied, her voice cool and monotonous.

Jordan watched her for a moment, trying to sus out what was wrong.

"Is everything ok?" He asked.

"You tell me." She replied, refusing to give anything away.

Jordan paused for a moment, cogs turning.

"If this is about me and Ciara in the bog last night …" he began, but his mum cut over him.

"No, Jordan, it's not about that. It's about the other thing you and your friends were doing in the bogs last night."

Realisation dawned on him, and Jordan swallowed guiltily, knowing he had been caught. He tried for a few minutes to defend himself, to come up with some sort of plausible lie to cover his tracks, but his mum wasn't having any of it.

"Ok, Mum, I'm sorry. My friends were experimenting with coke, and they asked me if I wanted some. I didn't want to look like a weirdo by saying no, so I tried it. Just once, but I promise it won't happen again. I wasn't even really that into it."

Georgia was doubtful about that last remark, but glad that her son had admitted to using the coke. She thought about pressing the matter, about drilling into him the dangers of taking class-A drugs and telling him how upset she was that he had tried it, but she knew that wouldn't help matters. Backing him into a corner would only make him more likely to rebel, and to keep things from her in the future. Instead, she simply said, "I just don't want you to end up like your dad; you're better than that."

"I know, Mum, I won't."

He sounded sure, and Georgia hoped he meant it. However, even if he was downplaying his involvement in the drug-taking, she felt reassured by the fact that come September, he would be engrossed in his Engineering course at uni and wouldn't have as much free time on his hands to get up to mischief. For now, though, all she could do was hope.

November of 2019 came around and, for once, the country had a real choice in the upcoming general election. In the red corner was a, once again, socialist Labour Party led by veteran left-winger, Jeremy Corbyn, promising to renationalise failing industries, an end to austerity, a repaired NHS, a better deal for the country's youth and security for the country's sick, disabled and elderly – to be paid for by the billionaires. In the blue corner was Tory leader, Boris Johnson, who promised to continue the country's suicidal Brexit policy, to build 40 new hospitals by 2024 and to 'level up' the UK – whatever the fuck that meant. One was principled, dedicated, caring and a lifelong anti-racist. The other was a bumbling out-of-touch, populist old Etonian, at the time best known for making hideous remarks about minorities. After nine years of Tory austerity, it should've been a Labour landslide. However, once again, not one major party had anything in its manifesto about organised crime or drugs.

The Smith household was genuinely split on the upcoming election. Georgia liked most of Labour's policies but had seen pictures on Facebook of Mr Corbyn attending IRA funerals, and posing with Osama Bin Laden at Highbury, among other things, so she had decided not to vote Labour, especially after hearing workplace rumours about Corbyn's links to the IRA and to Hamas. In vain, her son, Jordan tried to point out to her that the images that she had seen had been photoshopped and that the IRA and Hamas stuff was just part of a gigantic smear. Jordan was an ardent Corbynite, being both a student and a poorly paid part-time worker, he could be nothing else. Olivia, still only 17, had no vote, but was pretty vocal in her support of both Corbyn, the SNP and the Green Party – although none of the three members of the Smith household wanted Scottish independence – their family traumas had shown them what could happen when families split up.

Georgia's mum, Janice, had suffered a second heart attack and had tragically died a few hours later, on the last Saturday of September. Georgia had been at work, at her weekend job at SKY TV in Livingston, that day, and by the time that she had gotten word of her mum's collapse and had driven to the hospital in Lanarkshire, her mum was gone. Doctors later told Georgia, and her devastated Dad, Alex, that her mum had died from an arrest brought on by a leaking aorta. The loss of a parent to any human being is a watershed in life – entailing grief beyond comparison – and Georgia was no different. She blamed herself for her mum's death. If she'd been around for her mum and dad more, instead of always working, going to the gym or swimming and sleeping, maybe her mum would've lived a bit longer, she thought. She was sure that the business about Keith leaving the family home and his drug addiction and all of the local gossip that came with that had hastened on her mother's heart attack, too – the older generation always viewed drug-related problems through a far darker prism, after all – to Janice and Alex, the loss of their beloved son-in-law to these drugs was a bitter pill to swallow – a failure of their parenting, somehow, even though it probably wasn't. Moreover, Georgia had been working in Livingston at her second job on the actual day of her mum's death, that second job that she had been forced to take on in order to be able to afford to keep the family home and to pay off the crippling debts left behind by her errant, junkie absent husband. Those debts had meant that she was sitting in a call centre in Livingston when she should've been looking after her elderly mum, in Georgia's mind. Of course, there was a common denominating factor in all of those reasons why Georgia felt so guilty about her mother's death – that factor was local gangster, businessman and drug baron, Hugh Mann. But, by then, by late 2019, Georgia had long since stopped harbouring anything other than disdain for her one-time classmate turned drug dealer – she knew that if it wasn't Shug, it would doubtless have been somebody else supplying gear to her husband – that's just how Scotland was, now – the other stuff with Shug, the sexual stuff, that simply didn't matter now either, as he had left her alone ever since sending her the smutty video of her coked-up husband.

No, Georgia blamed herself for her mum's death, despite reassurances from the kids, her dad, other family members and friends that she was utterly blameless. Georgia, as ever, kept things together, though, on the surface at least, staying strong for her dad and for the kids. She didn't hit the bottle, she took minimal time off work and she kept to her normal routine, wherever possible.

Her mum's funeral was held in mid-October and was attended by hundreds of people – Janice and Alex had been an admired and well-loved couple for decades. Keith even showed up at the funeral, looking extremely gaunt, pale, and guilty, though dressed smartly in a dark Marc Darcy suit. He offered his sympathies to his estranged family in the crematorium and spoke to the kids outside briefly, but didn't appear at the Stuart Hotel for the wake and sandwiches, which kind of pissed off Georgia and the kids, without surprising them. During the wake, as the drinks flowed, Isla told Georgia some gossip. Mostly snippets about marital infidelity among couples that they knew. Georgia really couldn't be arsed listening to it all, but there was one stand-out nugget. Hugh Mann, had collapsed at a function in the Rugby Club the previous weekend and been taken away in an ambulance. Initial rumours had been that he'd suffered a cocaine overdose, but it had later been confirmed that Shug had suffered a terrible asthma attack – that illness that had killed his dad and that had plagued his own life, doubtless getting worse as Shug entered middle age and did nothing about his excessive weight and made all the more dangerous by whatever perverse sex-life he enjoyed with the much younger Alana Renfield – the plastic Barbie girl. On that momentous day, Georgia heard the snippet about Hugh Mann, heard that he had survived, and she felt, well, nothing. Nada. Zilch.

As well as the emotional trauma, the death of Georgia's mum also brought her a great deal of stress on a financial level. With her mum gone, her dad, Alex, was alone at home all day, and he already showed early signs of dementia, as well as suffering from arthritis, type 2 diabetes and osteoporosis. Alex was in his early 70s and was lost without his wife.

Back in the good days, Georgia and Keith had always planned to build a wee extension to their house for if and when one of Georgia's parents died and the other one needed more help with day-to-day living, but now in 2019, with Georgia still on a credit blacklist and just keeping the family finances under control, getting builders in and splashing out tens of thousands of pounds on a granny flat simply wasn't an option.

This meant that old Alex would need to be cared for in his own home. Jordan was busy a lot with university and work but promised to help all that he could. Olivia, too, was all too happy to pitch in to help look after her granddad, but that simply wasn't enough. Council carers went in to see him twice a day, but Georgia didn't want her dad getting lonely, or to be 30 miles away if and when the next tragedy happened, so, as she saw it, she had no choice but to give up her weekend job at Sky TV. Her main job at the council, being full time, could make allowances if she needed time off for family emergencies, but there was no real way that Georgia could keep the part-time job on going forward. She'd actually liked the job at Sky, both times she had been employed there, but from then on, she couldn't risk spending half of the weekend in another county, dreading a phone call or text bearing bad news. Georgia left Sky to concentrate on looking after her dad and though this reduced her stress levels, the loss of 16 hours a week of decent pay put further strain on the family finances. Olivia and Jordan helped out when they could, both financially – Jordan from his ASDA job and Olivia from the money she made from selling apps that she had coded – and practically, going up to see their granddad, getting his shopping, taking him out for a half pint or a coffee, watching old films with him and doing all that they could to keep him stimulated and to delay the onset of his dementia.

In decades past, it was cancer everyone feared. Nowadays, most people would rather take their chances with the big C than being told that their mind and memories are going to fade away slowly with dementia – dementia is the new cancer.

In the December election, a combination of relentless smears against Labour and the Labour leader's own lacklustre attempts to stand up for himself, plus a pack of Tory lies that went unchallenged by their bedfellows in the media, saw the Tories win a big majority in parliament and a fourth successive election. Scotland, and the UK's working class, faced a future of renewed virtual serfdom in the post-Brexit Conservative wet dream world consisting of deregulation, lower wages, freeports, special enterprise zones, and fire and rehire.

It was a downbeat Christmas for the Smith family. They all missed Janice, so badly, and the family Christmas dinner, with Georgia, her dad, Jordan, Ciara, and Olivia, was a sombre affair. They all saw the bells in together on Hogmanay, too. That was a more upbeat gathering, as Isla and her man, Cammy, were there, too, so, Georgia had someone to have an adult conversation with after everybody else went home or went to bed.

All in all, it had been a sad end to the year, but at this last family gathering of 2019, there was, remarkably, some family optimism. Alex was on a new drug to slow his dementia. Jordan seemed to be loving university. Olivia was still a bit of a computer hermit and a geek, but she was doing well in her highers and making a few bob from her side-hustle.

Georgia had never been one for new year resolutions, but this year, she made one. This year, her wee family would have a better year than last.

CHAPTER TWENTY-TWO

Don't You Want Me?

January of 2020 saw much of central Scotland plagued by dreary weather. The country itself seemed to be on an actual downer – collective depression.

No sooner had university gone back after the Christmas holidays than Georgia found herself dealing with yet another dreadful problem.

Jordan was expelled from the University of the West of Scotland that month. An informer on campus alerted the authorities that he had been selling drugs at the university, not just to fellow students, but to a lecturer and some staff members, too. When Jordan had refused to open his rucksack to be searched by staff, they phoned the police, who soon turned up and found about an ounce of grass and a quarter ounce of cocaine on him. Those weren't vast amounts of drugs in the eyes of the law per se, but the problem for Jordan was that the cocaine was all in single one gram wraps and the weed was in individual wee bags, each of them 3.5 grams – that wasn't just possession, that was intent to supply, too. Jordan had been led off campus in handcuffs by the police. He was banged to rights, yet may have been released with a caution if he hadn't steadfastly refused to tell the police from whom he had acquired the drugs, and on whose behalf he was delivering them. The police kept at him in an interview room for hours and kept him in overnight, yet in the morning, he still refused to say who the supplier was – refused to say much at all, in fact. With a lecturer and university staff involved in the purchase of drugs from Jordan, the university was in as much shit as he now was, but the police were only interested in nailing the laddie from the scheme. Because of the 'intent to supply' thing, and the fact that he was uncooperative with the investigation, Jordan was charged– the police knew fine well who the actual source of the drugs had been, and when she found out what had happened to her son, Georgia, too, was under no illusions. Hugh 'Shug' Mann, again. Jordan was given bail, as he had never been in trouble with the police before but, for the time being, his life was over. He was expelled from university and left with just his part-time ASDA job to look forward to, at least, for the foreseeable future.

Georgia had a blazing row with two CID officers in the police station on the day that Jordan was bailed. She even blurted out Shug's name to the officers at one point, who looked at each other and then asked Georgia if she had any evidence of his involvement, which of course, she didn't, so, there was nothing that the police could do. They did say that they had found messages on Jordan's phone indicating that he had recently begun working as a drugs mule, but the messages were from burner phones or from social media platforms – at that time difficult to trace, even more difficult to pin on one specific person.

Georgia and her son hadn't spoken on the drive home from the police station, and Georgia waited until the next day to talk to her son about the matter. After all, he was her boy, he was only 19, she knew someone had put him up to all of this. With a mother's persistence, though, she got the truth from him, or at least, most of it, as they had yet another heavy family chat in the kitchen. Jordan was adamant that the drugs that he had been delivering had been for another dealer, not Shug Mann, but when he eventually told her the guy's name, it didn't take Georgia many quickfire text messages to her friends to find out that this dealer, a Mark Woods, known as Woodsie, was a franchisee, a sub-tenant, a soldier, and general lackey of Hugh Mann.

"You have to tell the police, son, you'll go down for this, this is fucking serious." She spoke to her son firmly, making no attempt to hide her disdain for his actions.

"Mum, no, I'm not a fucking grass, right. I can't." He replied.

"A grass? You're worried about fucking street cred? You wouldn't last five minutes in prison, son, please, just tell the police who put you up to it."

"It's got fuck all to do with street cred, Mum, once you're a grass, you're a grass forever. I'll get stabbed, or shot, they'll maybe even come after you, or ma sister, too," he said. He'd obviously had time to rehearse this inevitable confrontation during his spell in the cells.

"Son, listen to me. This will ruin your entire life. What about your career? Being an engineer? An officer? What about Ciara? Tell the fucking polis everything you know."

Jordan shook his head. "I can't tell them, I'd be fucked."

"You're fucked now! If you won't do it for yourself, then, please, think of your family. I work for the fucking council, son, can you imagine the consequences of this for me? What about your sister? And granddad? How are you going to help him if you're in the jail? You might never see him again, son."

"*I fucking did it for my family*!" roared Jordan, before he sat down at the kitchen table, with his head in his hands. Georgia could hear him crying.

"What do you mean, son?" asked Georgia.

Jordan sighed then spoke, big tears rolling down his cheeks. He looked less the young adult now and more the frightened youth that he was.

"Someone offered me a chance to make money, Mum, real money. All I had to do was deliver a few parcels and after a few months, I'd have enough,

I'd be able to stop. I wanted to make enough money so that we can have that extension built onto the house so that granddad can live here, that's why I did it. If you don't believe me, go up to my computer and look at my internet history."

Usually, Georgia would take her son at his word, but not this time. She went upstairs into his bedroom and pressed a key on his keyboard. She opened his Mozilla Firefox browser and brought up the internet history. It was full of building companies, mostly local, and mostly pages about extensions. Georgia then went to his search bar and clicked on it, bringing up the most recent search terms.

House extension cost UK

Granny flat builder Scotland

How much does a single storey extension cost?

There were hundreds of similar searches, going right back to around the time of Janice's death, so, Jordan had been telling the truth about his motives for becoming a drugs mule. Georgia did wonder why the police hadn't bothered to seize his computer, but she supposed that they had seen everything that they needed to see via the Google drive on his phone when they had searched that. After about 5 minutes of noseying at her son's computer, she went back downstairs.

As she entered the kitchen, her mouth fell open, and she let out a strangled scream. Jordan lay slumped at the table, wrists cut open, kitchen awash with arterial blood spray. A knife lay next to his hand.

"NO, NO, NO!" screamed Georgia, grabbing her phone off the kitchen worktop and dialling 999. The commotion brought young Olivia down the stairs, who herself panicked at this gruesome, heartbreaking, terrifying sight, but at the same time she grabbed a tee-shirt and a tea-towel off the pile of laundry in the kitchen and did her best to tie two crude tourniquets around her big brother's upper arms.

"I saw this in a TikTok video, mum, we need to lie him flat, help me." Georgia and Olivia's hands and clothes were covered in blood as they laid Jordan out on the kitchen table. Olivia's makeshift tourniquets had slowed the bleeding but hadn't stopped it. Jordan was groaning, murmuring, "Just leave me, I deserve to die."

Georgia stood there, feeling helpless, watching the life and colour drain from that young man she loved so much, that child she had carried, taught to walk and talk, seen grow into a man, now, in an instant, reduced to a bloody, dying mess.

Olivia wasn't standing about. She was in her brother's face shouting at him to stay awake, urging him not to give up. "You're my brother and you're not going anywhere," she kept saying, then, noticing her mum momentarily standing there in shock, she shouted.

"Mum, open the front door for when the paramedics come. *Now!*"

Georgia did, just as the paramedics were coming to the door. Georgia's phone was still connected to the 999 call centre, and the operator was still talking down the phone, but in her shock, Georgia had dropped her phone on the floor – this may have expedited the arrival of the ambulance. The police had arrived, too, because a bladed weapon had been involved in the incident, but they didn't stay long. The paramedics used proper tourniquets on Jordan and soon had him on a stretcher and in the back of the ambulance. Georgia and Olivia went to the hospital, following the ambulance with the dying Jordan on board.

CHAPTER TWENTY-THREE

Disco's Revenge

Jordan didn't die, but he very nearly did. Olivia's makeshift tourniquets and the quick arrival of the paramedics saved his life. While Jordan was in getting emergency treatment, Georgia and Olivia sat on chairs in a corridor, crying, waiting, praying.

Once again, Georgia blamed herself. She'd been too hard on him. She'd scared him too much with talk of jail. Had she been a better mother she'd have known what was going on.

After a few hours, an exhausted-looking doctor appeared in the corridor and asked Georgia and Olivia to join him in a side room, which they did.

"Jordan is out of danger, for now, but we're keeping him in, he has some serious wounds, he has lost a lot of blood and toxicology indicates he's taken some Valium, too, street Valium, I think. We found a bag of them in his jeans pocket. "

"So, he's going to be alright?" pleaded Georgia.

"He's out of immediate danger, but it was a close-run thing. Had the ambulance been a few minutes later it wouldn't have been good."

"So, can we see him?" asked Olivia – still in her blood-soaked pyjamas and dressing gown.

"Not yet, he's sleeping, I should prepare you, we may have to detain Jordan under the mental health act..."

January of 2020 had been by far the lowest point of many lows that had plagued the Smith family of Lanarkshire in more recent years. For a good while their lives had been perfect, it had seemed like the family had everything. They had security, love, good jobs, money, hope, laughter, loving friends and relatives, a future, a lovely home and above all, they had each other. By early 2020, almost all of that was gone. Ill fortune had stolen a lot from the Smiths. Of course, ill fortune wasn't the main culprit, the real culprit was drugs.

February of 2020 saw the Smith family in dire straits. Young Jordan, about to turn 20, was being detained indefinitely under the Mental Health Act at Glasgow's Gartnavel hospital. The lad's brush with the law over the drugs he was selling at university had been the straw that had broken the camel's back where his mental health was concerned. Being charged with intent to supply had lit the tinderbox under all of the other issues that had been gnawing away in his head for the last couple of years. There was his dad's departure from the house, and the manner of it, there was the subsequent financial hardship at home and his deferring university for a year because of stress. The death of his beloved granny had hit him hard, too, and then his beginning to dabble with substances stirred up a mess in his head that was already quite messed up to begin with. Like most men, Jordan had never spoken to anybody about his problems, or about how he was feeling about all the sadness his family had encountered in recent years. His dad had shown virtually no interest in him or his sister since leaving home. Moreover, Jordan had also had to deal with comments and nasty gossip he heard from his peers regarding his dad's behaviour, both before and after he had left. All of these things had turned Jordan's head into a pressurised tank of hurt and confusion in recent times, each new blow and every new sadness ramping up the pressure inside. Jordan had tried throughout all the family's ordeals to appear strong and silent, to be a rock to his mum and to his sister, and he almost pulled that off, but that, too, put more pressure on him, and what happens to a pressurised tank when it becomes overloaded? It explodes.

Jordan's mental explosion had been compounded more recently by his girlfriend, Ciara, ending their relationship right after New Year. Ciara had given him some bullshit excuse about still being young and not wanting to be tied down, but in truth Jordan had known that she was going to dump him well before Christmas. He knew, in retrospect, that she had stayed with him out of duty when his Gran died, and then out of social awkwardness throughout the festive season and new year, before she called time on their relationship. She had probably done this so as not to give Jordan more sadness before Xmas, thinking she was doing the right thing, but Jordan had taken that very differently. When she ended their relationship just after New Year, Jordan knew straight away that the last three months or so of their relationship had been pure fraud – she'd only stayed with him out of pity, in his eyes. He had changed, a bit, given how his family life had been, and he knew it, and he knew she knew it, too. The end of that relationship was just one of many factors in Jordan's crisis, though.

While in the hospital, Jordan on more than one occasion had tried to reopen his wrist wounds but had been stopped by nurses. He was on a locked ward and under more or less constant observation, heavily sedated at all times. His mum and sister visited him regularly, always together as only Georgia could drive the car. When they visited him, they always smiled and tried to cheer him up, tried to get him to talk about his feelings, took away and returned his laundry and brought him in such goodies as he was allowed. There were so many limitations on what they could bring in for Jordan - no caffeinated food or drinks, no energy drinks, no sugary food or drinks – and for obvious reasons he wasn't allowed a mobile phone, either.

Every visit broke Georgia's heart. She and Olivia would sit there and talk away to him at first, he'd sometimes smile or make a half-arsed reply, but would then revert back to looking straight through them both for long periods, his Valium-eyes fixated on empty space behind them somewhere, or sometimes on nothing at all. Conversation would always end up mechanical, generic, even. What was for lunch? What did the doctors say? What was for dinner? All that pish.

Of course, Georgia was her son's next of kin, and she had been given the full picture of her son's condition by the ward consultants. According to them, Jordan had suffered an acute psychiatric breakdown and had been suffering from PTSD and depression for a considerable time, maybe even a couple of years. The ward had a strategy in place for treatment but that would take time, with talking therapies and with medication – mostly medication. It would take time for the Citalopram and the Sertraline to build up in his system to a significant level for there to be a noticeable difference. The ward doctors were also considering treating Jordan with new anti-psychotic drugs and staff were also continuing to heavily sedate him with Diazepam. The only good news, thus far, was that the police and the procurator fiscal had agreed to go slow on the legal case against him, under the circumstances.

By end of February 2020, Jordan had been incarcerated on the mental ward for over a month, with discharge not looking possible in the near future. Georgia blamed herself, and her husband, for what had happened to Jordan, and found herself unable to go to work. The doctor gave her a sick line for a month, and the council were very understanding and supportive of their employee – Georgia was to be paid full wages for the month-long absence. Luckily for Georgia, her brilliant, beautiful, strong, red-haired daughter stepped up to the plate, giving a back seat to her constant online and sports activities so that she could help her mum, and her increasingly lonely and confused granddad, at this time of great sadness.

March of 2020 began with Georgia off work and taking prescribed sedatives, doing her best to care for her dad and to be there for her daughter, while her daughter, in turn, looked after her. Young Jordan was locked in a mental hospital and still staring at a possible prison sentence for being a drugs courier, if and when he was ever discharged. Keith Smith was still nowhere to be seen and hadn't even bothered to visit Jordan in hospital – neither had Ciara. The Smith family was fractured and on the brink of collapse, bills were mounting, prices in the shops kept going up, granddad was becoming weaker and more and more confused, needing ever more visits and care. Georgia needed an intervention on a grand scale to save what was left of her family from complete and utter collapse.

On Monday, March 23rd, 2020, her prayers were answered - she got that intervention.

CHAPTER TWENTY-FOUR

Hideaway

When Boris Johnson appeared to the nation on television that day and uttered those immortal words, "you must stay at home", so began the most serious crisis to face the country since the Second World War. Despite what cranks and conspiracy theorists would say about Covid-19, or Coronavirus as it was initially referred to, the pandemic was an existential threat to mankind's existence on this planet. If left unchecked, it could have easily killed 20% of the world's population. Yes, at first, most of those killed were the sick, the elderly and the disabled, but mutations in the virus as it rocketed around the world at terrifying speed could easily have turned it into another Black Death, killing strong and weak alike. When military units suffer 20% casualties in combat, the unit becomes useless, as that's the magic figure which, when reached, usually means that everybody in the unit has lost a friend or someone they know. Likewise, when a workforce fires 20% of its workforce, the remainder invariably become demoralised and lose productivity or become insular and fearful. Humanity would have been no less hamstrung, had that awful virus simply been ignored by the authorities.

If you were middle-class or above that station, lockdown was, for many, a nuisance, an annoyance – you had to spend more time in the garden, you had to get your groceries and other purchases delivered, you maybe even had to do the dreaded Zoom-call Friday-night 'drinkypoos' thing with your friends, instead of meeting them for a pint or a glass of vino. Maybe you were furloughed, maybe you were working from home, maybe you went to work as normal – but unless you were self-employed, by and large, you still got paid.

For working-class and poor people, as well as elderly people who lived alone, single parents with young children, people in care homes, families with children living in temporary or overcrowded accommodation, older people who had no access to the internet, families in flats or other homes without gardens or any outside space, people trapped in abusive relationships or couples who had been on the verge of splitting up, the virus and its lockdowns were a fucking catastrophe – as bad as the 1940 Blitz – worse, in many ways.

For Georgia and Olivia, sitting at home eating a takeaway pizza when the prime minister announced the lockdown, the seismic announcement of the wholescale shutting down of UK society was initially just one more sad, unfathomable thing that had befallen them. Olivia couldn't go to school, while Georgia would have been expected to work from home, had she not already been signed off on the sick. Georgia decided immediately that nobody would stop her from going round to care for her dad, whatever the new emergency laws said, but that aside, the Smith household resolved to abide by the rules.

At first, as with many households at the start of the lockdowns, the kind of Dunkirk spirit that most people showed was enough to stop Georgia and her daughter from having too bad a time of things – the novelty of lockdown, ironically, got them through the first couple of weeks. Mother and daughter actually did some serious bonding over movies, wine, home karaoke sessions and even clearing out the loft. The dreaded banana bread was baked and enjoyed, turgid but well-meaning family quizzes of an evening on Facebook or Zoom were enjoyed, they even recorded a couple of sea shanties together for an online competition but didn't win.

In those first two weeks of lockdown, Georgia really connected with her daughter in a way that she hadn't before. She saw that her wee girl was now a young woman. She was emotionally mature, streetwise, witty, and had big plans for the future – most of them involving making a fortune through the internet and by computer coding. Olivia was by now almost the same height as her mother, too, and had blossomed into a beautiful, curvaceous, sassy, smart credit to femininity – just as her mother had been as a young woman and still was now. To Georgia, sometimes, looking at her daughter was like looking into a mirror at her younger self, and talking to her was much the same. Olivia had the look of her mum; Jordan looked more like his dad.

Jordan remained seriously ill in the psychiatric hospital and at first visiting wasn't allowed during the lockdown, which was hard for all concerned. Georgia and Olivia could only stay in touch by phone calls and by getting periodic updates from ward staff about Jordan's progress – though they were told that he was still heavily sedated anyway so the loss of the frequent, but largely soulless, in-person visits wasn't the family's chief concern. No, what really worried Georgia and Olivia was the prospect of the mental hospital suffering a Covid 19 outbreak. The news and online sources were full of horror stories about staff in hospitals having no PPE (Personal Protective Equipment - masks, visors, and gloves, etc. to shield them from the virus) and medical staff were dropping like flies. Many elderly people in care homes had already been killed by the virus, having been discharged from hospital with it into care settings where there was literally no protection against Covid, other than social distancing – mankind's weapon of last resort against deadly pandemics since Roman times. Alex, Georgia's dad, continued to deteriorate but his carers kept coming, at first using home-made PPE. Georgia visited him every day, too. She and Olivia agreed that it was best that only one of them went to see old Alex, to minimise his exposure to the threat of infection, so, instead, Olivia phoned her granddad twice a day, keeping up both his spirits, and hers.

CHAPTER TWENTY-FIVE

Feel The Same

Lockdown was initially supposed to have lasted for three weeks, but the rampaging virus, still without a vaccine and with little or no testing capacity at first, didn't relent, and a woefully unprepared government had no real choice other than to continually extend the lockdown restrictions.

By week six of the lockdown, the novelty had well and truly worn off for most people. Rich or poor, it was now, at best, a monumental pain in the arse, at worst, a long, dark, life-destroying nightmare. Olivia was missing her friends and her sports activities, but she did at least have plenty of time for working from home and online gaming and socialising. Georgia, by then, wasn't any less sad, but the downtime that she had enjoyed since the start of the lockdowns, even with the stress regarding her son and her dad, was the most rest that she'd had in many a year. Her sick line had been extended, too, and the council had assured her that her wages would still be paid, meaning that the debt wolf was still kept from the door.

Georgia was on Facebook a lot more as lockdown wore on, keeping up with friends and local news, enjoying nostalgia pages and hearing local gossip. Some people she knew from work were in the middle of extra-marital affairs when the pandemic began, and she found herself giggling at the plight of those who were the 'other woman' or 'the other man' in someone else's marriage, being forced by law not only to curtail their affairs but to endure the agony of worrying that their married lover might just reconnect with their spouse due to lockdown forcing them to be at home together- which, in Georgia's eyes, would serve the 'others' just right. Most dating apps scrambled their location settings early in lockdown, to discourage people from meeting up in person. Georgia found time to get talking to a nice guy from Bogota, Colombia, who spoke excellent English. She found him really charming, but after a fortnight or so she had given up chatting to him – it wasn't exactly going anywhere, so Georgia deleted her dating apps – she had also collected in that time quite an assortment of unsolicited dick pics and filthy messages from men all over the world, and had no wish to receive anymore.

By early May of 2020, she and Olivia had found a loophole which allowed them to visit Jordan in the mental hospital. His ward was on the ground floor and staff, provided social distancing was observed, very humanely allowed them to visit Jordan by talking to him through an open window. At times, though, it seemed that Jordan barely knew that they were there, he was so heavily doped up on meds, but that didn't stop them from coming – an in-person visit is worth a thousand phone calls, both to the visitor and to the patient. Jordan, by then, wasn't getting any worse, but wasn't really any better, either.

Auld Alex, by then, had become a bit quieter and withdrawn, as if he were a prisoner on a life sentence, but at least he hadn't caught Covid. By then, his carers had real PPE and one of them, who lived locally, was even calling in on her own time just to see him, too. Georgia did his shopping and visited daily, Olivia still phoned him twice a day.

At home, the 10am arrival of the Amazon delivery guy each day had become a highlight for Georgia and Olivia, as whatever shite they'd bought online was left on the doorstep by the tall, stressed-looking heavy-metal dude.

By this time, Olivia was spending almost all of her time in her room online for one reason or another, appearing now and then to get food or drink, to sunbathe in the back garden or to sit and talk to her mum in the living room. They still did wine and movie evenings now and then but nowhere near as often as they had at the start of the lockdowns. They did meet up in the living room most afternoons to do a home workout together, though, settling on Joe Wicks. With the swimming pools still closed, Georgia needed the physical release of cardio-vascular exercise, and Olivia knew that a good way to keep her mum's spirits up was to join her on these cringeworthy sessions of star jumps and squat-thrusts. To both of them, the annoying Mr Wicks was dreadful but was the least annoying of all the home-workout gurus who had appeared since the lockdowns began. When Mr Motivator had returned to breakfast TV screens earlier in the pandemic Georgia had considered putting her foot through the fucking television. To her, his reappearance epitomised the utter pishness of lockdown, as if the state were saying, "Hey, no swimming or gym for you, but here's an annoying berk from the 90s."

CHAPTER TWENTY-SIX

Superstar

On Friday the 8th of May in the evening, while Olivia was holed up in her bedroom doing online stuff, Georgia was sitting in the living room watching an old Sex and the City when her phone unexpectedly rang. The caller ID flashed up as WANKER – she'd used that name to save the number of the person who had sent her the dirty video of her husband cheating at a drugs party. With a knot in her stomach and her stress levels shooting up to critical, she answered the call.

"HELLO?"

"Georgia, long time no chat, it's me Shug Mann, do you remember me?"

Of course she fucking remembered him! What the fuck did he want? Georgia couldn't be arsed with any of his pish, but nor was she particularly annoyed to hear from the gangster creep – at least she knew whose number it was for sure, now.

"Hi, Hugh, aye, of course I remember you." She hoped he didn't think that was a compliment.

"Listen, Georgia, it's a mad time with this virus pish, tough times for many, I heard what happened with that laddie of yours and I'm really sorry. I was sorry to hear about your mum, too, Janice was lovely. Listen, I'm just checking in to see if you and that daughter of yours are ok? Do you need anything?"

Georgia had to bite her lip, but Shug did sound like he was in his 'nice' mode, so she remained calm – he was the dark past, after all.

"That's good of you to ask, Hugh, thank you, we're doing ok, though, all things considered. Has your Alana given birth yet?" That question was asked out of civil politeness, rather than out of genuine curiosity. There was a pause on the other end of the line before Shug answered.

"Erm, no, Georgia, we lost the baby and Alana just up and left me afterwards, just after this pandemic thing started. I don't know where she went."

That naturally tugged at Georgia's heartstrings ever so slightly. Though she hadn't really known Alana very well and had no fondness for Shug, it was still a sad thing to hear, and she had known him since school. Georgia's better nature took over.

"I'm really sorry to hear that, Hugh, that's a real tragedy. How are you bearing up?"

"It's not been great Georgia, that's all I'll say, she was my world, and I was looking forward to getting a second chance at being a dad, I'm just taking things one day at a time, y'know?"

Georgia thought that he sounded genuine and depressed, but it still irked her to have to reciprocate his earlier concern.

"Is there anything that I can do to help you, Hugh?" She asked, meaning it, but hoping he'd say no.

"Thanks, Georgia, that means a lot, but I don't think so. Just hearing your voice again and phoning other old friends to see how they're doing is keeping my mind off it a bit. Listen, if you or that daughter of yours are looking for work, or if you need anything at all, just call me. There's always jobs going in my organisation, especially for you and Olivia."

Georgia was both impressed and unnerved that Shug remembered her daughter's name.

"Thanks, Hugh, I'll keep that in mind. You look after yourself." Georgia was trying to subtly end the call. Shug didn't seem to hear her reply.

"Georgia, I know there's been issues in the past with us and I regret my part in them, as I'm sure you do, too, but I've changed. It gets lonely up here in this big house all by myself. Listen, say no if you want, but I'd like to stay in touch with you, just a wee phone call now and then to see if you're alright. It's so good to be talking to you – good to be talking to someone who doesn't want something. Would that be alright?"

Part of Georgia was livid. Shug implying that she was somehow partly to blame for their chequered past really was some serious mental gymnastics on his part, but she knew that was how his mind worked. Yet Georgia also felt genuine sympathy for him at the loss of his child and partner, and in a way, she empathised with his apparent loneliness and lack of real actual friends to talk to – Georgia had always been a sucker for a sob story. Maybe Shug had changed? The pandemic had changed a lot of people. More importantly, Georgia knew that Shug was her best chance of re-establishing contact with her absent husband, Keith, which would be good for the kids – provided Keith was sober.

"Look, Hugh, I'm really busy with looking after my dad and with this thing with Jordan in the hospital, and you're a busy man, too, but I tell you what, we have each other's numbers now, I'll check in on you now and then, not like every week, but I'll check in, how does that sound?"

"Thanks, Georgia, that really means a lot, thank you. And look, I'll see what I can do to help your laddie with this drugs charge thing – I have contacts."

That shocked Georgia, she hadn't been expecting to hear that, but Shug sounded genuine. She was unsure what to say, but Shug was in the middle of having a huge coughing fit down the phone, really chesty, dreadful gasping coughs. Then she heard two skooshes that she recognised as the sound of an inhaler. There were a few more coughs, then Shug apologised for the coughing, pointing out that it was asthma and not Covid.

Georgia didn't really want anything to do with Shug but his offer to help her son out in his predicament with the law naturally interested her – in life, she knew, there are certain maxims, but there's always a time to cut cards with the devil. When it came to helping her son get off the hook with the drugs thing, Georgia would have fucked Satan himself, just to get the charges dropped.

"Thanks, Shug, I'd appreciate any help you can give me with that, Jordan and Olivia are my world."

"No problem, Georgia, I'll see what I can do, I'll be in touch, God bless you all," said Shug before hanging up. Georgia's inner monologue continued.

"That was fucking weird. He sounds really different. The breakup and losing his wean must have made him find God, or something. Either that or he's had a guilt attack about what happened with Keith and the coke and he's trying to make amends. I'm pretty sure he ISN'T just trying to fuck me this time. Even if he is, would I do that to get Jordan off the hook? I hope he doesn't ask because I'm not sure I'd say no IF it meant Jordan got off the hook, even though he gives me the utter ick. Shug does know a lot of dodgy people, but he probably doesn't have any real friends. I should phone Isla.

Georgia spent the rest of the evening chilling, eating beef Hula Hoops and watching Sex and the City, while Olivia, she could hear, was doing another online home workout up in her bedroom, judging by the music creaks and thuds from above. The music was fucking dreadful. It was Dance Monkey by *Tones and I* – the tune had been massive a year earlier in May 2019 – by May 2020, most people felt like that earpiss annoying but catchy ditty had been around for a decade – for everybody, Georgia and her family especially, so much had changed in the last 12 months – the world was irrevocably different.

> *Dance for me, dance for me, dance for me, oh-oh*
> *I've never seen anybody do the things you do before*
> *They say, "Move for me, move for me, move for me, ay-ay*
> *And when you're done, I'll make you do it all again"*

CHAPTER TWENTY-SEVEN

Played-a-Live

On the Monday after that weekend, the Amazon guy dropped off a pile of eight parcels at the door of the Smith residence just after 10am, doing his, by then well-mastered, pandemic chap-door-run move. Georgia was still in her dressing gown and drinking her fourth morning coffee out of a Kitkat easter egg mug by that point – decaf, to cut down on stress. As she opened the front door and noticed the small pyramid of parcels on the step, she heard her daughter's footsteps thudding down the stairs behind her in the hall, almost running.

"Five of those are for me, Mum" said Olivia, as if she were giving instructions to a bloody servant. Georgia didn't bother about that, after all, servant is just one of the additional ad-hoc duties performed by most parents. She was curious though, as throughout the pandemic thus far mother and daughter had made a kind of event each morning of opening all their parcels together, joking that it was just like Christmas.

Olivia was wearing her dairy cow pattern onesie and big fluffy pink pair of slippers, with her long red hair tied back with a bobble. To Georgia, she looked just like a wee girl, and that warmed her inside her heart, remembering Olivia as a child. Olivia gathered up three parcels that were basically big near-flat envelopes – clothes probably, Georgia thought – one small square box parcel and one larger rectangular box parcel. She then smiled at her mum and squeezed past her in the hall, heading for the stairs.

Georgia joked to her, "Oh aye, what's with all the secrecy today?"

Olivia's pale cheeks went red as she stopped on the bottom stair, pausing for a second, turning to her mum and replying with a wink, "Just business stuff, Mum, a new headset and some clothes that I need – nothing top secret!"

Georgia laughed and asked her if she fancied some coffee. As Olivia plodded back up the stairs with her parcels she answered "Aye, lovely, with a bacon roll?"

"Ya cheeky bugger, aye, go on then, I may as well have one, too," said Georgia, in awe of her daughter's brazen cheek.

Business stuff. Georgia liked hearing that from her wee girl. She really admired what Olivia had done with her wee side hustle, her coding and web design – though like all parents, she did wonder if her child was spending too much time online. When Georgia was Olivia's age, the internet was a thing, but it was all dial-up and no social media, other than the dodgy chatrooms on AOL and Yahoo – it was mainly the preserve of geeks and perverts back then.

Georgia hadn't asked directly what was in Olivia's parcels, she knew that her daughter was careful with money, and she knew that it was probably all computer stuff and daft tee-shirts, as usual.

Twenty minutes later, after Olivia had come back downstairs to swipe her coffee and her bacon roll before taking them up to the media hub that was her bedroom, there was another knock at the door. Still chewing the last bit of her bacon roll with brown sauce, Georgia trudged from the kitchen to answer it.

In the doorway stood a smart young man in a suit – a salesman, by the look of it, wearing a surgical PPE mask. He spoke.

"Georgia Smith?"

"Aye, what is it?" replied Georgia in a muffled voice, still chewing her breakfast with her mouth half full. He was young, but he was handsome, she thought – from what she could see.

"I'm DC Iain Finlayson of Police Scotland CID, would you mind if I came inside to talk to you, please, Mrs Smith?" He flashed Georgia his warrant card.

The fear of God suddenly gripped her like a wave of icy terror, her thoughts running amok – it could be about her dad, or Jordan, or maybe even Keith. Then, Georgia hesitated, as she swallowed the last bite of her bacon roll. There was a pandemic on, with social distancing laws and regulations for all government agencies to keep them away from people's homes, save in case of emergencies. Why was a detective, on his own, asking to enter her home?

"Right, officer, would you mind coming round to the back garden, instead? I know you're a policeman, but I look after my elderly dad and don't want him to catch Covid. There's a wee bench you can sit on in the garden."

The officer said, "no problem," and turned left, making his way around the side of the detached house towards the back garden. Georgia would normally have been mortified at being caught still in her dressing gown answering the door at that time, especially to a young man, but she needed to hear whatever this cop had to say. She made her way through her house to the back door, wiping a smudge of brown sauce off her lips with the sleeve of her dressing gown before opening the back door. In the garden on the bench sat the cop. The bench was a good two metres from the front door, so Georgia just sat on the back doorstep, hurriedly putting on a disposable mask she had grabbed from a shelf in the hall en route.

DC Iain Finlayson started talking, but the mask muffled his speech, making him sound like one of the blah-blah adults in the old Charlie Brown cartoons, so he removed the mask. When Georgia didn't protest and slipped her own mask down around her chin, he tried again. It was a bright, sunny day, like most were during the first three months of the pandemic.

"Mrs Smith, it's about your son."

Georgia felt another agonising chill, this time in her stomach. The cop continued.

"There's been a development in the case against your son, Mrs Smith."

Georgia felt relieved, Jordan wasn't dead, or escaped from the hospital, at least.

"Some new evidence has become available to us which indicates that your son may have had the items in question (the drugs) planted on him by another individual. A new witness came forward and the person who planted the drugs in your son's bag has confessed, so, we won't be charging Jordan with anything – we will, however, be calling him as a witness if the Fiscal decides to prosecute this new culprit. I hope that this news brings some comfort to you and your family, Mrs Smith. We've already notified the staff on the ward where your son is being treated."

Georgia stared at the cop. He looked about 30 years old and was thin and wiry with big blue eyes and gel-slicked short black hair. The news made Georgia want to get up and hug him, but she thought better of it.

"So, Detective Constable, what new witness, what new evidence? That's great news!"

"Please, call me Iain," he said, before letting out a heavy sigh. After a beat he spoke again.

"Mrs Smith, officially I'm not here, do you understand? That's why I'm alone today at your house. Off the record, I can tell you that your son's complete lack of cooperation when under arrest and being questioned about this offence may just have saved his bacon. When we tested the bags of drugs we took from your son we found fingerprints, but not his. Do you or your son know a Mark Woods, or Woodsie?"

"I think Jordan mentioned him once, I assumed it was one of his pals," said Georgia, relieved, but still desperate to learn more.

"Well, Mrs Smith, if Mr Woods is the type of pal your son has, you may wish to try to keep him from renewing that friendship. Mr Woods is a bad egg – has links to drugs, prostitution, and organised crime, he has a history of violence, too, but we've never been able to collar him."

"So, that's who you've charged instead of Jordan?"

"No. I'm afraid we've charged your husband, Keith Smith. Keith's were the second set of prints we found on the drug bags. I'm so sorry, Mrs Smith. I understand that you've been separated for a while, though?"

Georgia's head was racing with manic thoughts, relief that Jordan was off the hook, but utter confusion regarding her long-absent husband's sudden appearance in the ongoing drama. "I don't understand, Iain," she said.

The cop continued.

"As I said, Mrs Smith, I'm officially *not here* today. We went to a house in East Kilbride on Saturday to find this 'Woodsie' and your husband happened to be there too. It was some sort of drugs and sex party. We broke up the party, fined everyone present for breaking Covid restrictions and arrested your husband and this Woodsie in connection with your son's case. When questioned, both of them said that your husband had put the drugs in the bag which your son was later found in possession of, your husband confessed, he was already out on bail for another drug-related offence, so he's now been remanded in custody until his trial."

Georgia was stunned. "That doesn't make sense. My son hasn't seen his dad in a long time."

"Oh, I know it doesn't make sense, Mrs Smith," said the cop, trying to remain calm and reassuring, but now unable to sound at least a little bit stern.

"It doesn't make sense to us, either. Our administration and backlog is crazy just now what with the pandemic and everything. However, senior officers decided that your husband and only your husband should be charged in relation to this matter, in light of the new evidence. All that scumbag Woods did was have his bag used by someone else. Your husband's confession fits the evidence, a bit too well, truth be told, Mrs Smith. But, there we have it. It seems like your husband has taken the rap for your son. We can't ask your son about it at the moment as we're told he'll be unwell for the foreseeable future. Mr Smith said nothing after his confession, didn't implicate anyone else and refused to say where he had obtained the drugs, so, it's all on him."

Georgia was unsure what to say and her emotions were mixed. Though estranged from Keith, his degeneration into becoming a drug- and drink-fuelled loser and now a petty criminal made her so sad – on the other hand, if given a choice of having either Keith or Jordan saved from going to prison, she'd choose her beloved son all day, every day.

"Ok officer, I mean, Iain. Why are you telling me this off the record? I'm grateful and relieved, I really am, but why?"

The cop sighed again. "Mrs Smith, your husband keeps very bad company indeed. Some of that company is of interest to other branches of law enforcement for very serious offences, that's all I'll say, except ... I know, from talking to people *on the square* that you and your daughter are good, law-abiding decent people, as is your son, despite recent events. You've all suffered a lot in recent years, through no fault of your own."

The cop's guarded reference to freemasonry was reassuring but Georgia's mind was still racing, and she said, "I have a question. Who was the new witness that alerted you and how do they know my son?"

"It was an anonymous tip-off by phone, an untraceable burner mobile number. Scottish Male. Whoever it was gave us Woodsie and your husband late on Friday night."

"How long will Keith go to jail for?" asked Georgia.

"A year, maybe two – maybe nothing at all – the justice system is near collapse because of this Covid thing," replied the cop, adding, "Your son's not a bad lad, Mrs Smith, I hope he gets better soon and makes the most of this second chance. Make the most of your family, Mrs Smith. Look, I better be going." The cop got up and checked his mobile phone, briefly, then spoke again.

"Needless to say, Mrs Smith, I was never here today, and you can never repeat any of what I've told you – though if you did, I'd just deny having been here," He smiled at Georgia.

"Thank you, Iain, thank you so much."

The cop smiled and turned to leave the garden, but then looked back, just as Georgia was getting up off the step.

"Just one more thing, Mrs Smith."

Georgia didn't think it appropriate to say, 'yes, Mr Columbo' so she just answered "Yes?"

"Do you know anything about a guy called Hugh Mann? Goes by Shug? Since I'm not really here, there's no harm in my asking, is there?"

Georgia glanced at the floor, then looked up and answered.

"We're both from Blantyre and we went to the same school. I don't know him that well, though. I've heard he's dodgy, my husband used to work for him."

"Still does, Mrs Smith, still does. Thank you. You might want to avoid him, too."

And with that, DC Iain Finlayson turned and walked out of the back gate.

Georgia let out a deep breath. Her inner monologue raced once more.

"*What the actual fuck? That was like something out of Homeland or the Sopranos. Still, he seemed nice, a decent guy. My Boy! My boy is going to be ok!*"

Georgia knew immediately that this was all Shug's doing, somehow. True to his word, he had tried to help, however, Georgia was livid that it appeared that her estranged husband had been sacrificed in order to save her son – typical Shug, everything always came with strings or twists. Then again, given the choice, she'd have had Keith in jail in place of her son in a heartbeat. Sometimes justice comes in many forms, after all. She wanted to phone Isla to tell her all about her visit from DC Finlayson and the new developments, but she knew that she couldn't – she could never mention any of this to anyone. Georgia made herself another decaf coffee and popped one of the 2mg diazepam pills that the doctor had given her for anxiety, then plonked herself down on the sofa for a couple of hours, until it was time to go and see to her dad. She used her phone to cast some decent tunes from Youtube to her TV. INXS, Disappear.

> *Say I'm crying*
> *I'm looking at what's on TV*
> *Pain and suffering*
> *And the struggle to be free*
> *It can't ever be denied*
> *And I never will ignore*

But when I see you coming
I can take it all

Georgia turned the TV up to drown out the RnB music blasting out of Olivia's room – *Buttons* by the *Pussycat Dolls*. Georgia was relieved that her son was free from the prospect of a criminal record. She felt guilty, too, though, that her once loving husband appeared to be taking the rap, yet she also admired Keith for going along with that, whatever his motives or reasons for doing so. As the diazepam kicked in, Georgia started to doze off on the sofa, but then her phone buzzed. She glanced at the screen and saw that it was Shug who had WhatsApped her.

The message simply said, 'ALL SORTED? X'

Emotionally drained, Georgia wasn't sure what to reply, but she knew what he was on about. All she could do was politely and grudgingly reply, "Yes. Thank you." Shug didn't send a reply, he simply 'liked' her post with the thumbs-up emoji.

That afternoon, Georgia went to see her dad, took him round his dinner, home-made mince and tatties crammed into an empty Chinese takeaway carton, and the two of them had a lovely time, watching a dreadful Burt Lancaster Western on Channel 5 – Lancaster playing an Indian chief wearing blackface, or rather, redface – something common in movies in the 50s but that would rightly get the producers of films pilloried if they tried to do it today. Georgia had left her phone in the car when she went in to see her dad and when she got back to the car, she noticed another message from Shug. 'CALL YOU LATER X'.

Georgia rolled her eyes and proceeded to drive home.

CHAPTER TWENTY-EIGHT

Loneliness

"Georgia, how are you doin'? It wasn't easy but I was able to pull some strings through business associates to get the polis to look at your Jordan's case again, turns out your ex, Keith, and another guy were behind that drugs thing, so your boy isn't going to jail. You never know, those useless cops might even lose the evidence or the witness statements next, they're not the brightest. Is that a big help to you, Georgia, does that ease your burden? Are your prayers answered?"

To Georgia, on this phone call, Shug sounded like a builder calling a customer to tell them what had been wrong with their sub-floor and how he had managed to fix it, rather than a dodgy gangster tacitly admitting that he had, somehow, been enough of a 'Billy big balls' to interfere in an ongoing police investigation. She was pleased that it looked like her son was out of trouble with the law; the fact that it was Shug who had dug her out of this particular hole troubled her greatly, yet she was still grateful, to a degree – in her eyes, he fucking owed her, owed her family – it was the least that he could do, but she remained diplomatic.

"Thank you, Hugh, whatever you did, thank you."

"Don't mention it, Georgia. Listen, so how is your laddie now?"

"There's been no real change, Hugh, but this thing with the police being dropped will help I think, but his problems were as much to do with family issues as they were this business. I'm allowed to be his named visitor now, so I have a pass and can visit him at the hospital properly now. The NHS also gave him an iPad so my daughter and I can videocall him every day, too, it'll be a long road for Jordan, though, he's basically had a full nervous breakdown."

Shug sounded empathic. "I'm glad, Georgia, nothing more important than family, is there?"

"That's true, Hugh, that's true," agreed Georgia. It felt good for her to talk about it with someone, even this creep – despite his indirect role in her family's woes and his periodic, crass, sleazy attempts to seduce her, she had known Shug for a very long time. Still being off work sick, and with the pandemic still ruining everybody's social lives, most of Georgia's social interactions since February had been with her teenage daughter or her elderly, sick father – asides zoom calls with Isla and the odd blether to folk on Facebook. She was also fully aware that Shug, too, had suffered loss of his own, of late, with the loss of his unborn child and the departure of his partner, Alana Renfield.

"So, Hugh, how are you bearing up? What happened? she asked.

Shug went on to tell Georgia in more detail about what had happened. After her miscarriage, Alana had become understandably withdrawn and wouldn't talk to Shug, let alone let him near her. But with the pandemic being on, the couple had been stuck alone at home together with their grief – most of Shug's staff across his many businesses, including Alana, were still on furlough because of the pandemic. Isolation together under those circumstances had created a bad atmosphere at home and one morning Shug had woken up to find Alana gone. Shug said that he felt like Alana blamed him for their losing the baby, so they had been unable to grieve together. He ended his sad tale by saying, "We were both so heartbroken, Georgia, it was like we had a future, then, boom, it was gone."

Georgia was sure that Shug was near tears on the other end of the phone. His tale of woe made her pity him, in spite of everything – nobody deserves to go through that. She offered Shug some kind words, and some advice, suggesting that he should perhaps talk to a professional counsellor – she suggested that partly through genuine concern for a fellow human being, partly so that he might feel less need to be phoning her up – she still held him indirectly responsible for many bad things that had befallen her family. Shug said that he would give counselling a try and again asked Georgia if she and her family needed anything, to which Georgia politely said 'no'. Shug then said he had to go and have a Zoom call with his employees. Both of them had a quick bitch to one another about how tediously irritating the whole Zoom thing was, before they both thanked each other again, and said goodbye.

The call reminded Georgia that throughout the near 30 years that she had known Hugh Mann, sometimes he could be ok, pleasant, even. He was a familiar voice and those were few and far between in mid-2020 – though he still gave her the ick. She was pleasantly surprised that Shug hadn't asked for anything in return for helping her – it just seemed he'd wanted someone to talk to, after all, even rich gangsters get lonely, she reasoned to herself.

CHAPTER TWENTY-NINE

Swamp Thing

For the remainder of May and June, Georgia plodded on through the dystopian weirdness that was the pandemic. She was still signed off from work but started to join the council's weekly zoom conferences with her colleagues, so as to remain in the loop for when she did feel well enough to resume her duties. She continued to look after her ailing dad – seeing him every day really lifted her spirits, despite his obvious decline. Olivia had taken up jogging in an attempt to stay fit while her preferred sports were still prohibited by pandemic restrictions. When she wasn't out jogging or sunbathing in the garden, she was up in her room, either coding, gaming, or chatting to friends online. Mother and daughter still spent a couple of hours together most evenings in front of the TV together in the living room, watching the news and the soap operas, before Olivia would disappear upstairs again to live her life in cyberspace – like all young people had to do during the Covid 19 lockdowns. Olivia even got so bored one weekend in late June that she decided to tidy her room, though she wouldn't let her mum help her with that potentially disgusting task. When she was finished, all four of the family wheely bins were overflowing with cardboard and other junk. Several mugs and plates that Georgia had noticed long-term absent from the cupboards also reappeared after this monumental room-gutting. Though Olivia was messy, she was not a pure mink, like her brother when it came to his smelly-sock aroma bedroom.

Throughout that time, Jordan remained on the locked mental ward at the hospital in Glasgow. His condition didn't really improve in those months, despite being told about the developments regarding his drug-dealing charge. Georgia and Olivia took turns using the pass to visit him and they both called him daily on Skype, too, though on one day that they called, another patient answered on the iPad, a young guy who told them that Jordan wasn't available that day because Tony Blair had sent Jordan to Afghanistan to negotiate a ceasefire with the Taliban – Jordan had actually been in the toilet at the time. Throughout their painful visits to see Jordan, his mum and sister saw changes, some good, some bad. The staff had reduced his sedatives, so he was at least a bit more talkative when they went to see him. On the other hand, he seemed to have embraced his new surroundings, like he was meant to have been there all along. He had studiously memorised the ward and staff's schedules and practices. Georgia could see that institutionalisation was a threat, even after such a relatively short stay in hospital, and both she and Olivia prayed for the day that he was well enough to be cared for and to recover at home with his loved ones, where he belonged. The Smith family soldiered on.

Throughout this time, Shug had called Georgia most weeks, almost always on a Friday evening. The phone calls ran to a pattern. Shug would ask how Georgia was getting on, then enquire as to Jordan's health, and ask Georgia if she needed anything, to which Georgia would politely say 'no, thanks'. The conversation would then switch to Shug's woes, and he would open up to Georgia about the loss of his child and his breakup with Alana and her subsequent ghosting of him. Georgia would console him and offer advice, then their conversation would switch to the pandemic, and their mutual thoughts on the catastrophe which was currently engulfing the country. They both agreed that the government's response had been shite and had made things worse. Shug would always mention that his asthma and generally fluctuating respiratory health made him terrified to catch the virus, Georgia could empathise there as she was afraid to catch it in case she gave it to her elderly, vulnerable father. They would wish each other well, and that would be 'it' for another week. Georgia found the phone calls tiresome but saw it as the price she had to pay for Shug's helping out with Jordan's case. She was, too, relived that his creepy long-standing desire to get her into bed seemed well and truly gone, at least, he hadn't mentioned that again.

CHAPTER THIRTY

Beachball

July 2020 came, and the first chinks of light began to break through the barrier over society that was the pandemic restrictions. Masks were the order of the day, but outdoor seating areas at pubs and cafes were allowed to reopen. People could hug their grandparents again and limited social bubbles were encouraged among families – though Georgia had ignored the restrictions when it came to visiting her dad at home, anyway.

On Monday July 6th, Georgia was able to go out and meet her best friend, Isla, in the outdoor seating area of the local Brewer's Fayre place, for a coffee. Georgia wore a black jumpsuit and did her makeup for this long-overdue social gathering – before leaving the house she looked at herself in the hall mirror and thought to herself, 'I've still got it'. As ever, Isla upstaged her, turning up to drink coffee in the beer garden in the afternoon wearing a black evening dress and heels, showing so much cleavage that every male in attendance couldn't help but sneak a longing stare – she looked like a movie star on the red carpet at the Oscars that day. The two friends drank coffee and giggled and had a proper catchup – both were genuinely relieved to see each other again. Zoom and Skype were, and are, no substitute for seeing someone that you care about in person. Georgia filled Isla in about how the kids were and how her dad was and how she was feeling on the meds the doctor had given her for stress. It turned out that Isla, too, had been given a prescription for anxiety recently – Covid 19 was boomtime for whoever manufactures Sertraline. Isla confessed that she and her partner, Cammy, had struggled with the lockdown, like many couples had, being suddenly forced to spend every waking hour together. There'd been tetchy, petty arguments, there'd been full-blown rows, even a few spells of them taking turns to give each other the silent treatment. To make it worse, Isla said, the Sertraline had made it more difficult for her to reach orgasm on those occasions when she and Cammy still jumped into bed together. There, in that moment, for the first time that she could recall, Georgia felt glad that she had been single when the pandemic began – asides the external stresses to do with debt, her dad and Jordan, Georgia realised that her relatively chill quiet time at home with just her daughter since mid-March had been almost a breeze, compared to the Covid ordeals of others. Georgia and Isla drank three lattes together and had some cake, before parting ways to go home – no kiss on the cheek or hug, this time, just a cheeky elbow bump between them. Georgia got home feeling renewed – the trip out to meet her friend had nourished her soul and she hadn't laughed so hard in a long time – there's no substitute for warm, familiar human company.

When she got in, Georgia poured herself a small glass of whisky and plonked herself down on the sofa, flicking on the TV. She then grabbed her phone and cast some music to the TV from Youtube – '*If you'll be mine*' by Babybird – she'd always loved that song.

> *I tick like a bomb*
> *A little bomb with feelings*
> *In every single country*
> *Under every ceiling*
> *There's no feeling, there's no feeling at all*

There's no feeling, there's no feeling at all
If you'll be mine, I'll be yours
If you'll be mine, I'll be yours
If you'll be mine, I'll be yours
If you'll be mine, I'll be yours

As she sat back enjoying the song and her wee dram, her phone began to buzz.

She sighed and took the call. It was from Shug – who'd never called on a Monday before. The conversation went much the way that their other recent chats had – these calls tended to last for around 40 minutes. Though Georgia was in a good mood and went through the motions of talking to this nutter about his problems, she could've done with the 'me' time and wished that she had turned her phone to silent when she got in. She did notice that Shug seemed a bit more upbeat, he told her that he was on steroids now for his chest and that he had regained his mojo – whatever the fuck that meant.

"Oh, that's great, Hugh, hopefully that improves things for you," she said.

Shug then threw her a curveball by asking her to meet him for a coffee somewhere tomorrow, now that some Covid restrictions had been lifted. With every fibre of her being, Georgia wanted to say, 'Absolutely not. I don't mind listening to your problems over the phone, but I've no wish to be in your presence regardless of what you might have done for my son,' but she didn't. He wanted to meet her at a coffee place in Hamilton tomorrow afternoon, so at least it was a public place. For the sake of a quiet life, she agreed to meet him. What swung her decision was Shug's insistence that he had some news about her husband, Keith, that he said he could only share in person.

The next day, Georgia's wee Renault Clio car finally gave up the ghost and refused to start, only eventually spluttering into action after a jump start from her neighbour. The garage that she usually used was in Hamilton so she dropped the ailing vehicle off there, did her best not to flinch when the mechanic did the trademark inhaling whistle and told her the extortionate rough cost of the repair, then made her way on foot to the coffee place to meet Shug.

Shug was already there waiting when she arrived. He was sitting at an outside table. He was now completely bald and was wearing his business attire – a Marc Darcy suit and a pair of shiny new black brogues. Georgia thought that he looked scary, monstrous, even. He was greedily stuffing his face with a huge panini dripping with ham and cheese, and on the table sat his huge coffee, his inhaler, and his mobile phone – which had a claret and amber shockproof cover on it for his team, Motherwell.

"Georgia, good to see you, pal," he said, still chewing his messy panini, talking with his mouth full – something that was one of Georgia's pet hates. He had put on weight again, too, Georgia noticed. Shug continued.

"Yours is a latte, right? I've ordered you a large one on the app, should be here in a minute. Here, sit down."

Georgia sat down opposite him, just as the young barista lassie plonked her latte down on the table before scurrying off.

"So, Hugh, how are you?" she said.

Shug kept on chewing as he spoke. All around his mouth were crumbs, flecks of cheese and what looked like smears of mustard.

"Aye, no bad, Georgia, listen I heard some news yesterday, that I didn't think was appropriate to share on the phone." He continued stuffing his face, stopping eating to noisily slurp a glug of his coffee, the brown liquid dribbling out of the corners of his mouth. He then burped loudly, Georgia did her best not to wince as the unspeakably awful waft of his burp reached her nostrils. Georgia didn't really care about the waft, she just wanted to hear Shug's news. Her inner monologue was saying '*It's not the fucking X-Factor, stop doing 'the pause', you're not fucking Davina McCall.*'

"So, what's the news, Hugh?" she asked.

"Mmm, aye, sorry." Shug put down the last bit of his panini. "Fuckin' good grub, by the way. Aye, where was I? Your Keith pled guilty last week, he got 18 months, he's in Shotts Prison. He might get out in nine or ten months. He doesn't work for me anymore, but as we're pals and he was my employee for years, I thought it best to tell you in person. His court thing was all done on Zoom, by the way."

Georgia was heartbroken and annoyed at the same time. She knew Keith had been on remand but hadn't expected him to be dealt with so quickly. She knew that a guy like Keith would struggle in prison. She was annoyed because Shug really could have just told her this over the phone.

"That's sad, Hugh, but the kids and I have kinda gotten used to him not being around. I wish he'd made better choices, for his sake."

"What does that mean?" asked Shug calmly, devouring the last piece of his panini.

"Hugh, he gave up a good life for the sake of some white powder, some junkie slags and the jakey party circuit. If he hadn't chosen that path, he wouldn't be in prison now."

Hugh looked a bit surprised at Georgia's directness, but his ego didn't let him take it as a dig at him.

"Look, Georgia, I've got people on the inside, I'll make sure his time is as easy as possible."

"Thank you, for that," said Georgia, politely but with no warmth or enthusiasm. Shug continued.

"I want to thank you for taking my calls when I've been down of late, Georgia, this must be a tough time for you and the kids, and your dad. Is there anything I can do to help you out? Anything at all?"

Georgia was tactful. "I can't think of anything right now, Hugh, but thank you, if I think of anything I'll let you know". What she really wanted to say was *'please fuck off',* but because he'd helped Jordan, she didn't. As Georgia took a glug of her coffee and absorbed the news about her husband, Shug's phone rang, and he answered it.

"Aye, sure. Where? Ok, when? Right, fine," and the call was over. Georgia realised that she'd left her own phone in her car and would need to walk back to the garage to get it before getting the bus home.

"I'm really sorry, Georgia, but I have to go," he said. He took two puffs on his inhaler then thrust it into his pocket, pulling out a set of car keys, adding, "Where's your car, do you need a lift?"

"No. I mean, no thanks, I'm just off to pick it up from the garage along the road, actually," she lied. Then she had a brainwave and blurted something out that seemed to come from nowhere.

"Hugh, did Keith still owe you any money?"

"About twenty grand," replied Shug, matter-of-factly. "Why do you ask?"

"So, how will you get it back now?"

For once, Shug seemed to know what she meant.

"Don't you worry about that, Georgia, that's nothing to do with you, forget about that. You should concentrate on your own life and those kids of yours. Jordan is a good kid from what I know, he'll pull through, and your daughter's a brainbox, she looks just like you did at her age – like I said, Keith's debt isn't your problem."

Georgia paid little heed to Shug's comforting words about her kids; they were mere well-meaning platitudes – after all how on earth would he know what her kids were like? She was, however, delighted and relieved to hear that there'd be nobody coming to the door expecting her to cover Keith's drug debt.

"Ok, well, thanks, Hugh, I hope your business thing goes well," said Georgia, getting up to leave.

"Cheers, Georgia, I'll be in touch – look after yourself," said Shug, as they parted company, heading in opposite directions. Georgia felt like taking a bath after being in his company. She made her way back to the garage and retrieved her phone from the mechanic's. To her annoyance, it was off and when she switched it back on it went off again – the battery was dead. The bus journey home took an hour or so. Georgia was sad to see so many shops and business units in Hamilton to let or boarded up and wondered to herself how many had closed because of Brexit, how many had closed because of the Tories and how many of those remaining were really just fronts for money laundering?

CHAPTER THIRTY-ONE

Inner City Life

When she got home it was about 3pm. She made herself a decaf coffee – the big strong latte she'd had with Shug had blown her head off, almost giving her a panic-attack on the bus home, then she went to the kitchen table, where there was a charging cable that snaked over from the plugs at the kitchen units. She put her phone on charge and sat down. She could hear Olivia's music from upstairs – she was blaring something decent for a change – *Blinding Lights* by The Weeknd.

> *I've been tryna call*
> *I've been on my own for long enough*
> *Maybe you can show me how to love, maybe*
> *I'm going through withdrawals*
> *You don't even have to do too much*
> *You can turn me on with just a touch, baby*

Georgia really liked The Weeknd because he was a fairly new artist so she, as a new forty-something, was still, evidently, hip and with-it for her age just by liking this artist, even though, of course, nobody under 40 actually uses terms like 'hip' and 'with-it' – middle-aged people do. Then again, 40s are the new 30s for many. The real reason she liked The Weeknd was that his stuff sounded a bit like A-Ha! and other 80s bands, from when she was a child.

After about ten minutes Georgia knew that it was now safe to actually switch her phone back on without it being overrun with notifications and shutting down again, so, on it went.

She really hoped that there were no more messages from Hugh Mann – and there weren't.

As her notifications started to come in, she noticed eight missed calls – one from her dad's mobile number, which he barely knew how to use. One from Gladys – her dad's lovely West African carer, one from a number she didn't recognise and five missed calls from a withheld number. The withheld numbers might be spam, but they might also be calls from work or from a hospital, so Georgia was a tad concerned. She rang her dad's mobile, but it just rang out. She rang his carer back, but that number was engaged. Then she Googled the number that she didn't know and saw that it was a notorious scammer number. Next, she looked at her texts. There was one from Gladys. "Please call me back ASAP." She tried ringing Gladys again, but it was still engaged. Then Georgia heard a sound that she hadn't heard in months – the bland monotone of the landline – that ornament that nobody uses anymore. With some suspicion she went to the hall and picked up the receiver, wondering who on earth this might be.

The call was from a Northern-Irish staff nurse at the local hospital. Alex, her dad, had become breathless earlier that afternoon and his carer had called 999. Paramedics had come, had examined him and then taken him to hospital in the ambulance. The nurse said that they had been trying to call her but got no answer – which explained the missed calls. The nurse indicated that Alex was very poorly and advised Georgia to make her way to the hospital quickly. Georgia became frightened and angry with herself, for had she not been in Hamilton meeting Shug for coffee and had she not left her phone on the dashboard after dropping it off at the dealership, she'd have heard about her dad's illness straight away – her battery had clearly been drained while her phone sat idle in the car without her, so, the worst had clearly happened while she was actually supping a latte with Shug. Georgia panicked then rushed upstairs to bang on Olivia's door. There was a rummaging sound, but no answer, so she barged straight in. Olivia, who was lying on her bed in her dressing gown chatting to one of her geeky friends on the computer, jumped at the sudden intrusion, snapping, 'Mum, it's called privacy!', and slamming her laptop shut. But when her mum said what was wrong, Olivia's mood changed, and she quickly got dressed. With no car, Georgia rang a taxi, and within 20 minutes they were at the hospital. The taxi driver sensed that they were both upset and didn't hit them with any of his shite patter. The hospital entrance had far more security guards than usual, because of the pandemic, but they made it to the desk and were told that Alex Dooley was being treated in the red zone – the emergency area of the hospital reserved for Covid patients and suspected Covid patients.

Mother and daughter made their way anxiously, hurrying along the corridors until they reached the double doors that were the entrance to the red zone. There was a desk beside the entrance, staffed by two masked nurses – Georgia and Olivia had already masked-up in the taxi.

To their dismay, they were told that only one of them could see Alex, who was being treated in a side room, but only from the corridor through that side room's glass panel – nobody, save the nurses treating him, could enter his room – and they were to wait for now. There was a waiting area next to the desk with chairs spaced two metres apart as per regulations, and on one of those chairs sat a chubby but friendly looking black woman wearing a carer's tunic and trousers, and a mask. It was Gladys. They both walked over towards her then stopped two metres away.

Gladys told Georgia that her dad had almost collapsed that afternoon after eating his lunch, but Gladys, thankfully, was there when it happened and had called for help – she'd made her own way to the hospital in her little Fiat 500 work car and had tried to call Georgia. Then Gladys told Georgia that her dad had tested positive for Covid.

Georgia and Olivia's hearts both sank – for them, the pandemic was no longer an abstract thing on the news that stopped you having a life, as it was to many people – it was trying to kill their loved one.

A tall male doctor in what looked like a painter's facemask – those tales about PPE shortages were clearly true – then came out of the double doors leading to the red zone and stood two metres from Georgia and Olivia. Georgia couldn't see his face but could tell by his eyes that he was both extremely sad and stressed out to breaking point.

"Mrs Smith, I'm afraid your father has pneumonia and has also tested positive for Covid 19. He's deteriorating very rapidly – we've done all that we can. You should prepare yourselves for the worst."

"Go on, Mum, in you go, I'll stay here with Gladys," said Olivia, calmly.

Georgia, stunned, went with the doctor through the big double doors, stopping, yet again, to sanitise her hands at the sanitiser station beside the doors.

"Your father is in the last room at the end of the corridor, on the left, follow me, please," said the doctor, as they walked down the long corridor. On either side of them, all the way down were a mixture of individual side rooms and four-bed mini wards. Doctors and nurses buzzed about the ward at frantic pace, dressed in hazmat suits, or aprons with dust masks, some even had proper NHS PPE. To Georgia, it was like something out of a science fiction movie – a horrible one. In each ward and side room lay patients. Many were unconscious and breathing through ventilators, some were conscious and coughing like World-War-One victims of mustard gas, while some were laid out flat on their stomachs – which was initially the NHS's only real way of treating victims of the virus. Contrary to what she had heard on social media, Georgia noticed that around half of the patients weren't old-age pensioners – some were young – but there were no children.

As she and the doctor walked along that hospital corridor with nothing but death and suffering on either side of them, and with little more than plasterboard walls and glass windows between them and the most dangerous virus to threaten humanity in over 100 years, it flashed through Georgia's mind just what a fucked-up situation the country was in. At home, in the safety but tediousness of lockdown, it could almost seem like the virus wasn't real – something that happened somewhere else, to other people. There were even some people in the UK and around the world – former LSD and other illegal drug users mostly – who, through various forms of tinfoil-hat idiocy and perhaps as a coping measure for the stress of the pandemic, had decided that there was no such thing as Coronavirus at all – such was their delusion. Georgia had seen their nonsense on social media; there were even a handful of celebrities turned cranks who had bought into the windup 'scamdemic' narrative and thus lost all credibility. Georgia knew that one stroll down the terrifying, ghastly steampunk horror that was this hospital's red zone would soon put any doubters right – this was fucking real.

They reached the end of the corridor where the side room housing Georgia's dad was, next to another set of big double doors, guarded by yet another masked security guard. Those doors led further into the red zone, but Georgia had reached her destination and stopped at the side room window to look in. She looked through the large glass pane and saw her dad. He was barely conscious and was hooked up to all sorts of drips and monitoring devices. She could see that he was also wearing an oxygen mask but wasn't on an actual ventilator – Georgia was utterly horrified but also knew that his not being on a ventilator was a good sign. The doctor soon robbed her of that comforting delusion.

"I'm so sorry, you can only stay for five minutes, your dad is in very bad shape indeed, as you can see – we're doing everything that we can – we're giving him oxygen, fluids and some IV antibiotics for the pneumonia, but the problem is the Covid and the pneumonia being concurrent."

Georgia was well-informed enough to know that the doctor had basically just told her that her dad's life was in God's hands now, she knew there wasn't an effective treatment for Covid yet. "Thank you, Doctor." she said in a monotone voice. A bedside alarm on the ward went off and the doctor had to rush away back up the corridor. Georgia put her face as close to the glass separating her from her dad as she could and stared. It was the first time that she'd ever seen her dad so ill, or looking so old. She remembered the stoic old industrial worker and trade unionist that he had been when she was younger – strong, athletic, fearsome, yet so kind, too. Now she still saw that, but she also saw a skinny, elderly, fragile bag of bones in a hospital gown gasping for life, his only company an overworked nurse wearing full PPE. Every fibre of Georgia's being screamed at her to say 'fuck the rules' and to burst into his room to take his hand, but the proximity of the security guard and the fact that there was a nurse in the room with her dad made her override that very natural instinct. When human beings see a loved one in danger, fight or flight kicks in – yet Georgia, like thousands of other people in her position in 2020, had to suppress both of those instincts, so, she just watched helplessly through the pane of glass. When her dad turned to the left and could see the pane of glass, making eye contact with her, she burst into tears and smiled at him at the same time. He knew she was there! Her dad stared up at her through the glass, seeming to somehow register her presence. He continued staring, then Georgia was sure that she saw him smile a bit. Then, he shook his head. It was as if he were telling Georgia, 'I'm glad you're here, but it's pointless, hen."

With tears in her eyes, Georgia held his gaze for a few minutes – there was so much that she wanted to say to him, she wanted to thank him, she wanted to tell him how much she loved him, and she wanted to say goodbye – but she couldn't. All she could do was cry and look through the glass. The fucking glass. The nurse in his room came outside to fetch something from a trolley, looked at Georgia and tilted her masked head to one side. Georgia could see from her eyes that she was trying to be sympathetic, but even a hug from a nurse was out of the question under the current circumstances. The nurse spoke.

"I'm really sorry. I've been with your dad since he came in, he's a fighter. Look, why don't you go and have a cup of tea? We're doing all that we can."

"Has there been many in my dad's condition who have recovered?" asked Georgia, again, in a monotone voice.

The nurse took a beat before answering, unenthusiastically, her voice muffled by her mask.

"One or two. The issue with your dad is the pneumonia and Covid at the same time – he's not getting enough oxygen, no matter what we do – but he's a fighter."

The nurse took what she needed from the trolley and went back into Alex's room.

Fighter or not, Georgia knew that her dad already had a bad chest from his time in the tyre yards and in his career in heavy industry. With his age, his dementia and myriad other conditions, Georgia knew that the game was up for Alex – her dad was going to die. She remained, her face wet with tears, standing at the pane of glass watching her dad gasping for breath – watching him die, until the doctor reappeared and apologetically told her that she had to return to the waiting area and leave the ward.

Georgia's instinct was to wave to her dad, which she did, her dad gave a single nod of his head and blinked at her, Georgia was even half-sure that his mouth had curled up at the corners to try to smile, but then he rolled his head back so that he was staring at the ceiling again. Stunned and in tears, Georgia reluctantly made her way back along the corridor of death and suffering, sanitising her hands again at the double doors before rejoining her daughter and Gladys in the waiting area. She imparted her saddest of news to Olivia and her dad's carer, thanked Gladys then gave her daughter a hug. The three of them then sullenly made their way back along the hospital corridors – which, when deserted that way, looked like a scene from A Clockwork Orange – Georgia's dad's favourite film. The hospital coffee shop had closed for the night, so they had to make do with vending machine tea – half a cup of minging dark brown tea-flavoured hot water with sugar – for the shock. There was a sign up at the canteen indicating that it should be open, but there was also a hand-written note pinned to the pulled down shutter – closed due to staff illness.

The three of them went outside to drink their vile brews, it was still summer and very warm outside. Other patients' relatives were gathered outside, too, some also enduring the torture of bogging vending machine beverages, as if seeing loved ones living their last moments in a dystopian hospital setting wasn't bad enough. Everyone there had the thousand-yard stare.

Gladys had to go home after around ten minutes – she'd been on her feet for 12 hours by then. Georgia and Olivia wanted to give her a hug, but because of the rules, they couldn't, so they just said thank you. Gladys had been taking new experimental lateral flow tests every day since they had become available and was tested again by staff at the hospital when she first appeared there to support auld Alex, and she didn't have Covid – Alex had clearly caught the virus that appeared to have sealed his doom from one of his other carers – possibly one of the young Scottish ones who weren't taking the pandemic as seriously, nobody would ever really know who.

Unsure what to do next, Georgia and Olivia made their way back to the waiting area outside the red zone. There were now two different masked nurses manning the desk outside, and two new security guards were on the door.

This time, Georgia was told that there was no way that she could see her dad, because he had deteriorated to the point that he had been put onto a ventilator. Both mother and daughter knew what that meant. The nurses suggested that the best thing that they could both do was to go home, get some rest and wait for news from the ward – the nurses also promised to set up a video call with auld Alex. Going home and leaving her dad to die alone surrounded by strangers, albeit heroic ones, wasn't what Georgia or indeed any other human being wanted to do – but there was little choice. In truth, Georgia had been lucky to see her dad through the glass pane, at all. Drowning in a Tiber of sadness, they called a taxi to go home, but had to wait over 90 minutes for one to arrive – there were far fewer taxis around, because of Covid, after all. They arrived home in the evening, tired, dejected, frightened, and full of sorrow. Olivia, ever a tower of strength, sat with her mum in the living room all night, that night. She was Georgia's rock, her strong daughter, making her tea and sandwiches, helping her to phone round relatives to tell them that poor auld Alex was on the way out, and generally keeping her from losing her mind. To top it all off, though, both of them had forgotten to visit Jordan on the psychiatric ward in Glasgow that day and they both felt guilty about that. They resolved to go the next day, though they'd have to get the bus as Georgia's car was still at the garage.

They ended that Tuesday evening drinking wine and watching old music videos, talking about how amazing auld Alex was. An obscure 90s cheesy pop song did get them both crying again, though. It was by Swedish songstress, Amelia.

I'm a big, big girl
In a big, big world
It's not a big, big thing
If you leave me
But I do, do feel
That I do, do will
Miss you much
Miss you much

Before bed, mother and daughter prayed together for the first time in years – beseeching a higher power to intercede on behalf of auld Alex, on behalf of Jordan, and on behalf of his dad, too – after all, here was one fractured family who truly needed a miracle.

CHAPTER THIRTY-TWO

In and Out of My Life

The next day, they decided that Georgia would get the bus into Glasgow to visit Jordan, while Olivia would wait at home in case the local hospital, where auld Alex was, tried to get in touch via the family landline. Georgia hated the bus – the noise, the farts, the nippy wee bastards listening to techno music on their phones without headphones, everything - though, like many adults, Georgia knew that the future in our crowded and polluted world was a return to public transport for most people. Limited numbers were still allowed onto buses because of Covid and mask-wearing was still required. The bus trip into Glasgow would've taken about an hour but for an incident in the city centre, when a fat guy in a baseball cap and reeking of weed tried to get on the bus without either a mask or a pass saying he was exempt from wearing a mask. The guy wasted about twenty minutes slavering to the driver that Covid was a hoax, that Bill Gates was trying to take over Scotland and that everyone wearing a mask was a sheep for doing so. The guy then accused the bus-driver of being part of the 'illuminati' and being employed by a race of lizard people who, he claimed, now controlled Scotland's bus network and had possessed the first minister, Nicola Sturgeon, who had now 'become one of them'. This moron kept ranting at the driver and as he refused to get off the bus, they were all stuck there for some time, in only moderate traffic.

Eventually, Georgia got up out of her seat and walked along to the front of the bus until she stood just a few feet from this crackpot, who was about her age – early 40s.

"Look, pal, I'm trying to get to Gartnavel Psychiatric Unit to visit my son, is there any chance you could just fuck off?" Georgia then folded her arms and stared at the crackpot.

He was slightly overweight for his average height, he stank of green, he hadn't shaved and he was wearing baggy denim shorts, white sports socks, blue Nike trainers and one of those '*Take me to your dealer*' tee-shirts – in other words, he looked like a fanny – and he was.

Obviously having not expected to have been confronted in this manner, the crackpot looked Georgia up and down, looked at the elderly male bus driver again, sighed, then got off the bus with an "Aye, ok, sorry. Fuck's sake," as he alighted from the vehicle. The driver, who had been on the point of radioing for the police, thanked Georgia, then, when she turned around to walk back to her seat on the bus, the 11 or so other passengers gave her a round of applause and a wee cheer. That felt good to Georgia, despite her worries about external matters – she had stood up for herself and had won – something she was guilty of rarely doing in her life thus far. As the bus pulled away, the passengers saw three neddish teenagers – two boys and a girl, all under 14 – approach and surround the crackpot who had just left the bus, knocking off his hat and bullying him – which gave them all a lovely warm glow inside. Georgia sat down and took out her phone, she wanted to post on Facebook and on Twitter about what had just happened with the bus guy and the round of applause, but she thought better of it, knowing that it would probably be filed under 'things that never really happened' by most people on social media.

The hour-long visit with Jordan at the hospital went as well as could be expected. Jordan was still very unwell, but a little bit of his old sharpness was fighting to get out of him again, Georgia could see and feel it from behind his sedated blue eyes. Jordan understood that his granddad was seriously ill and was lucid enough to realise that he probably wouldn't see the auld guy again. Georgia and her son cried together at this visit, probably for the first time ever, but it did both of them good. As their time together drew to a close, Georgia was heartened to hear her son say that he had a plan – get better, get home, get back to work, go back to studying – it wasn't exactly complex but to Georgia, to hear her sedated son even say that, after what they'd all been through, it was music to her ears.

Georgia headed home on the bus afterwards. It was early afternoon. Waiting in the bus stop for the journey home, when she reached it, was a lassie in grey joggers, white trainers, and a grey hoodie with the hood up – despite it being a hot summer's day. Georgia could tell that it was a woman because her enormous tits and arse couldn't be hidden by the joggers. Georgia leaned against the opposite side of the bus stop, got out her phone and started scrolling. Then, she heard a woman's voice.

"Georgia? Georgia Smith, right?"

Georgia turned to look at the woman in the grey joggers who had just addressed her and replied "Aye, who's that?"

The woman pulled back the hood of her grey hoodie and Georgia at once recognised her.

"I'm Alana Renfield, we've met before, do you remember me?"

Georgia was stunned. It was Shug's ex, the one who'd suffered a miscarriage and had left Shug afterwards – the one who gave the good business presentation to the council, the one who'd had all the plastic surgery.

"Of course I remember you, Alana," said Georgia. She could see that Alana looked far less the business-savvy glamour-puss and more like a jakey-ned today – the blonde hair was unwashed and tied back, with the dark roots coming back in. She wore no makeup and had a scar down one side of her face. Under her eyes were big dark rings indicating exhaustion, stress, substance abuse, or perhaps all three. As the bus wasn't due for another 30 minutes, Georgia, out of curiosity, sympathy and genuine concern for her fellow woman, asked Alana if she fancied a coffee – Alana accepted unhesitatingly. The pub on the corner of Kelvindale Road had outdoor seating, and as it was midweek and daytime, they had no difficulty in finding a table, even without booking. Georgia ordered them each a latte . The drinks appeared a few moments later, brought by a young male staff member who seemed annoyed that they hadn't booked ahead but also seemed too much of a snowflake to confront them about it – he wouldn't be getting a tip.

Georgia took a sip of her latte then spoke.

"So, Alana, look, I was talking to Hugh, I heard about what happened – I'm really sorry, that must be so heartbreaking."

Alana took a sip of her own coffee and looked back at Georgia apprehensively. Georgia could see from the look in her eyes and her general manner that Alana had indeed gone through major trauma – another human being with the thousand-yard stare – the plastic surgery she'd clearly had on her nose and lips looked even more odd, now.

"Let me guess. Shug told you I lost the baby, I became weird and then I left him, drowning in grief?" said Alana.

"Aye, he did, Alana, I'm so sorry, you must be devastated, Hugh is too. Can't have been easy."

Alana seemed to ignore that statement and continued.

"Listen, Georgia, why the fuck do you call him Hugh? Literally nobody else calls him that, I've seen him hospitalise folk who did, or stop their drug supply, or get them sacked."

Georgia was surprised by the question but answered.

"Oh, I don't know, really. We're from the same town and went to the same school, he was just Hugh at school, so I've always just called him Hugh, it doesn't seem to annoy him, or at least, he's never said anything about it."

"You should avoid Shug Mann like the plague he is, Georgia, keep him away from you and your family – he's bad news," said Alana, looking around in a paranoid manner before taking a pack of cigarettes out of her hoodie pocket. Glancing around again, she lit one, offering the packet to Georgia, who hesitated for a second before saying 'no thanks'. Alana put the cigarette packet on the small round table they were sitting at, took two long draws from the fag, exhaling upwards at an angle away from Georgia's direction, then spoke again.

"I did 'lose' my baby, but I lost it because of Shug. One night he came in from a day sesh with his dealer cronies and demanded a blowjob from me. I said I would after he'd showered, cos he'd been out all day and was stinking of sweat and drink. He got really angry then demanded food instead, when I asked him what he wanted to eat he started being a pure fanny, calling me names, running me down, calling me a fat cow for being heavily pregnant, saying that he had plenty of younger women he could go to for the blowjob, instead. I took the huff and went upstairs to watch TV, but he soon followed me upstairs. Long story short, he couldn't *make* me suck his cock, no matter what he said or did, so he just battered fuck out of me instead. At first it was just a few slaps to the face and head – his usual thing – but when he booted me in the ribs I got scared and tried to escape. He got worse and worse, swearing, insulting, threatening, as I started to pack a bag with some of my stuff. Eventually, I had enough of it and told him to speak up, so that his unborn child could hear him. He froze for a second and I went to go down the stairs, he then ran after me and with both hands between my shoulders he shoved me down the stairs.

I must have lain there for about half an hour at the bottom of the stairs – that cunt did nothing, didn't even phone me an ambulance. When I came to, he was sitting drinking Stella on the sofa and doing lines, like nothing had happened. The cunt's first words to me after waking up were 'do you want a line?'."

I hadn't broken any bones but my back had gone into spasm, and I was bruised and cut all over, and bleeding between my legs."

Georgia looked open-mouthed at Alana – all she could say was, "Fuck. I'm so sorry."

Alana continued, still smoking. She fingered the cut on her cheek.

"That was Shug's watch, by the way, a missed blow."

Georgia really didn't know what to say, so she said 'fuck' again, adding 'then what?'

"Then what? What do you think? We all lived happily ever after?"

Alana scoffed, then apologised, her eyes beginning to water a bit. She wiped them on the arm of her hoodie.

"Then, he phones an ambulance, says he'll kill me if I don't tell the paramedics that I just fell down the stairs, so, scared and injured, fearing for my baby's life, I did just that, then I passed out again. I had a catastrophic haemorrhage in my womb from the fall and lost the baby at seven months. The baby's body was removed when I was unconscious, so I didn't need to give birth". Alana lifted her hoodie up a little to show a sickened Georgia a caesarean scar. "I then, stupidly, bullshitted the police away when I was still in shock, so Shug got away with it. There was also damage to my cervix meaning that it's unlikely that I'll ever conceive again – Shug told me in the hospital that I'm damaged goods now and told me to get to fuck, so when I got out of hospital I had to go and stay with my auntie, just around the corner from here. Shug even sent one of his goons round with black bags containing my clothes, well, apart from any designer stuff he bought me. He treated me like a piece of rubbish, Georgia. He made sure I had nothing, no money, no job, he even kept my valuables, my jewellery and all that."

Georgia believed every word that Alana had said and tried to be constructive.

"He can't do that, weren't you business partners? He can't leave you with nothing," said Georgia, trying to lift the girl's spirits.

Alana scoffed again. "He's Shug Mann, he's a psychopath, he can do whatever he wants. He used me for sex, as arm candy and to exploit my employment background in order to get council contracts for his businesses – he's a bastard, make no mistake. He did pay me a wage but once I moved in with him, he set up a joint account for us and had both our wages paid into it – but only he had access to it – from that moment on, I was fucking trapped. At first it was ok, plenty of money, cocaine on tap, parties, he promised the Earth and I got a thrill from being with a rich gangster, but then his mask slipped, and my noticing that his mask had slipped just made him even worse. I was just the front for that business, by the way – the one you gave the council contract to, he fooled you as well with that, didn't he? My getting pregnant probably saved me from what he usually does to his women, though."

"What does he do, Alana?" asked Georgia, dread beginning to creep over her once more.

"Ever since that lass of his, Karen, escaped him with their twins, he runs to a pattern, I've found out. He meets a new woman, impresses her with the money, the power and the gangster thing, they end up addicted to coke if they weren't already, just by hanging around with him, then when he gets tired of fucking them he turns round and jars them for the money they 'owe' him, for all the coke they've taken when with him – gear they assumed was free as they were his 'girlfriend'. When they can't pay, he gets them to work it off as escorts in manky flats in Glasgow or Edinburgh, owned by a business associate of his, or if the lassie is a real looker, they first have to work it off doing webcam for him online – he has a LOT of girls working off their coke debt that way. By the time I realised what he's really like it was too late, I was in too deep, but I got pregnant, which weirdly protected me from his excesses, until it didn't anymore, of course. He's bad news, Georgia, BAD news."

Georgia was stunned but not surprised – she felt for Alana even though she hadn't really liked her before and still didn't now – gangster's moles were usually tedious, but she was also a woman in need, a sister in distress.

"Alana, look, I'm really sorry that all of this has happened to you, is there anything that I can do to help?"

Alana finished off her coffee, slurping the last few drops loudly, then looked Georgia in the eye.

"You can't really help me but thank you. I've got Anti-Ds from the doctor, I've got a trauma counsellor who I have to lie to, I'm living rent free with my elderly auntie and I'm fucking skint. If you really want to do something for me, stay away from Shug if he tries to contact you – don't let him ruin your life, like he's ruined so many others – and please, tell nobody you've seen me."

Georgia tried to give Alana £80 from her purse, but Alana refused it point blank. They exchanged phone numbers and went back to the bus stop, where Georgia felt obliged to give her a Covid-law-busting hug. Georgia's bus came first and soon she was on her way back through Glasgow, towards home. There were no calls or texts on her phone throughout the trip home, so she had some rare time to think. One thing that poor, broken Alana had said to her kept repeating in her head.

"Don't let him ruin your life."

The streets of Glasgow still seemed so quiet – not quite the dystopian levels of desertion seen at the start of the pandemic, but eerie nonetheless.

Georgia knew for certain now that Hugh 'Shug' Man was a complete and utter psychopath whom she needed out of her life for good. Her blood boiled at her own gullibility for being his 'counsellor' recently, wasting her time listening to him lie, in depth, about a fantastical breakup where he was somehow the victim, rather than poor, broken Alana. She cringed that she'd been fooled by his latest game and wondered to herself why he had chosen to play it. If it was because of his longstanding need to fuck her, he hadn't actually said or done anything to even suggest it. Then Georgia reminded herself that psychopaths and sociopaths don't need any reason to say or do the fucked-up things that they do – they just do them – other human beings are just toys to such people – collateral damage. Her interactions with Shug over the last twenty years or so had been sporadic and also never really beneficial or pleasant – he always had an agenda, it seemed. Georgia started to wonder if her husband Keith's descent from a family man into a tedious coked up loser jailbird may even have been part of a deliberate long-game by Shug, to make Georgia single and financially vulnerable and thus easy prey to Shug's attempts at seduction – but then she dismissed that thought in her head – Shug was clearly scum, but Georgia thought such an elaborate scheme to be beyond his intellect and his temperament. On that bus journey home, Georgia resolved never to answer another phone call from him and never to speak to him if she saw him around town, it was time to forget who Hugh Mann was – Georgia had far more important people and problems to deal with.

When Georgia got home, the front door was slightly ajar – Olivia's annoying habit of not closing the door properly when she was in a hurry at play, again. Georgia shook her head and walked into her house, making for the landline to see if there were any messages, but the hall floor was covered in another mound of opened Amazon packages. Georgia sighed and shook her head, then shouted "OLIVIAAAA", summoning her daughter. As there was no answer and no music coming from her teenage daughter's room at club-sonic volume, like there usually was, she assumed that Olivia must have popped out. She began to tear up the Amazon boxes into smaller pieces so that they wouldn't clog the recycle bin too much. As she tore, she looked at the sub-labels on each parcel which indicated the seller whom Amazon had supplied the item from. Olivia's online and coding side hustles were clearly doing well, and this pleased her mother – her daughter was a bright spark.

There was a package stamped Samsung, one was stamped Nike, one was stamped with Japanese letters so was probably another one of those 'Hello Kitty' things that Olivia seemed to love so much. The last box was stamped 'Lovehoney'.

Georgia raised a concerned eyebrow as she realised that her wee girl, who was almost 18, was buying things from a sex toy and clothing company. As far as Georgia knew, her lovable geek daughter had no boyfriend, had little or no interest in finding one and lived most of her life online – what was she doing buying items from a sex toy and lingerie supplier? Georgia was a bit confused and went into the kitchen to make herself a cup of decaf coffee. As the kettle boiled, she pondered.

What was her teenage daughter buying from Lovehoney?

Did Olivia have a secret boyfriend?

If so, why was he a secret? Was Olivia too embarrassed to tell her mum?

Perhaps it was a girlfriend? If it were, Georgia was pretty sure she'd be fine with that.

Was she buying toys or clothing?

Maybe she was buying kinky uniforms or underwear because of her online gaming and cosplay things that she always seemed to be doing?

All of a sudden, Georgia turned and went upstairs to Olivia's room. She respected her children's privacy, but on this occasion, something didn't feel right, at all. Moreover, respecting Jordan's privacy had been catastrophic for him and for the family. She took a deep breath and pushed open Olivia's bedroom door, hoping her daughter wouldn't come home and catch her spying on her in such a manner.

On the left as Georgia entered the room was a white IKEA Malm drawer unit and a wardrobe in the same colour. The floor was charcoal grey carpet. Against the far wall was Olivia's dressing table – she'd bought it herself and it had real Hollywood vibes, surrounded by spotlights and dotted with photos of her friends and Hello Kitty stuff. The dressing table's matching chair was being used as an ad-hoc clothes rack, piled high with discarded clothing . The tabletop was a typical teenage mess of makeup, toiletries and various cables. On the wall were movie posters for Trainspotting and Hello Kitty and a massive The Weeknd poster. Georgia could not believe her eyes.

The bed was on the right-hand side of the room, with a small bedside table at either side of the headboard.

Olivia was on her bed with her back to the door and to her mum and she was wearing a headset, that's why she hadn't heard her mum shouting on her or heard her bedroom door opening.

Olivia was on her bed, grinding and gyrating on one of her hands like a stripper. She was wearing a cheap PVC nurse's outfit – the type of tat you get from cheap online retailers – and she had pulled down the top of the outfit so that her breasts were on show.

And somebody was watching her via her webcam!

CHAPTER THIRTY-THREE

The Legacy

Olivia's laptop was on the bedside table facing the bed at an angle, the white light coming from the webcam indicating that it was indeed broadcasting live to someone. Olivia, unaware that her mother was standing a few feet behind her, was talking down her headset microphone, in an almost sultry voice which belied her young age, devoid of all innocence.

"Ooh yes, Daddy, I know you love it, wanna see more?"

Georgia knew straight away what was going on and she instinctively blurted out "What the fuck are you doing?"

Olivia didn't respond and continued wiggling her body and giggling down her microphone, still oblivious to Georgia's presence – due to her new Samsung noise-cancelling headset.

There are times for respecting your older children's privacy. Georgia mulled that over for a split second and reasoned to herself 'fuck that'.

She stood right behind her daughter and roared "O-L-I-V-I-A!".

Olivia very nearly jumped out of her skin but instantly composed herself, somehow simultaneously managing to slam shut the lid of her laptop *and* pull her nurse outfit back up so that it covered most of her chest again, all in one sweeping movement – just like a million or more other women have learned to do in the 21st century . Before the laptop shut,

Georgia caught a split-second glimpse of what looked like a pasty-faced middle-aged man, his face framed by a small square window in the screen's bottom corner. Olivia turned around, her face scarlet with embarrassment, yet the red-haired teenager went straight onto the defensive.

"What are you doing, Mum? I was busy, you're supposed to knock before coming into my room, why are you spying on me?" She tore the headset away from herself and placed it on top of the closed laptop.

"What the fuck is this, Olivia? What's going on?" asked Georgia, sternly but without aggression – this had to be handled carefully.

"What does it look like, Mum? I was working!" said her daughter, defiantly.

"You were working? Showing your bits on cam? Who was that you were talking to? I thought I raised you better than to be a wee whore!"

Georgia instantly regretted using the 'W' word.

"Mum, it's 2020. I'm no' a wee lassie anymore, I'm 18 tomorrow, remember?"

'Oh fuck' thought Georgia, with all the recent stress and family dramas she'd forgotten it was indeed her daughter's 18th birthday tomorrow. Olivia continued.

"Mum, it's not a big deal, most of my pals have been doing it, too. My body, my choice."

"And how long has this been going on?" asked Georgia, trying to be calm.

"A couple of months. Honestly Mum, it's no biggie, I go on cam, I tease guys – most of them are older or foreign – they pay me. It's good money, by the way."

Georgia shook her head in disbelief, but then suddenly everything about her beautiful daughter's apparent agoraphobia began to make sense. The long hours spent in her room, the revealing clothes she bought online, the new headset, the dreadful stripper music that was usually blaring from her bedroom, and the fact that she always seemed to have plenty of money.

"Look, hen, I can't take you seriously in that bloody nurse's uniform, I'm making a brew, come downstairs and we'll talk about this, ok?" Georgia turned and left her daughter's bedroom and went downstairs. Olivia joined her in the living room a few minutes later, now wearing her fluffy pyjamas and slippers. Olivia sat in the armchair, Georgia on the sofa, as they both drank mugs of steaming coffee. Georgia put some music on via the TV – Wet Wet Wet.

My love has taken a tumble
Oh, but I'm still standing
You're such a natural, sing
'Cause that's what you are
Say I wouldn't steer you wrong now baby
I wouldn't steer you wrong
It's just that sweet little mystery that makes me try, try, try, try
and makes me try

Georgia opened the conversation.

"Ok, so my daughter is a cam-girl and an underaged one at that – so, was all that stuff about coding and web design a load of shite, lies?"

"Look, Mum, no. I work from home. I design apps, I get paid. I design websites, I get paid. I go on cam, I get paid. I can show you all of my payment receipts for all three, if you like. Honestly, Mum, please don't overreact, it's not a big deal – everyone is doing it."

Georgia wanted to say, 'what would your dad say?' but given her absent father's sleazy lifestyle of late, that wouldn't have done much good.

"What do you mean everybody is doing it? Who else?" asked Georgia.

"Most of my female friends do it, Jordan's ex, Ciara, too, and someone you know, too."

"Hen, most of your friends are 18, Ciara is old enough to do what she wants and … wait a minute, who? What are you talking about? Someone I know? Who?"

Olivia went a little bit red again and giggled. "Mum, Isla does it."

"Fuck off, not Isla, no way – she wouldn't," said Georgia, doubting her own words as she spoke them. Olivia started punching something into her phone then got up and held her phone screen up for her mum to see.

Georgia found herself looking at a website called Onlyfans, the username on the profile was 'Foxy Roxy MILF' and the profile picture, although filtered to make the scantily clad woman in it look younger and more polished, was indeed Georgia's best friend, Isla.

"Fucking hell,' exclaimed Georgia.

"See," said Olivia, "everybody's doing it."

Georgia actually felt a bit amused at seeing her best friend's secret alter ego and felt compelled to send her a quick WhatsApp.

"Hey 'Foxy Roxy' you kept that quiet LOL"

She immediately got a reply from Isla.

"LOL. Rumbled. How the fuck do you know about that? X"

She replied, "Tell you later. All good x"

"So, does Isla know you're a camgirl?"

"Of course she doesn't, she'd have told you. She uses Onlyfans, I can't use Onlyfans because I'm not 18 until tomorrow. I use Adultseeking, it's a kind of dating site where rich men and younger women connect. Adultseeking doesn't check or verify our ages."

Georgia took a sip of her coffee and seemed to relax a bit.

"Tell me everything," she asked her daughter – and she did.

Olivia explained that because of lockdown there were millions of horny men suddenly alone and without access to women, all over the world. To her, it had been a business opportunity, nothing more. She'd made a profile on Adultseeking early in lockdown at first to try and meet a nice, mature older guy to talk to in lockdown, but as soon as she'd put a few photos on her profile she'd been inundated with hundreds of messages from men from all walks of life, many ages, many locations, all ethnicities – all bored, lonely, rich and horny. One of her online gaming techy friends had been using the website for a while to supplement her own income and had shown her the ropes.

Olivia was open and honest and admitted that she did get a buzz from these older guys lusting after her – and they weren't paedos, because Olivia had listed herself as being 19 on the website – they were just lonely perverts. She usually charged £50 for a cam session, which could last anything up to ten minutes, though at first very few of them were on the cam for more than two minutes – despite paying for the full ten. Olivia told her mum that she did go topless sometimes but never flashed her fanny and had soon found a niche on the website – a lot of men just wanted to look at her feet, and just her feet!

There had been guys who wanted cam stripteases or various outfits – like the nurse one – but Olivia had actually made most of her money simply from showing her feet. There were other guys, too, she said, who paid money just to talk to her online, not asking for or expecting anything else. An Arab guy had once tipped her £500 just to talk to her for an hour, as he was fascinated by her red hair – a lot of men on that platform were. Olivia didn't do anything more extreme on cam and admitted to her mum that her webcam activities had helped her immensely in recent months – by providing her with an escape from lockdown, from family trauma and from the world in general. She got paid for the camming by bank transfer using her Monzo account and had eight thousand pounds in the bank because of that kind of work. She then reiterated that 'everyone was doing it' and subtly suggested to her mum that she shouldn't be prudish about this, reminding her that her best friend, Isla, was also doing camming as a side-hustle.

Georgia listened to what her daughter had to say, then got up and went through to the kitchen to make more coffees. As she stirred the hot brown aromatic liquid, she realised that her daughter's explanation made perfect sense and, given all that had occurred in Olivia's life in the last few years, she concluded that this wasn't so bad – it could be a lot worse. She was safe webcamming at home, behind a pseudonym. If she was busy doing that, she wasn't out somewhere doing drugs or associating with those who took or sold drugs, she wasn't selling her body – just an abstract concept of it in pixel form. Even if she were, that was better than an unplanned pregnancy or a drug habit brought about by some local loser guy. Georgia reasoned that her daughter had, in fact, become quite the entrepreneur, cashing in on a once-in-a-century business opportunity as most of the world stayed at home and existed online. Georgia even reasoned that, were she her daughter's age during a pandemic she'd have tried exactly the same thing- after all she'd always been beautiful, too. She carried the two coffees back through to the living room and spoke to her daughter again.

The main things that still worried Georgia about Olivia's side hustle were her safety and her age when she started doing it – Georgia was also interested to learn how Olivia had found out that Isla was webcamming, too, given that they didn't use the same platform to earn money.

"Right, hen, how did that website let you on if you were only 17 when you joined?"

Olivia explained that at one point when registering on Adultseeking, a pop up had asked her to click 'yes' if she was 18 or over and 'no' if she wasn't – that was it.

Georgia knew that nobody in history, male or female, when trying to access an adult-only site has clicked 'no'.

"So, these guys you cam for, are they local? You don't know them, do you? Do they know where you live?"

Olivia shook her head, smiling, and answered – she knew her mum wasn't angry anymore – just concerned.

"My profile says I'm in Edinburgh, Mum, I don't *think* any of my subscribers are local, most are overseas, but if they are, I don't know them and they think I'm in Edinburgh, anyway – it's totally safe, Mum. Oh, the old guy who asked for the nurse uniform is kind of local, I think, but whoever he is, I've never seen him before in my life and he thinks I'm in Edinburgh, anyway."

"Right, ok, do these guys ever ask you to meet up in person, Olivia? 'Cos that's a road you're not going down, let me assure you."

"Mum, it's fine. No, I mean, yes of course they ask, but there's a fucking pandemic on, so nobody can moan when I say 'no'- and I always do. I'm not an escort, Mum, I'm just a model – there's a world of difference."

Georgia was seriously fucking relieved to hear that.

"Right, ok, well, you're 18 tomorrow, hen, so even if I did object to your doing this, I can't really stop you, you seem to know what you're doing, do you promise me you'll stay safe and won't meet up with any of those men?"

"Of course, Mum, that was never going to happen in a million years, anyway. Hey, you've still got it, Mum, you could make a few quid selling selfies and videos, too." Olivia was joking and Georgia got the joke. They both started laughing, Georgia almost spilling her coffee.

"Oh aye, hen, I can see it now, me on Onlyfans as "MILF Jessica Rabbit."" Georgia saw her daughter go red.

"Mum, that's my username, JessyRabbitScotXXX, how did you know?"

"Oh my god, that's what some fellas used to call me when I was younger, hen. How time flies."

They both laughed again.

"Olivia, listen if this is what you want to do for now then fair enough – milk all those perverts dry of their cash, if you want – the last few years haven't been easy for you."

"Not been easy for any of us, Mum."

"Aye, I know. Do what makes you happy, Olivia, you're not a wee lassie anymore – just stay safe, ok?"

Olivia smiled and nodded. "Anyway, it's my 18th tomorrow and I've got nothing planned, so why don't we go out for lunch and coffee, maybe even a wine?"

Smiling, Georgia replied. "Aye, sounds brilliant we can do the hospital visits in the morning after I collect the car from the garage, then we'll have some 'us' time. In fact, why wait? Fancy doing a movie and a pizza tonight?"

"Oh Mum, I've got to watch my figure, I'm a model now. Only joking, sounds brilliant, yes! I love you, Mum."

Mother and daughter laughed and then embraced in the living room, Olivia asking her mum to order the pizza while she went for a shower – another unfair distribution of labour in the Smith household. That evening they streamed 'Django Unchained', at Olivia's recommendation. They loved it and laughed their arses off throughout it – Georgia had been a bit sceptical of watching a western, but had soon realised it was no ordinary western, plus she also got to finally find out the source of that smug sneering Leonardo Di Caprio meme that everybody always used on social media. They ate pizza, relaxed and went to bed late. There were two phone calls and a text message that evening for Georgia. The hospital rang the landline to say that Georgia's dad had improved slightly and seemed to be over the worst. There was a WhatsApp call from Hugh Mann which Georgia rejected – she wouldn't be listening to any of his mind games shite ever again. And Georgia got a text message from Alana Renfield, saying how great it had been to meet up, reiterating her request that nobody should know where she was, and moaning about feeling unwell while hoping to meet up next week. Georgia didn't respond to any of the calls or texts – she was happy about her dad, annoyed about Shug and largely indifferent about Alana, so, she had a digital break that evening, eating pizza and scoffing ice cream with her almost adult daughter – her beautiful wee lassie. 'Family is all we have' was Georgia's mantra, that evening, and her daughter said exactly the same thing. It was the first really happy evening in the Smith household for a very long time indeed.

CHAPTER THIRTY-FOUR

Lola's Theme

Both family hospital visits the next morning went ok. Georgia was still only allowed to see her dad through the glass, that square window which separated the safe from the endangered, the healthy from the ill – the loved ones from each other. The exhausted, stressed-out nurses always said hello to Georgia when she came in to see her dad through the glass. He was still ventilated, but the doctor told Georgia that his blood oxygen levels had increased and it may be possible to take him off the ventilator soon. She gazed through the glass window into the side room. Her dad, auld Alex, actually looked peaceful, aside from the tubes and the wires attached to various points of his body.

Next, Georgia and Olivia visited Jordan, at the psychiatric ward in Glasgow, after Georgia had collected her car in Hamilton first. To both of their surprise, on arrival at the ward Jordan handed his wee sister a 'Happy 18th' birthday card that he had made in the ward's therapeutic arts and crafts class the day before. Olivia had a tear in her eye as she read it and Georgia knew that it was a good sign that Jordan was thinking about the outside world, again. Jordan was, still, however, heavily sedated. His big blue eyes still looked so sad. The three members of the Smith family sat and drank bland NHS coffee and ate off-brand rich tea biscuits for an hour together, and it did their souls a world of good. Georgia was now sure that Jordan would make a complete recovery – given time.

The repair bill for Georgia's veteran car had been over £700, so, short of cash on her daughter's 18th birthday, she asked her if the local Brewer's Fayre would be fine with her for Olivia's birthday lunch. Olivia knew that the repair to the car had wiped out her mum's bank account and that money was tighter than ever right now, so en route back from Glasgow she countered with an offer of her own – she would pay today, after all, she was minted from her webcam, coding and web-design bedroom empire, but she still wanted to go to the local Brewer's Fayre anyway, because she really liked the sticky toffee pudding that they served there. Mother and daughter thus enjoyed a hearty birthday lunch of burgers, chips, and sticky toffee pudding together and laughed together for a good two hours – both delighted that Auld Alex and Jordan seemed to be doing better, both feeling closer and more connected to one another after their heart-to-heart about Olivia's webcam career. Neither bothered with alcohol with the meal, settling instead for diet Pepsi, water and lattes. After paying their bill and getting up to leave the Brewer's Fayre, they walked straight into the path of none other than Hugh 'Shug' Mann on the way out. Georgia was determined that bumping into this nasty, lying creep wasn't going to spoil her or Olivia's day, so she looked him in the eye, did her best to smile and managed a, "hi, Hugh".

To her annoyance he stopped to talk. He was wearing business attire, another flash Marc Darcy suit and pointy leather shoes, covering his greasy bald head with a Peaky-Blinders-esque newsboy hat – Georgia noted mentally that nearly all gangsters became who they are by first watching too many fucking gangster films and TV shows, as a child and into adulthood.

Shug looked like a greasy bear in a nice suit. He didn't seem his usual self when he answered.

"Oh, hi, Georgia, and this must be Olivia? Wow, are you two gorgeous rabbits out on the lash?"

"Birthday lunch, Hugh, Olivia's 18th," Georgia corrected him, hoping he'd just go away.

"Oh, wonderful, happy birthday to you, pal, all the best, listen folks, I can't stop to chat I've a meeting – have a great day!" Shug then walked towards the back of the restaurant and sat down at a booth. Georgia was relieved that she hadn't had to speak to the horrible cunt for any longer.

Mother and daughter got the car from the carpark at the side of the Brewer's Fayre but Georgia realised that she'd forgotten to have her parking validated as a restaurant customer, so, she pulled up outside the restaurant door and parked, leaving Olivia in the car while she quickly popped back into the restaurant foyer to scan her parking ticket at the front desk. As the helpful young waitress was sorting that, Georgia saw Shug rise from his table to greet a very young woman, who kissed him on the cheek. When she turned around, Georgia was horrified to see that the young woman was Ciara, Jordan's ex-girlfriend. Though Ciara was an adult and it had been almost eight months since she had split from Jordan, ultimately hastening his nervous breakdown, Georgia took the attitude that if Shug was sniffing around Ciara, then he wasn't phoning her or thinking about her, and that was just fine by her – Shug had a new victim, a new thing to torment. Georgia had always thought that her son could do a lot better than Ciara, anyway – after all, to most mothers, no woman is good enough for their son.

It wasn't until Georgia was back in the car with her daughter and heading home that Georgia's mind started going into overdrive.

"*Wait a minute, what if Hugh was the reason she dumped Jordan when she did? And why did Hugh just refer to me and Olivia as 'gorgeous rabbits'?*

Didn't Olivia yesterday tell me that Ciara had been doing webcam work, too? Oh fuck no."

Georgia turned to Olivia as they waited at the big roundabout beside the M74.

"So, listen, you ever hear from Jordan's ex, Ciara?"

"No, mum, she's pretty much ghosted me, too, she's been seeing some rich old man."

"Oh, has she now? Listen, how did you know that Isla and that Ciara were also doing webcam modelling?"

"Why?"

"I'm just curious."

Olivia explained in depth that there was a local private Facebook group where lassies from Scotland who did webcamming and other remote sex-work could chat, share advice, have laughs and, most importantly, share the details and account names of any dodgy, threatening or scammer punters. That's where Olivia had first found out that her mum's pal, Isla, and Jordan's ex, Ciara, were both doing cam work.

Georgia continued "See that big man we spoke to on the way out of the restaurant there, do you know who he is? Have you ever seen him before?"

"No, Mum, who is he?" replied her daughter.

"Nobody, hen, just a ghost from the past," lied Georgia, both relieved and certain that her daughter was telling the truth.

"He called us rabbits. Her webcam username has rabbit in it. When I was younger guys said I was like Jessica Rabbit. Holy fuck, I bet that prick has been perving at my daughter on cam in lockdown and she doesn't even fucking know it. That's creepy as fuck – he can't have me, so he sneakily wanks himself off to my wee girl instead? Or worse, what if he's sitting with a load of his coked-up cronies watching her? If he has been, he'll be fucking sorry – oh shit what the –"

Georgia's inner monologue was interrupted by the loud horn of a Ford Focus in the outside lane. She'd been so deep in thought for a second that she hadn't noticed her car drifting out of her lane a bit. She caught the sound of the Ford Focus driver shouting 'STUPID COW' before he pulled in front of her as the bypass began to narrow down to one lane.

"Mum, for God's sake," exclaimed Olivia, somewhat hypocritically as she'd been totally absorbed by Instagram on her phone at the same time that her mum had started to drift.

They made it home safely and Olivia made them both a coffee. They sat together in the living room chatting for a while, listening to a random playlist on the Alexa device.

All the other kids with the pumped-up kicks
You better run, better run outrun my gun
All the other kids with the pumped-up kicks
You better run, better run faster than my bullet

Georgia wanted to set her mind at ease about her daughter's online activities and to allay her possibly delusional paranoia about Hugh Mann. She was also genuinely interested in how her daughter had carved out such a varied and lucrative career from home, so she asked Olivia if she could see the books. Her daughter scoffed and reminded her that online businesses didn't really have books, as such, but she went up to her bedroom and fetched her laptop back downstairs.

She showed her mum the receipts from the web design, five clients had paid her a combined total of £3750 in the last 18 months.

Then Olivia showed her the receipts for the apps that she had coded and sold to Apple and to Google in that same period – just over £4400.

Georgia felt pride as a mother as she viewed those figures, knowing that it was her clever, talented, beautiful daughter who had earned these relatively big bucks.

"What about the webcamming stuff? She then asked Olivia.

"Oh aye, that's all done privately, by direct bank transfer into my Monzo, but here, look".

Olivia brought up her Monzo statement. Georgia took the laptop onto her own lap and began to read. Sure enough, her wee girl, or not so wee now, had made just over £8000 from the webcam work.

"Over 16 grand, Olivia, from all three jobs, well done you. Here, I'll be asking you for a tap soon," joked Georgia.

Olivia looked sad for a second, then spoke.

"It's for you, Mum."

"Eh? What do you mean it's for me?" Georgia asked.

"The money I've earned. I earned it for you, for us, for the family. Use it to pay off that debt dad lumbered us with, or maybe we can go on holiday together as a family when Jordan is better, or you could get a new car – you bloody need one. I want to do my bit, Mum. Money isn't everything, I know that, but we've struggled since dad and his drugs thing and the bank debt, I did what I could to help."

"No way, Olivia, that's your money, that's really sweet of you, but no, you keep it, we'll manage – that's your money."

Georgia had never been prouder of her daughter, but no way was her wee girl's hard-earned cash being used to plug gaps in the family finances caused by her arsehole dad.

"Mum, listen. You say it's my money, right? Well, ok, it's my money, I'm an adult now and I choose to use it to help my family. I was going to wait until there was £20k in the account, but, well, here we are. Please, mum, that money is to give our family a new start, or at least to go towards it. And before you say no again, remember, I had to say all kinds of filth to sleazy guys online, show them my body, dress up in costumes and had Arab Sheikhs paying to wank over my clips of my bloody feet. I basically whored myself out online just to get this money, and I want that money to be useful, not to just be spent on frivolous shite by me. Please Mum, take it – our family needs it."

Georgia started to cry. It was a sad state of affairs to be accepting cash from her children to keep the family going: on the other hand, Olivia's gesture was so beautiful and compelling that she hadn't the heart to refuse her.

"Look, I'm not saying 'no', but it's your birthday today, let's discuss this tomorrow, deal?"

Georgia then resumed looking at Olivia's Monzo statements on the laptop.

She was mightily impressed with the figures, even though she wasn't quite as ok with her daughter's new line of work as she had let her think she was, after all, there's a great difference between toleration and approval. Here, in front of Georgia, were the names and bank account details of scores of sad, sleazy lonely horny men, all of whom had sent cash to Olivia. She noted that Olivia had a few regulars.

Omar Hassan, Bank of Egypt, had paid her almost £800 spread over just three payments.

Rachel Gordon, Skipton Building Society, had paid over £500 – clearly, Olivia didn't mind catering to women as well as men. Buddy Hawkes, Bank of America, £450.

Hugh Mann, Clydesdale Bank, £1000. One-off payment. Reading that item on the statement from just a few weeks ago chilled Georgia's blood and filled her with rage. At first, she felt angry at Olivia, but she also remembered that Olivia had said that she'd never seen Shug before in her life and Georgia believed her. Moreover, when they had bumped into Shug at the Brewer's Fayre earlier, Olivia hadn't known who he was, from what Georgia could remember of her daughter's demeanour at that moment.

"It's my daughter's 18th birthday and she's chosen to spend it with me, rather than see her pals, I'm not about to ruin the rest of the evening with her by asking about that Shug bastard. Why can't he fucking leave us alone? I'm 99% certain Olivia doesn't know who he is. The sick fucker, can't have me so he pervs on my daughter? That's why the cunt made the rabbits reference earlier, he's making a cunt of me, and my family, again. Why do I put up with this? I've a good mind to phone him up and let rip, but, no, that'll just excite the prick, and I'm not letting him spoil this precious evening with my daughter. He'll keep. He'll be getting a piece of my mind soon, though. Ah, I know..."

Georgia's inner monologue gave way to her voice.

"Who's this one who sent you a grand as a one-off, hen?"

Olivia was looking through her mum's old CD collection, stacked beside the TV still on one of those zig-zag tall CD racks that were cool back in 1998.

"Oh, just a perv, Mum, Scottish middle-aged guy, it was him who asked for the nurse uniform when he first got in touch through the website. He's actually pretty harmless, basically just likes to look at me while talking to me, respectful, easy to talk to – his webcam isn't very good, though, too dark to really make out his face – here's hoping it's not someone who knows us, eh Mum?"

Georgia ignored the joke. "What's his name?"

"Hugh, I think. Why?"

"Has he ever asked you to meet him?"

"No, he hasn't, Mum, but he did say he's setting up a cam studio shortly soon and asked if I'd be interested in going to work for him – that was a bit weird, to be honest, but I politely declined and it wasn't mentioned again. He thinks I'm in Edinburgh."

"That's right, so he does," lied Georgia.

"Before you interrupted me and him on cam he had actually just said that he'd be online less because he had a new girlfriend, I was like 'yeah, whatever'."

Georgia decided to act on her anger at a later date. She was now certain that Olivia didn't know that it was Shug Mann she'd cammed for. She'd confront Shug later – tonight was all about her daughter.

The rest of Olivia's 18th was a joy to mother and daughter both. They drank wine, ate takeaway pasta, listened to music, and set the world to rights together. They reminisced about the good times; they lamented the bad and laughed about the weird. They even got the karaoke mics out towards the end of the evening, standing together drunk on the living room carpet, Georgia's arm around her daughter's shoulder as they belted out a song that was a childhood favourite of Georgia's and a much-loved streaming track for Olivia.

And so I wake in the morning and I step outside
And I take a deep breath and I get real high
And I scream from the top of my lungs
"What's going on?"
And I say, hey-ey-ey
Hey-ey-eyI
said "Hey, a-what's going on"
And I say, hey-ey-eyHey-ey-eyI
said "Hey, a-what's going on?"

Throughout the evening Olivia's phone had been going non-stop, as friends called and texted to wish her a happy birthday. She promised them all they'd have a proper party once the Covid restrictions were over.

Georgia's phone was relatively quiet all evening, WhatsApps from Isla, another text from Alana Renfield, in which she again was very nice and seemed to want to be friends, while also moaning about not feeling well – Georgia knew that Alana had been through hell at Shug's hands and sympathised completely, but couldn't really think of much else to say to the lassie. She also got a call from a withheld number, which she declined, assuming it was Shug or a foreign scammer.

Georgia and her daughter both went to their beds tipsy and happy that night, despite everything going on in the world and in the background, Olivia's lockdown birthday had been fun, all things considered.

CHAPTER THIRTY-FIVE

Lethal Industry

Mother and daughter both overslept the next morning and were still in their beds when the postman came. Georgia got out of bed when she heard two thuds on the inside doormat. She got downstairs and picked up the two boxes of Covid 19 lateral flow test kits that she had ordered online, putting them on the kitchen table, then she made coffee, shouting upstairs to ask Olivia if she wanted any, to which her cool daughter replied, shouting *'Obviously'*.

After coffee and then some breakfast, Georgia headed to the local hospital to visit her dad, or at least to try to see him. She planned to pop in there and then go back to collect Olivia so that they could go and visit Jordan together.

Georgia, masked up, made her away along the long, deserted corridors of the local hospital to the big double doors that marked the entrance to the hospital red zone. To her surprise, there were no nurses manning the desk at the entrance and there was no security guard at the doors, either. She was a bit early, so Georgia just sanitised her hands then opened the doors. She made her way alone along that same hospital corridor, trying not to stare at the patients in the wards and side-rooms to her left and right as she walked. The ward was still much the same as before. Medical staff in PPE, patients on ventilators, other patients lying on their fronts, still more lying in bed groaning and doped up, some breathing through oxygen tanks, some young, some old, but there were still no children.

This NHS dystopian nightmare really got to Georgia as she walked towards the end of the corridor where her dad's side-room was the last one on the left. She hoped that he'd be conscious, but she knew that, even if he wasn't, he was in good hands and it would do her a lot of good just to see him, even if it was through the glass.

When she reached her dad's side room and looked through the glass pane, all she saw was an empty, stripped bed. There was no name written on the white board next to the bed anymore.

"Can I help you?"

The male voice behind her made Georgia jump as she was already chilled to the bone with utter dread. She frantically spun around to see what she assumed was a doctor – a guy in his early 30s, judging by the sound of his voice and what she could see of him through the PPE.

In a forlorn, desperate voice, Georgia asked, "Where's Alex Dooley?"

The doctor scratched his forehead nervously and said, "Come with me, please."

Georgia followed the doctor back along the corridor and through the double doors to the spaced-out seats of the waiting area. The two nurses on the desk and the security guard were back on duty. She already knew in her heart what the doctor was about to tell her, but she hoped beyond hope that she was wrong.

Auld Alex had been improving until the previous evening when he had suffered a stroke. He had lingered on until the early hours of the morning, but had passed away at around 4am, despite the valiant efforts of the medical team on the ward. Georgia's dad was dead – the Covid 19 and the pneumonia together had simply overwhelmed his body, and he was gone forever. Georgia couldn't believe it. Her dad was a fighter, and he had been getting better.

As the bad news sunk in, Georgia asked the doctor why nobody from the hospital had been in touch, either to tell her that her dad had suffered the stroke, or later on to tell her that he had passed away. The doctor told her that someone had tried to call her the previous evening, but he also apologised that more effort hadn't been made to keep her in the loop – the hospital staff had been decimated by Covid, several nurses had already died and there were many other members of staff off sick. Knowing that it was pointless getting angry at the doctor, who was but a mere messenger, Georgia simply thanked him for his and his team's efforts, answered a few questions from the two sympathetic nurses manning reception, and then turned to leave. Tears began to fill her eyes as she walked back down through the long corridors of the local hospital – to Georgia, it was a nightmare – she never got to say goodbye. Now she would have to go home and tell her daughter and then her son and then the whole fucking world that auld Alex Dooley was no more – and she never got to say goodbye. On the drive home, Georgia went over and over in her head what it must've been like for her dad in the end, alone in an isolated room, attended only by masked strangers, with the occasional visitor peeking through his side room window now and then, but for a few fleeting moments. Georgia cursed Covid 19, she cursed the government, she cursed life itself, yet in her anger and disbelief, she cursed Hugh 'Shug' Mann most of all, for she knew in her heart that the withheld number call that she had ignored last night, thinking it was from him, was actually from the hospital switchboard, they *had* tried to call her – but because it was an evening call, she'd assumed it was Shug. She in no way blamed Shug for her dad's death, but just like when her mum died, she was in the wrong place, indirectly because of him.

Georgia drove home and told her daughter the sad news, and the remainder of the Smith family grieved.

Auld Alex Dooley had always hated funerals, so there was to be no burial, cremation or formal service to mark his passing – he'd been very specific about that both in his will and when talking to his daughter about the future. He had opted for one of those new cremation-only things. At the height of the pandemic there were long delays for families wishing to hold a funeral, often made worse because of a shortage of wood for coffins, caused by increased demand due to pandemic deaths. This meant that Georgia and her kids, their extended family and auld Alex's friends and old colleagues didn't get to gather to celebrate his memory. All agreed to hold a proper memorial celebration later, after the pandemic, which made sense practically, but that also meant that Alex's friends and family were, for the time being, left to deal with their grief alone. Phone and online chats are no substitute for the necessary ritual of a formal funeral and the support network such things can create or strengthen. Her dad's death hit Georgia hard – the doctor had to increase her meds, and she started to drink a lot more, trying to numb her pain. Due to the pandemic restrictions and her dad's own wishes regarding not having a funeral, it was kind of hard for her to accept that her dad was gone, even though she knew that he was. Georgia didn't do much else for the rest of July 2020, except visit her son in hospital, watch TV, and drink wine and whisky.

Chapter Thirty-Six

Binary Finary

On Saturday the 1st of August, on a bright summer's day, her dad's birthday, Georgia took delivery of an urn containing her dad's ashes – it was only then that his death really hit home. Georgia placed the silver urn in the middle of the living room coffee table, until she felt up to deciding what to do with them. Georgia only had the one glass of wine that evening, as she knew that sometimes it did the body good to hurt, to feel real, tangible emotion, as part of the healing process. It helped in a way that she was feeling a bit out of sorts that day as she had a splitting headache and was taking Cocodamol for it.

Olivia had been self-isolating in her room for the last three days after testing positive for Covid 19. It had started as a simple runny nose earlier in the week. Olivia wasn't seriously ill with it, she'd said it was just like the flu, but Georgia had tested negative, so she didn't want to pass it on to her.

That Saturday evening started off dull for Georgia, as usual. She put her feet up on the sofa and was messaging Isla on WhatsApp while also vaguely paying attention to Paddington 2, which was showing on TV. She and Olivia both had Chinese for dinner that evening, Georgia leaving Olivia's spare ribs, beef chow mein, and sesame prawn toast on a tray outside her room. Georgia had recently started watching the BBC drama, 'Life on Mars', on Netflix, since her dad's death. She found it comforting to escape into a drama set in the world where her mum and dad had been younger and stronger – and alive. By around 8pm she was beginning to doze off around halfway through season two, when her phone buzzed. It was a WhatsApp from Hugh Mann which read:

"Hey sorry to hear about your dad anything I can do to help just ask. Shug"

This seemingly innocuous message seemed to pluck a string in the back of Georgia's mind. That cunt was the last person she wanted to hear from, or to have anything else to do with. After all, directly or indirectly, she finally realised that Shug was the common denominator in almost all of her families woes and troubles, and she was fucking sick of it, sick to the back teeth of it, sick to her stomach of that fat, manipulative, mingin', lying, scheming, drug-dealing, sleazy, woman-beating gangster.

Shug followed up his message. 'What are you up to tonight?'

And with that, something in Georgia snapped. Suddenly her eyes were open.

This cunt had harassed her in her youth, helped turn her husband into a junkie loser, ruined her marriage, got her husband's pal jailed, facilitated her husband's infidelity, ruined her family's finances with drug debt and bank debt, made an arse of her at her work, tried to make her fuck him in lieu of debt, almost deprived her children of food and clothing, got her son arrested for drug dealing, causing his hospitalisation in the nut-house and then started seeing his girlfriend, he'd gotten her errant husband jailed in place of her son, and because of Shug she had been working a second job in Livingston when her mum died and had ignored a phone call from the hospital when her dad was dying, too. He'd been perving at her precious daughter on webcam and had even offered to become her webcam pimp, too. Shug had plausible deniability for some of those things, but Georgia knew to her very core that *he* was the culprit. In her grief, in her rage, in her sadness, suddenly all that she could see was Hugh Mann as the cause of all of her woes. On top of all of that, she knew that he was a gangster, a drug dealer and a money launderer, prone to dangerous bouts of violence and there were hundreds of families and people in the local schemes who lived a life mired in addiction, suffering and exploitation, all because of *him*. He was an organised crime kingpin, a dodgy businessman, and a fat, sleazy, nasty cunt, and Georgia Smith had finally had enough of him.

She took a deep breath and messaged Shug back.

"Hi, not much, want me to come over? I'm only coming over if you're alone x"

He immediately replied, "Aye just on ma lonesome tonight, Georgia, that's magic xxx wear something slutty, by the way."

"See you in an hour x," she texted back.

Georgia went upstairs and got changed into her low-cut tight blue dress and her long coat, after showering and doing her hair. She knew she looked hot. She really hoped that Shug was alone. She shouted to Olivia that she was going out for a while, then nipped to the kitchen, picking up her Japanese razor-sharp fish knife and putting into the bottom of her blue handbag, before setting off in the car to see Shug at his big house in Bothwell.

Georgia listened to the radio quietly as she drove the short distance to Shug's place. *Underdog* by Kasabian was playing on Planet Rock.

See the local loves a fighter
Loves a winner to fall
Feels like I'm lost in a moment
I'm always losing to win
Can't get away from the moment

Seems like it's time to begin
Kill me if you dare
Hold my head up everywhere
Keep myself right on this train

As she drove, Georgia's expression was blank and emotionless, save for the occasional glance at herself in the mirror, but her mind was doing somersaults, boiling over with emotion and rage.

"He's been part of my life for so long, lurking in the background, sometimes unseen for years at a time. He was a nice boy once, it was life that twisted him, as life can twist us all, but most people don't become a horrible cunt, like he has. Truth is he's never been able to handle the fact that I refused to get off with him when we were younger, and I've kept knocking him back ever since and that's bothered him more or more as the years have gone by – he eventually got everything in life that he thought he wouldn't, except me – his money, his power, his drugs, none of that could make me do what he wanted with him. I suppose I should be flattered that in my 40s I'm still someone's fantasy, but I'm not. His borderline obsession with me over the years has cost me almost everything – but never my self-respect. I wonder - if I had given in and shagged him all those years ago – would he have left me and my family in peace? Well, today, I give up, sometimes you just have to bow to the inevitable and give people what they really need, do what needs to be done. I have to do this, for all our sakes."

She glanced across to her handbag on the passenger seat and could see the handle of the knife just visible in the corner beneath the zip line.

"Am I really going to do this? Fucking sure I am. He's wanted me for a such a long time, well, tonight he's going to get more of me than he ever dreamed was possible, beyond all of his expectations. Georgia Smith is going to be one of the last things that Hugh 'Shug' Mann is ever going to see, so, he'd better

drink it all in, while he can – he's getting more Georgia Smith than he can possibly handle..."

CHAPTER THIRTY-SEVEN

Closer

Her car pulled into the posh cul-de-sac where Shug lived in a huge four-bedroom house with large front and back gardens, and a driveway that could easily have accommodated four vehicles. His big SUV was parked on the driveway beside a white old-school Toyota MR2 – his hobby car. Georgia parked up next to that little white flying machine, looked at herself in the car mirrors one more time and walked up the monoblocked path towards the front door. She was already disgusted by what she saw, drug money – which is really blood money – had bought Hugh Mann a sweet place to live indeed.

The door was slightly ajar when Georgia reached it, so she pushed it open a little bit more then half-shouted, 'helloooo'.

Shug's voice shouted back, "Just come straight through."

So, she did.

The hall floor was done in trendy charcoal laminate and on the wall was a large full-length mirror with the Motherwell FC crest on it – Shug's team. At the far end of the hall, through an open door, she could see the kitchen. To her left, was a spacious dining room with table and chairs for eight people – but the dining table was piled high with paperwork, and it looked like nobody had been in that room for some time. Further along the hall on the left was the bottom of a wide staircase – the stairs were carpeted in a darker grey. To her immediate right, through an archway, was clearly the lounge area, as she could hear televised sport commentary emanating from within.

"Come on in," said Shug's voice, though she still couldn't see him. She walked into the lounge area.

Sure enough, on the wall was a 75-inch smart TV showing a football match from an empty stadium. The sound of two bored commentators trying to make soulless fan-free Covid-era football sound interesting filled her ears at first, as her eyes scanned the main living area of Hugh 'Shug' Mann's house – a place Georgia hadn't ever thought about before, let alone envisaged visiting for a reckoning.

She could see that the long, wide lounge area turned off to the left at the far end where a breakfast bar marked the beginning of the kitchen – it was an open plan living space, despite the kitchen door in the hall. On the walls, were various Motherwell FC framed fan memorabilia and a couple of framed Metallica posters – at first glance, it was like a huge teenage boy's bedroom – which didn't surprise Georgia, at all, even though until recently Shug had lived with Alana.

The room contained a huge new four-seater red leather sofa along the main wall, with big red armchairs in the same style, at either end. There was a chrome coffee table in front of the big red sofa, on that were some remote controls, a couple of packets of medicine, a leather wallet, Shug's asthma inhaler and four Motherwell FC coasters. The floor was charcoal grey laminate, like in the hall, and the walls were a plain grey, too. Georgia could see that the kitchen units and worktop appliances were also bright red, showing that Shug was at least like other normal guys in one respect – he had no taste in decor – grey and red – what a tragic fucking male stereotype.

Georgia also noted that Shug had no photographs of family, friends, or pets on display anywhere, again, not to her surprise. The room was spotlessly clean and tidy, like the hall was – Shug clearly had a good cleaner.

Shug himself was sitting at one end of the sofa. He hadn't bothered to even get up to greet his guest, as he was busy shovelling what looked like curry from a tinfoil takeaway container into his mouth. An open bottle of Miller beer sat beside his feet. Shug was wearing grey 'jobby catcher' joggers, white trainers and one of those TOFFS retro Motherwell FC shirts. Both the shirt and the joggers bore fresh curry stains. Shug hadn't shaved and had what looked like a few days of stubble growth on his chin.

Georgia thought that it was ironic that the millionaire drug dealer and businessman was dressed more or less just like the legions of minions who took, sold or trafficked his drugs for him – the ones who took all the risks. That at least proved that you can take the boy out of the scheme but you can't take the scheme out of the boy.

"Georgia, do you fancy a beer? They're in the fridge through there, grab me one, too, there's a good girl."

"Aye, I'd love one, no sweat," said Georgia warmly as she walked to the fridge, noticing that the rest of the kitchen was as immaculately clean as the rest of the house. She took off her long coat and draped it across one of the breakfast bar stools as she passed into the kitchen area but kept her blue handbag close. She opened the big fridge door and looked inside. It was pretty Spartan – some blue milk, a bag of grated cheese, a large packet of bacon, a bottle of fresh orange juice, a bottle of Moet champagne and about 20 bottles of Miller, all neatly stacked. No fruit, veg, or salad, which wasn't a surprise.

Georgia stood in front of the open fridge gazing inside, wearing her short, low-cut blue dress and matching heels. The beers were in the fridge's bottom compartment, so she had to bend down to pluck two of them out.

She could feel Shug's eyes on her body as she did but didn't flinch. Instead, she held that pose, knowing he'd be transfixed by her Rubenesque, firm bum and her shapely legs as she did. Sure enough, as she straightened up and turned to carry the beers over to the sofa, she noticed him avert his stare briefly, as if he'd been 'caught'.

"You're looking good, Georgia; you've always looked good, Georgia," said Shug with a wink and a grin, which Georgia merely smiled back at, handing him a beer.

"That's the Pilates, Hugh, it keeps me fit, but I can't wait until the pools and gyms open again so I can get back into my old regime." She could see Shug ogling her as she sat down on the sofa beside him, two seats down from him and sitting side on, turned to her right so that she was facing him. She'd brought her handbag with the knife in it back over, too, and it sat at her back.

"Aye, this pandemic hasn't been easy, Georgia. I have my weights bench and the cross trainer out in the garage, thankfully."

Georgia could see from Shug's flabby physique that he hadn't been using those items, despite his implying that he had. He still looked bearish and big, though.

Georgia took a drink from her bottle of beer and leaned forward a little, so that Shug could see more of her ample cleavage.

"To tell you the truth, Shug, I'll just be glad when it's all over and things can get back to normal." She saw his eyes divert to her chest briefly as he replied, trying not to look like he was ogling her tits – those beautiful bouncy breasts that he'd spent the last 20 or more years wishing were bouncing in *his* face – breasts that were now so tantalisingly close, so very nearly *his*. Georgia's change of pose had the desired effect.

Shug had a short rant about his own pandemic woes, mostly about his business problems and his big lie about his breakup with Alana Renfield.

When he repeated his cock and bull story about why he and Alana and split, without mentioning his beating his own child to death while still inside the poor lassie, Georgia felt like grabbing the blade from her handbag and lunging at him there and then – how many lives had this guy ruined? But no, she held back. He was a big guy and could easily block her and that wouldn't end well for Georgia or for her family. She had to wait until she was closer, when Shug was more vulnerable – she only had one chance.

Unwilling to carry on the bullshit conversation regarding Shug and Alana's 'breakup', Georgia instead asked Shug to put some music on. He reached for the remote control and turned off the football on the big TV, then told Georgia to ask the digital assistant device for whatever music she wanted.

"Alexa, play Erasure" she called out, and the tunes began to play.

"Good choice, honey, retro, love it," said Shug, draining the contents of his first beer and starting on the bottle Georgia had just brought him.

Georgia smiled back at him. "Lovely place you have here, Hugh." She meant that.

"Oh thanks, aye, I worked hard to get where I am."

Every fibre of Georgia's being wanted to scream at him, to yell at him about how his house was bought through blood money, profits from milking his fellow human beings in the schemes, but she didn't. Shug spoke again.

"So, look, Georgia, you know why I invited you here tonight, we both know, don't we?"

Georgia smiled and winked at him as he continued.

"I know we've had our ups and downs over the years, but you know I've always carried a candle for you, and with us both being single now I thought we might give it a go, what do you think?"

"I always thought you were interesting," said Georgia.

The sociopathic cunt took that as a compliment and, his eyes still out on stalks ogling Georgia through her sexy blue dress, he edged his way along the sofa so that he was sitting next to her. Erasure's cool electro-pop filled the room.

> *And the lovers that you sent for me*
> *Didn't come with any satisfaction guarantee*
> *So I return them to the sender*
> *And the note attached will read*
> *How I love to hate you*
> *I love to hate you*

Georgia remained cool and calm as he sat beside her, holding his gaze. Shug then pulled a little bag from his jogger pockets; it was full of cocaine – the stuff which had helped destroy Georgia's family. She looked at the bag and she felt nothing. Her handbag with the blade in it was right next to her.

"Well, Hugh, they say sex is better *with,* don't they?" said Georgia playfully, taking another sip of her beer, still holding his gaze, fully aware of the power that she had over him in that moment.

Having had the green light to get the coke out, Shug put the bag of powder on the coffee table in front of them and fished a £20 note and a bank card out of his wallet, quickly chalking up two fat lines. He offered Georgia first sniff, so she took the note and promptly hoovered up one of the lines. Shug couldn't believe his luck and quickly snorted his own line. As they both sat back and reeled for a moment, the drugs shooting towards the pleasure centres in their brains, Georgia noticed that Shug had a bit of curry sauce smeared among his stubble. The underarms of his retro

Motherwell shirt were also wet with a minging sweat rash and his B.O was bad. His bald head was beaded with smelly sweat, too, he was repulsive. Despite all of that, Georgia felt good to be desired, even by him.

Soon they were kissing passionately on the sofa while still sitting up, their tongues writhing together, Georgia doing her best to ignore the curry sauce, his B.O and his dreadful halitosis as they snogged like horny teenagers. After a few moments, Georgia stopped the kissing and placed a finger on Shug's lip – he eagerly waited to see what this meant.

In a flash, with a giggle, Georgia pulled down the shoulder straps of her sexy blue dress and exposed her beautiful, full, pert 38DD breasts to his transfixed gaze. Shug looked like an excited kid on Christmas morning – finally, they were his!

Shug let out a groan and buried his face between Georgia's magnificent tits, moaning and gasping as he kissed, licked, sucked on and gently bit them, covering them in his drool and spit, Georgia moaning softly as he had the time of his life down there, getting what he'd always wanted, what he'd have done almost anything to get – and all the while Georgia's hand was next to her handbag, that blue handbag containing the Japanese blade. She could've easily stuck him with the knife there while he was transfixed by her tits, but she didn't.

She looked down at Shug, this fat, greasy, bearish scumbag enjoying her tits, and decided to up the ante. When he stopped practically suckling her breasts to kiss her again, Georgia stood up and stepped out of her dress so that she was naked – she'd worn no knickers, knowing the effect that would have on Shug, all men loved that, after all. Shug looked wide-eyed with excitement as Georgia rejoined him on the sofa. Predictably, he resumed sucking on and kissing those breasts of Georgia's that had long been but a wank-fantasy to him. As he moaned, licked, kissed, and sucked on her ample globes, Georgia moaned and in her sexy voice asked, "How long have you wanted this, Hugh?"

His muffled reply was a mixture of *aws, oohs, fucks* and other incoherent lust-filled nonsense, but Georgia got the gist of it – a long time, then.

Hugh then kissed his way down Georgia's naked body and started to give her oral. He was still wearing his Motherwell shirt and his joggers but had kicked off his white trainers, leaving his feet in white sports socks – proof that money cannot buy class.

Georgia moaned a little then suggested that they should move to the bedroom, to which Shug instantly agreed, and they both made their way upstairs, Shug taking his beer and the coke stuff, Georgia taking her beer and her handbag. She placed the handbag containing the deadly knife on the corner of the bed upon entering the bedroom.

Shug's master bedroom was big - bigger than Georgia's living room. He had a king-sized bed with a wrought-iron frame. The floor was charcoal grey carpet and both sides of the bedroom had mirrored fitted wardrobes. The bedroom, like the rest of the house, was immaculately tidy. There was a door to a plush en-suite bathroom on the right-hand side of the room too.

Shug called out to the bedroom Alexa, 'play my sexy time playlist'. *Kiss you all over* by Exile came on, the cheesy 70s sexual track making Georgia wince inside a bit, almost as much as she winced inside at hearing the playlist name 'sexy time'.

> *You can see it in my eyes*
> *I can feel it in your touch*
> *You don't have to say a thing*
> *Just let me show how much*
> *I love you, need you, oh babe*

I want to kiss you all over
And over again
I want to kiss you all over
Till the night closes in
Till the night closes in

It was an apt song as the pair resumed their sexual activity on the big bed. Georgia made sure that she did indeed kiss Shug all over. Upon entering the bedroom, he had removed his slobbing clothes and plonked himself down on the bed, wearing only his white sports socks. Naked, Georgia got on top of him and the pair kissed passionately and deeply for a good ten minutes, exchanging saliva, their tongues exploring every inch of the other's mouth. Georgia put her tongue into each of his ears, too, making Shug whimper with pleasure. Then Georgia kissed her way down his neck, shoulders and chest, moaning as she went, then running her tongue down his hairy flabby belly. In the wardrobe mirror she could see Shug, clearly enjoying himself and placing his hands behind his head, with all the smugness of a guy who just knows he's about to get an epic blowjob.

That's exactly what he got, too. Georgia started slowly at first, using the tip of her tongue and her lips to tease him, but within a few minutes she was slobbering and spitting all over his hard but distinctly average-sized, mediocre penis. Its middling size made it easy for Georgia to take him all the way down her throat and soon Shug had lost all composure, howling and gasping in utter delight as she sucked his cock as if blowjobs were an Olympic sport and she the world champion. After about ten minutes of that, Georgia snaked her hand towards her blue handbag on the bed and pulled it closer to her, feeling its additional weight caused by the sharp, heavy blade within. She stopped sucking Shug's dick for a moment but continued stroking him with one hand, as she playfully asked.

"Mmm, is this what you expected, Hugh? How long have you wanted this for?" She started to deep throat him again.

Shug's reply was breathless and garbled as he was still howling and gasping with joy, but Georgia made out, "All my life, even better, so much better."

Now she had him at her mercy. Her blade was at hand. She could castrate the fucker if she wanted to. There had never been a better time to strike. She reached into her handbag.

Georgia had grabbed a condom from her handbag, which she slipped onto the still dazed and ecstatic Shug's mediocre cock, before taking him inside her, riding him in cowgirl position. She started slowly, moving up and down, back and forth with him inside her, arching her curvaceous body so that Shug got a real eyeful. All his adult life, Hugh 'Shug' Mann had fantasised about fucking Georgia, about seeing her beautiful eyes and pretty 'girl next door' face staring down at him lustfully, as her big perfect tits bounced inches from his face – now his fantasy was reality and Georgia could tell from his gasps and moans and by his tightening balls that it would all soon be too much for Shug. As she sat astride Shug riding him, Georgia stuck out her tits even more, hoping to drive him insane with lust, and started to ride him harder and faster, moaning like a whore as she did so. She made eye contact with him as they fucked and reached one hand around behind her, to rake his balls with her nails as she rode him. She spoke again.

"How long have you wanted this, Hugh?"

This time, Shug couldn't answer properly at all, the best he could manage amid his groaning and panting was an incoherent, *"Awwwwlll yeeessshhh, baby".*

Georgia's asking him that, her nails on his balls as she rode him, the sight of her naked and fucking him and the general buzz of having finally, after so long, seduced and fucked Georgia Smith, was enough to send Shug over the edge and he soon cried out in joy, Georgia feeling him fill up the rubber bag inside her with his cum. Georgia collapsed next to him on the bed, breathless and sweating, partly from the cocaine, partly because of her earlier headache. She then instinctively curled up next to his grotesque, flabby frame, all the more smelly now after the drugs and sexual exertions. She rested her head on his chest and ran her hand over his torso, as the dreadful human being that she had just fucked senseless began to get his breath back. After a few minutes he spoke.

"That was amazing. Here, grab my inhaler and my steroids from downstairs, will you?"

Georgia got up and went downstairs naked, returning momentarily with Shug's inhaler and pills.

Shug thanked her and took four huge puffs from his inhaler, then washed down some steroid pills with the dregs of his beer. Then he spoke.

"I'm starving, fancy a pizza?"

Despite the coke, Georgia was a bit peckish, so Shug used the Deliveroo app to order them both some food. Georgia then went into the en-suite and locked the door behind her, before closing the toilet seat, sitting down on it and letting out a big sigh.

Had she really just done that? Fucked the man who was largely to blame for ruining her life and the lives of so many others. And why hadn't she used the knife yet? She had certainly thought about it, but actually doing it, here, in the flesh, was another matter.

Their food soon arrived. A 16-inch meat feast pizza, garlic bread, chicken dippers, two cheesecakes and a big bottle of full-fat Irn Bru. Over the next hour or so, the two unlikely lovers ate the food in bed together while watching *Game of Thrones* on Shug's bedroom TV. It was the episode where Ramsay Bolton castrated Theon Greyjoy, which made

Georgia feel a little uneasy, not least because she'd earlier been considering doing exactly that to Shug.

It was Shug who ate most of the huge food takeaway, Georgia only ate two bits of pizza, a chicken dipper and the cheesecake, after all, there's always room for cheesecake. She wasn't surprised to see Shug gobble up most of this vast banquet – he'd always been a fat, greedy bastard, it stemmed from when he was deprived and abused as a young child. Georgia knew that being overweight, particularly during the pandemic, was dangerous, and she had, mostly, tried to keep her own weight down as much as possible since March – by contrast Shug was still very overweight.

CHAPTER THIRTY-EIGHT

You Take My Breath Away

The two stayed in bed together all night, cuddled up, talking at length. Almost to her horror, Georgia found that post-orgasmic endorphins actually made Shug a much calmer, nicer person to talk to – it was as if by making him cum she'd inadvertently brought out his nice side. Part of her wondered how he'd become so twisted, part of her even wondered, had she gotten with Shug when they were younger, before Keith, if he would've become a better person, but, most of her still hated Shug's guts for all that he had done – she was only there with him for her own reasons – tonight was all about her. Georgia empathised a lot with Shug that evening, though, about the shitty life that he'd had prior to, in his eyes, 'becoming successful' by morphing into a drug-dealing gangster. Shug's impoverished childhood in Blantyre, had greatly shaped who he was. The drunken, abusive father. The useless mother. The siblings who had left town to get away, abandoning him in the process. To Georgia's surprise, Shug agreed that Thatcher and the Tories' de-industrialisation policies after 1979 had fucked over Lanarkshire and the UK working class irrevocably. Where they both differed greatly was on how they had chosen to approach adult life, in light of the desolation that was Tory and then New Labour Britain.

Georgia and Keith had, until Keith's cocaine habit ruined him, followed the sensible, decent path to navigate life together – good jobs, buying a house, having a family, watching the pennies, essentially trying to ape the young adult lives of their own parents when they had young families. The Labour win in 1997 had brought things like tax-credits and child trust funds, along with better public services, higher wages and more workers' rights, to help out young couples with families, as Georgia and Keith had been – there was still a sense that if you played by the rules, you could still get on in life – do better, even.

Shug's world view had been very different. He'd had no good adult examples to follow in life, other than the fictitious characters in the gangster movies that he had watched as a child up in his room, hungry, angry, and afraid. He had worked for a fucking pittance as a decorator's apprentice until his time was served, enduring four years of having far less pay than his peers who had just left school and gone straight to work in factories or call centres, rather than taking up a trade. As people started to have a bit more money in their pockets from the mid-1990s onwards, Shug had chosen to do his best to get other people's money from them, rather than grafting hard to earn his own – and the only way for a young guy in a scheme to do that quickly was through selling drugs and he'd been good at it – very good at it. The way he saw it, he didn't need to work hard, even when he set up his own businesses. A legit business was good to have, but Shug had always liked being a dealer more. Why slog your guts out in a legitimate line of work when you can earn big bucks by employing a few trusted lackies and taking over the local drugs trade? At least half of the people in the schemes were drug users. If he got a monopoly on that trade, then he was effectively receiving 10 to 20% of everybody in the scheme's wages or benefits, almost a tax on working class suffering - paid directly to him, and the best part was, as it was the illegal drugs trade, he didn't have to worry about competition or big corporations eating into his profits, as legitimate businesses do. Likewise, he was immune from external shocks, too, like the 2008 global financial crash – safe in the knowledge that organised crime and showbiz are the only two recession-proof businesses – he'd learned that snippet from an episode of the Sopranos. The 2008 crash had increased demand for drugs in the schemes, not reduced it, and the timely arrival of 'pure' cocaine in large quantities shortly after the financial meltdown had ensured that Shug's customers stayed addicted and Shug got richer.

The Tories getting back into power in 2010 hadn't really affected Shug's drugs empire, either – folk gave up their expensive nights out on the lash but kept buying their weed and their ching. Shug's view was that the world was shite and that drugs were inevitable as a result. He didn't care how much suffering his dealing caused to addicts and families or how the druggy lifestyles of parents he preyed upon fucked up the life chances of their children. Shug's attitude was that his life had been shite, but thanks to drugs, it was good now – fuck everybody else. In that respect, Georgia could see that Shug, like most dealers, whether they realise it or not, was the personification of neoliberalism and Thatcherism – 'I'm rich and that's all that matters.'

This post-coital chat about the world showed Georgia that Shug wasn't born bad – he was a product of his harsh environment. She even found herself admiring his single-mindedness regarding his drugs empire – even though she abhorred the trade. After all, as a wise Chinese man once said, 'you can appreciate the beauty of a tiger even as it leaps to devour you'.

Once their very late dinner was digested, Georgia led Shug into the en-suite where they showered together for almost 30 minutes, rubbing soapy suds all over one another – Shug fulfilling another one of his teen fantasies by soaping up Georgia's big tits. After that, it was back to bed.

Georgia racked up a big line of cocaine on her tits and got an ecstatic Shug to snort it directly off them, though this time she didn't partake of the white powder herself. She then demanded that Shug give her head, which he eagerly did, filled with cocaine lust. Georgia quite enjoyed Shug's oral, he was good with his tongue, and she enjoyed covering his mouth in her wetness as she came. Then, she got Shug to fuck her in missionary, so that they could keep kissing deeply. That he wasn't so good at. He just lay on top of her, riding her blandly as they kissed passionately, he was too fat to do 'mish' properly, but Georgia didn't mind. After a while she put her right index finger up his ass and asked him breathily "How long have you wanted this?" which, as she knew that it would, soon made him explode again with a guttural groan, filling the condom inside her.

They sat up chatting again, cuddling, stroking, kissing, Shug looking as if all his Christmases had come at once, Georgia doing her best to make their time together as nice as possible, doing her best to block out her enmity toward him.

Around 6am, Shug fell asleep in bed. Georgia looked around the opulent designer master bedroom, and at the fat, nasty but content gangster snoozing beside her, and felt nothing. Her headache was back. At last, Hugh 'Shug' Mann was completely helpless, asleep. She could be like Delilah with a sleeping Samson – all that she had to do was reach for her handbag and strike.

She reached for her handbag and gazed once more at the prostrate, sleeping nasty mess of a man upon the bed, her senses heightened by finally having this man at her mercy. And then, she got dressed and drove home.

When Georgia got home, she put the unused knife back in the kitchen drawer and went for a snooze on the sofa – Olivia was still asleep in her bedroom upstairs. At around 10am, Georgia made toast and bacon with coffee for herself and for her daughter, left her daughter's breakfast outside her bedroom door, and went to bed herself. Georgia slept a full six hours, that Sunday. When she awoke and went downstairs, her phone was full of Whatsapp messages from Shug.

```
'Hey, last night was amazing x'
'Hey, fancy round two tonight x?'
'Hey, I really think something good happened
last night x'
'Hey, are you ok? x'
'What's wrong? x'
```

Twisted sociopaths absolutely hate it when people don't immediately respond to their communications. Georgia knew this all too well and on that Sunday evening she didn't want to be hearing from Shug again – she didn't feel well – probably from the cocaine she'd taken earlier at Shug's, which had gotten rid of her headache for a while but now seemed to be making her head throb more as the poisonous drug left her system.

As she sat alone in the living room on the sofa that evening, alternating between cups of tea and glasses of water as she recovered from what had been a very sleazy evening, Georgia wondered what the fuck she had just done, but didn't regret a second of it.

Why had she gone over to seduce and fuck a man for whom she held so much disdain?

Why did she think that giving him what he had always wanted would finally get him out of her life?

How on earth had she been able to reach orgasm with this man?

Why had she not used the knife?

To stop Shug's incessant WhatsApps, she tactfully messaged him "Thanks for last night, I had a great time. Olivia isn't feeling well so I'm running around after her, I'll text you tomorrow."

Shug replied with a kissy smiley and sent no more messages that evening.

Georgia went through to the kitchen to make another cup of tea, shouting to see if Olivia wanted one, which she did. Georgia left the mug of tea outside her daughter's bedroom door, knocking, then went for a long shower, washing away the sweat, scent, seed and slavers of Hugh Mann from her body, from her body's every nook and cranny. After her shower she meticulously cleaned her teeth and gargled with Listerine. She then went back downstairs in her dressing gown and realised that she hadn't drunk her tea. Cold tea is the devil's way of punishing laziness, so she stuck the kettle on to make a fresh cup. She felt exhausted, drained. As the boiling kettle rumbled away, she tidied away some letters and other junk from the kitchen table. Bills, mostly – she was still in over £20k worth of debt – her living husband's legacy. She put the letters into the little rack atop the breakfast bar and binned their envelopes. Then she got a piece of kitchen roll and carefully scooped up the surprisingly large amount of waste and debris caused by used Covid 19 lateral flow testing kits. At last, the table was clear and she could sit down and rest.

CHAPTER THIRTY-NINE

Saltwater

It wasn't until late on the Tuesday night that the call from the hospital came. Georgia took the call, thanking the nurse for taking the time to call her, and made her way there in the car. Once there, she headed to the ward in her mask, walking those familiar long, empty corridors until she reached the big double doors into the hospital red zone. The two nurses on the desk recognised her and were genuinely sympathetic that 'that poor woman' was here to see another seriously ill loved one. The nurses apologised that the doctor was busy and told Georgia, 'just five minutes, last on the left,' to which she nodded. She pushed open the double doors and walked back down that familiar passage of death and suffering, doing her best not to look through the panes of glass on either side, trying not to see the PPE-clad staff or the suffering patients gasping for breath. When she reached the last room on the left at the end of the corridor, that same male doctor appeared from another side room and asked who she was there to visit. He then explained that the patient was conscious but ventilated and had thus been given a tracheotomy, so, they'd know she was there but would be unable to speak. They had Covid 19 and it 'didn't look good' – doctor speak for 'probably going to die' - but before they had deteriorated to the point where they needed ventilation, they had asked that the hospital notify Georgia of their plight, saying she was their next of kin. Georgia could stay for five minutes and no more. Georgia nodded at the doctor, who then left her to it. Georgia approached the glass windowpane which looked into the same side room in which her dad had died.

She was clad in as much PPE as she could find, but having twice already visited the hospital's red-zone she knew the route off by heart and was certain that she could complete her journey with only one of her elbows touching anything – minimising the risk of her spreading the deadly virus – besides, this was important – someone else of great significance to her life was in that hospital bed and she wasn't about to let them possibly die without saying goodbye.

She gazed through the glass at the pathetic shell of a human being lying on the hospital bed, conscious but ventilated, their skin almost pure white, their bed surrounded by machines. Shug Mann.

Georgia glanced around and saw no nursing staff in the corridor, and something made her walk into the side room.

The big wooden hospital chair next to the bed was a bit close so she opted to stand at the end of the bed instead. Besides, the chair had a plastic bag full of patient's belongings on it.

As she stood there, Shug lifted his head slightly, and Georgia gazed at his ghostly, confused, breathless face, a ventilator tube sticking out of his mouth.

"Oh, Hugh, how did it come to this? Are you alright?"

Shug was unable to answer, but Georgia could see that he knew who she was and could hear her, too. She noticed tiny patches of colour appear on his cheeks and his mouth curling upwards at both ends a little – he was pleased to see her.

"You told the hospital that I'm your next of kin, Hugh, that's a bit presumptuous after just one shag, is it not?" joked Georgia, adding "But don't worry, Hugh, I'm here for you – nobody else is, are they?"

Shug was looking at her as the ventilator hissed and puffed to keep him breathing, trying to counteract the deadly virus which was doing its best to deprive him of oxygen. He was still trying to smile. Even in his near delirium, he was happy that *someone* had come.

Georgia moved closer to the bed and picked up the bag of patient belongings from the bedside chair. She opened the bag and hung Shug's curry-stained retro Motherwell shirt on his headboard. When she did that, he seemed to smile again.

For a moment, Georgia was silent, looking down at the breathless Shug, as a doting mother looks down at a newborn baby in a crib. Then, she spoke.

"Look, Hugh, or do you prefer Shug? Listen, Shug, I could lecture you about your weight and your use of alcohol and drugs and how they've made you more susceptible to Coronavirus, and they have, but that's locking the stable door after the horse has bolted, it's important that we focus on the future," Shug managed a nod, still trying to smile, the staccato repetitive noises of the ventilator still filling the room.

"There is a future, Hugh, but it's a future without you in it. You see, after you got my Jordan arrested for drug-dealing I decided to get rid of you and by doing so I knew that I was benefitting my family and the wider community. I realised that violence wasn't an option, nobody would act against you, and even if I had asked someone, you'd have found out. I also knew that the police wouldn't do anything about you without hard evidence, so grassing on your activities wasn't an option, although I did get a visit from a DC Iain Finlayson, during which his manner suggested to me that, were something to happen to you, the police would view it as good riddance. Then it came to me, after I caught you trying to become my teenage daughter's webcam pimp. There's a global pandemic of a deadly respiratory virus, a virus which is even more dangerous to asthmatic, fat, unhealthy people like you, all I needed to do was make sure that you got this virus, and fate, nature, and karma would do the rest. But how could I make you catch the virus?"

Georgia reached into her handbag and pulled out the lateral flow test cassette which still showed the two red lines of her positive test result from the Saturday afternoon and held it up close so that Shug could clearly see it. Shug wasn't smiling anymore.

"Our Olivia caught Covid, and I knew I'd get it from her; it was just lucky that you invited me round on the day that I'd tested positive myself. All I had to do then was, well, give you everything that you've always wanted – me."

Shug emitted a groan, and his face screwed up a little, but there was nothing else that he could do except lie there and listen, impotent with rage. Georgia continued.

"See, Hugh, you may be a businessman, gangster, and criminal mastermind, but you're still a man – your true weakness is between your legs and for once it was you who got exploited, not me. I made sure we kissed and fucked so much, so that my Covid-infected bodily fluids were all over you. You were so ecstatic and buzzing that your lifelong ambition to ride 'Jessica Rabbit' was coming true that you didn't stop to think about why I had suddenly given myself to you so easily, especially after all that you've done to me and to my family. In your arrogance, you thought it was all fate, but you see, it wasn't fate – it was Karma."

Shug's right hand weakly tried to reach for the nurse-call buzzer a few inches away from it, but Georgia picked that up and hung it safely out of reach, far down the cot sides of Shug's hospital bed. Shug's face began to twist with anger; his breathing started to go against the ventilator until he realised how painful that was. All he could do was lie there, helpless and immobile, as a smiling Georgia talked away to him.

"Where were we? Oh aye, Karma. My dad died of Covid in this very room, Hugh, did you know that? I missed seeing him at the end because I dropped a phone call from the hospital one night thinking it was you on the phone. I didn't see my mum before she died, because I was away working a second job to pay off all that debt you let my husband run up, knowing it would break our family.

My husband became a cokehead loser, because of you.

My husband cheated on me, because of you.

My family to this day is drowning in debt, because of you.

My husband left the family home, because of you.

My son beat up my husband, because of you.

My son got busted as a drugs mule, tried to kill himself, and is still incarcerated in a fucking mental hospital, because of you.

You tried to recruit my daughter, to be her pimp, after perving at her while she was under 18 on webcam.

And all because I wouldn't get with you years ago. Well, you've had me now, had me all ways, actually, had my spit and wetness all over you, at long last, how does it feel? Was it worth it, Hugh?"

Shug's hands were gripping his sheets tightly and he had gone red, shaking with helpless rage, despite his weakened state – yet he could do nothing.

"Of course, Hugh, the karma you're experiencing isn't just for me and my family.

What about that poor Alana, you beating her and killing your own child?

How many lives have the drugs you sell destroyed?

How many lassies are selling their bodies to feed addictions, because of you?

How many guys have hanged themselves after drowning in coke debt, because of you?

How many families have the drugs that you and your cronies sell destroyed?

How many communities have you destroyed? Your own fucking communities?

The list goes on, Hugh. During our cosy wee chat on Saturday night in between the bouts of rubbish sex with your useless wee baby-dick, you expressed no remorse at all the suffering that you have caused, in fact, you didn't even acknowledge that you've caused any. Well, ok, that means I can feel ok about feeling no remorse for deliberately giving you, a fat cunt, a deadly respiratory virus which kills fat cunts. See, as a drug dealer, you've had yourself wrong. You're not a necessary evil, you're just an evil fucking parasite – and we all know what should happen to parasites – much like viruses, actually, they have to be cleansed, eradicated, done away with."

Georgia looked down at Shug's pathetic flabby frame in the hospital bed, his hate-filled breathless face twisted and contorted, staring right at her. Georgia then put on the fake sexy voice she'd used on him when she seduced him, but instead of 'how long have you wanted this', she stood at the end of his bed, took off her face masks, put her hands on her hips and sexily drawled.

"How long have I wanted this?"

Shug, incandescent with rage but immobile and unable to speak, could only grunt and gurgle, his face contorted with hate. She said it again.

"How long have I wanted this?" Georgia then replaced her facemasks and slipped out of the side room, leaving Shug helpless, enraged and critically ill on the bed, alone.

None of the staff on the frantic ward had noticed her go in or come out of the side room. She stopped one last time to look back into the room through the pane of glass, that same window that she had looked through when watching her beloved father die of the same disease that was now doing its best to kill Shug. She reflected on that, then tapped on the window. Somehow, Shug was able to turn his head to the left and to stare hatefully up at the windowpane, where all he could see was the masked face of Georgia Smith, the fantasy woman who had ultimately been his doom. Georgia blew him a kiss, and gave him a little wave, and then a cheeky wee wink – before staring expressionless at him for a few moments, seeing the hatred and fear in his face as he stared back at that one woman that he had pushed too far. As he breathlessly slipped into unconsciousness and medical alarms in his room began to sound, Georgia turned and walked back down the corridor, as nurses hurried into Shug's side room. The last sound that she heard as she left the ward was the noise of Shug's monitoring devices go from a steady beep to a flatlining, constant wheeeeeeeeeeeee.

With a kiss of death, Georgia had defeated her tormentor. The Blantyre Girl had won.

CHAPTER FORTY

CODA

Georgia phoned Alana Renfield on her way back to the car and arranged to pick her up in Glasgow. It was around 11pm when they reached Shug's big house in Bothwell. En route Georgia had explained everything to Alana, who had seemed relieved but not overjoyed by an upbeat Georgia's recounting of the last few days. When Georgia had hung Shug's Motherwell shirt up on his bed during their final showdown in the side room, she had also taken his house keys from the small, pathetic pile of Shug's belongings.

Georgia had only taken the keys so that she could get Alana her belongings back, as Shug had only given her back a few items of clothing after throwing her out. Once in Shug's house, Georgia helped Alana to recover everything that was hers – jewellery, shoes, good designer clothes, makeup, electronic devices, even her old family photo albums and box of memories – Georgia and Alana had both known that Shug was too mean by nature to have thrown these out. They loaded four of Shug's big holdalls into Georgia's car and were about to leave when Alana said "Wait. We need to do this, come on."

Alana went back inside the house and Georgia followed, intrigued. Alana made for the kitchen drawer and pulled out a large sharp knife.

She then proceeded to slice open the big red four-seater leather sofa in the lounge, and then, it all made sense to Georgia.

Wedged in between the wooden lower frame of the sofa were two huge black and white adidas holdall bags, the ones with wheels on them at one end.

"Come on, help me" said Alana, trying to use all of her strength to unwedge the bags from the innards of the sofa.

"Is that the drugs?" asked Georgia.

"No. 300 grand in cash – Shug's rainy-day fund – he'll not be needing it, will he?" said Alana, huffing and puffing as she tried to drag the holdalls free, going red in the face and sweating.

"Hello?"

They both heard a man's voice and the front door being pushed open.

Both women turned around and were greeted by a solitary figure. He looked about 30 years old, was dressed smartly in a Marc Darcy suit and he had big blue eyes and slicked-back short black hair. He wore a medical grade facemask.

"Oh, Mrs Smith, Ms Renfield, hello, I'm sorry to disturb you, one of the neighbours phoned to report hearing a commotion coming from this address as the occupant was in hospital.

Georgia was almost glad to see DC Iain Finlayson, the copper who had paid her an unorthodox visit at home that time, to talk about her son. The cop continued.

"Do you still live here, Ms Renfield?"

Alana went red but remained otherwise cool.

"No, Shug and I broke up, he said I could come round to collect my stuff. He's in the hospital."

"Oh, is he? Nothing serious, is it?" asked Finlayson.

"Covid," said Alana. "We're going in to try and visit him tomorrow."

The cop raised an eyebrow, then held his facemask away from his mouth slightly.

"Do you think I'm fucking daft? Look, I recognised your car, Mrs Smith. We were worried the disturbance here was maybe Shug's cronies grabbing his stash, but that's clearly not the case. Look, I'll tell my colleague out in the car that it's just Shug's ex getting her stuff back, like you said, lock up the house when you're done, please".

With that, the cop turned to walk back out. Georgia called after him.

"DC Finlayson, thank you, for everything."

Turning back for a moment, the cop just smiled, winked and then left.

Alana and Georgia both let out huge sighs of relief as the unmarked police Volkswaggen Passat left the street.

"Shit, Alana, I didn't think. I've got Covid, I'm sorry," said Georgia, panicking as she remembered.

"I had it just after that time we met up in town, so did my auntie, it's fine." Replied Alana, finally freeing one of the holdalls and dragging it onto the carpet. The second holdall came out easily after that and, carrying one each, they locked up Shug's house, put the holdalls into the car and headed for Glasgow. Once at Alana's auntie's house, Georgia helped Alana take her belongings into the house, bag by bag. When there was just one holdall left, Georgia went to lift it out of the back of her car, but Alana put a hand on hers and stopped her.

"There's about 150 grand in there, look, that's yours, no arguments – I know what he did to you and your family – take it."

Georgia was shaking. "That's not mine, I can't take that."

"It's not mine either, is it? But that cunt is dead, and we're due compensation, one way or another – take it. You're a good person – you deserve it, Georgia. Use it for your family."

For once, Georgia was in no mood to do the 'aw shucks' thing. She took the bag and the 150 grand, hugged Alana, promised to stay in touch and then drove home. Here, dear friend, our story almost ends.

The £150,000 was enough to give the Smith family a new start and they were reunited a year later, with Jordan getting out of hospital. Shortly after, Keith was released from prison, clean for the first time in a long time, and vowed to make amends for all the pain he had caused his family. Little by little, they all found their way back to happiness.

Most of neoliberalism's innocent victims in housing schemes don't get that happy ending, that lucky break, that fresh start, most of life's Broken Biscuits aren't so fortunate.

But, as our tale comes to its conclusion, I ask you, dear reader, to picture the beautiful forty-something redheaded woman driving her Renault Clio eastward along the M8 towards home, her wee car carrying a holdall containing enough money to help to give her shattered family a brand new start, having just used sex and Covid 19 to get rid of her cunt of a nemesis once and for all.

As she drives, she's happily singing along to her favourite Nick Cave song in the car – and it's so apt.

Still your hands and still your heart
For still your face comes shining through
And all the morning glows anew
Still your soul and still your mind
For still the fire of our love is true
And I am breathless without you

The End

About the author

Ian is originally from Livingston, West Lothian. He had a nine-year career in warehousing before losing his legs in a fire, aged 24, in 2002. After that tragedy, he became a writer, historian and actor. In 2023 he was diagnosed with AuDHD.

9 781919 364803